MW00561481

The Misfit Society Vol. 1

Written
by
Aaron Carlos

Copyright Aaron Carlos Jones 2020

Published in 2020 by Cinemagical Productions

Edited by **Final Look Editing**

All rights reserved. No part of the book may be reproduced
without formal permission

1

Dedicated to:
The Lost Ones

The Misfit Society Vol. 1 (Generation Babylon)

Contents

CHAPTER I: MY BIG BROTHER MANNY

His voice has become horse from screaming so much over the past twenty-eight hours he's on the edge of insanity as he continues to see pitch black, he only hears the sound of rap music blaring through two twelve-inch speakers playing on full volume. Mobb Deep – *Get Dealt With* has been playing nonstop for the past twenty hours. He's losing the feeling in his wrist, his hands tied tightly behind his back. Suddenly the music stops, and the voice of what sounds like a teenager appears. He almost chokes on the water from drinking it so frantically. He begins to plead with the teenager who he can hear but not see, "Look, you seem like a nice kid. Just untie me before they get back, and I promise no one will ever find out. You can say I got myself free and attacked you. Please, kid, I have a wife who's pregnant at home. I want to see her again."

"Oh, don't worry, you'll be seeing your wife real soon," a young voice states.

"Wait! What? What does that mean?" "Get Dealt With" once again blares through the speakers. The man sits another thirty minutes, The song continues to play.

The blindfold suddenly is snatched off of the man. He becomes discombobulated. It takes a minute for him to adjust his eyes. Once his eyes fit to the light, he sees who's standing in front of him and immediately tries to explain himself. "Manny, please, you know I didn't know things would go that far. I had no idea what they were going to do. I don't know where my brother is. I swear to God if I did, I would tell you." Manny looks at the man with a stone-cold face and then breaks into a smile, "You know I figured you would say that." Manny puts his index and pinky fingers to his bottom lip and whistles towards the open door. "Juice! Bring that bitch in the room!" Juice walks the woman in the room blindfolded, gagged, and her hands tied behind her back. "Now I'm going to ask you one more time, and if you don't tell me where your brother is, I'm going to have my little man over there blow your girlfriend's brains out all over that brick wall. Why are you over there making that face, Juice? Because he said this bitch was his wife. I bet you he told you she was pregnant too?"

6

Manny steps closer to the man who has his head down as tears drip from his nose's bridge. Manny begins to countdown from ten. When he gets to six, the man screams out. "Okay, I'll tell you just let her go after I do. My brother is hiding out in the country in Lancaster, Pennsylvania!"

"What's the address?" Manny asks.

The man finally admits, "It's two-two-seven Yellow Mills Drive…"

"Tell my little man how to get there," Juice walks over to the man writing down the directions given. "Now see that wasn't so hard!" Manny looks over at Juice, waving him off and telling him, "Tell Ernesto to come in here!"

"But I told you what you wanted!" the man desperately exclaims.

"I know you did, and just like you've been lying to me, and how you lied to the kid. I lied to you. Plus, I knew Jose was in Lancaster; I just needed the address."

"WAIT! MANNY PLEASE NO!" Manny snaps his finger and then Ernesto puts a bullet in the woman's head, and then three rounds in the man as he screams, tied to the chair.

"Most of us go through life with simple desires, a roof over our heads and food in our refrigerators, and hopefully something to pass on to our loved ones when we perish. But far too often, we pass on the trauma we've individually suffered to the ones we feel we love the most."

-Misfit Z

Manny Alexander Castro was born May 9th, 1972, in Caracas, Venezuela. From the day Manny was born, he was thought to be a special child. His parents Adrian Castro and Blanca Castro, immigrated to the United States in 1976 from Venezuela to New York. By the time the family immigrated, Manny had a younger brother named Pablo. Pablo was Manny's world! Manny and Pablo were three years apart in age, but the two brothers were inseparable. Pablo favored his father while Manny looked like his mother Blanca, inheriting her jet black hair, light-brown eyes, and infectious smile. The Castro family was happy living their life in Mount Vernon, New York. That is until a tragic Christmas Eve in 1981. The wind blew ferociously. It was six-degrees with the wind chill. It was Thursday morning, and Blanca was doing some last-minute Christmas shopping she left out of the gas station after filling up the gas tank on her forest green 1979 Station Wagon and getting Pablo a snack. Blanca was headed towards the mall when she was violently blindsided by a drunken truck driver. The impact killed Blanca instantly, along with her six-year-old son Pablo. Adrian was a citizen and obtained a substantial settlement, but no amount of money could repair the damage done to his psyche or his eldest son's psyche. Manny would never be the same after that life-altering December day; his father would relocate to Daytona Beach, Florida, leaving Mount Vernon New York in 1985. Manny was thirteen at the time, and his father thought a fresh start would keep his delinquent son out of trouble, but the move to Florida only enhanced Manny's criminality. Manny moved out of his father's house dramatically at the age of fifteen. He told himself that he would never look back. Manny and his father went years without speaking to one another after his departure. Outside of the altercation between father and son, Manny's demeanor and the fact that he was dismissive of his father's opinions made Adrian dread that his son may be a lost cause. After three years of rising in the ranks of a criminal organization run by The Perez brothers based out of Miami, Florida, Manny was promoted and eventually settled down in the DC, Maryland, and Virginia areas. He built up a network of connections throughout the area and abroad. Manny would eventually speak to his father again after his baby brother. Adrian Luis Castro Jr. was born on July 4th, 1992, in Bethesda, Maryland. Adrian Sr. remarried a woman who was thirteen years younger than him named Isabella. The newlyweds moved from Miami to Fort Washington, Maryland, before Adrian Jr. was born. Adrian Sr. opened up an auto repair shop with a business partner, and Isabella was starting her career with the "Environmental Protection Agency." Manny didn't attend the wedding in 1988, but he was there for the birth his baby brother in 92'. Manny stayed alive in the jungles of America through the '80s and early '90s. He did receive his fair share of scars in his vanity conquest. From getting into shootouts to being stabbed, and doing a year prison sentence. The once-lost boy became a cold-hearted man passing on money and knowledge, but it's accompanied by pain! One day this kid and his friends decided to rob one of Manny's business. Manny allowed two out of the three boys who robbed him to stay alive; one of the boys would even become his protégé. Manny appreciated the teenager's cleverness who he would nickname Juice. The kid didn't rob Manny's café strong-arm style. He was patient! Something that Manny thought was rare for a kid his age.

Manny's Gold 1997 Cadillac sits idle as the sun shines on his freshly washed car. Water drips of the white wall tires a slight summer breeze blows through the front car windows. Manny waits for Juice to come out of the Exxon gas station; they're picking up his baby brother Adrian Jr. from his father's house in Fort Washington, Maryland. Adrian's fifth birthday is just one day away, but Manny will be out of town for business, so he's taking Blue to the movies. Manny calls Adrian Jr. Blue because of his reaction when he is upset and can't get his way. Juice hops in the Cadillac, gently shutting the passenger side door as he slides into the cream leather seat holding a bag that contains waters and candy. Manny sports a New York Knicks Patrick Ewing jersey with a hat and Reebok shoes to match. He talks to Juice about some of his behavior. Manny is growing impatient because Juice is still dealing with people he has told him to stay away from. Some of Juice's friends were the worst of what the Ronald Regan, war on drugs, "Just Say No" era birthed. Manny was a man who rarely second-guessed himself, but there have been moments where he felt that he may have made a mistake with Juice. The kid was special. No doubt about it! Juice had never made a mistake when it pertains to business, and he actually showed Manny how to get money through legitimate means that he never considered, but Juice was still young! A young, old head who thought living past twenty-five was living to fifty. Manny parks his Cadillac behind his father's black 1993 Lincoln town car. All four car windows are now rolled up. The five percent tinted windows block out the evening summer sun as Manny removes his Knicks hat wiping sweat from his light-brown-skin forehead with a small cloth face towel. He puts the cap backward onto his curly jet black hair as he looks over at Juice, who was rapping along with the Jay-Z's "Reasonable Doubt" album. The AC blows as Manny turns down the music; he removes his five-hundred-dollar pair of sunglasses and says, "Juice, I know you might think that I don't like Ken because of who he runs with. Yeah, them niggas is hot, and they only gonna attracted bullets or badges, but it's not about them. It's about Ken! I'm telling you this because what I see in Kenny is the same thing I see in some of the comrades I use to trust!" As Manny is talking to Juice, someone knocks on his tinted window. Manny rolls down his window. The smell of too much colon and leftover cigar smoke seeps into the driver-side window. A tall, middle-aged man stands outside of the car. He's wearing blue-jeans-shorts and a Dallas Cowboys jersey. His badge and pistol on his waist can be seen when his undersized jersey shifts, the man is a heavy set Black male with a gray beard and balding hair. He greets Manny's with his amorous offensive lineman like right-hand. "How you doing today, Manny?"

"I'm good! How you doing?" Manny responds. "I'm feeling good, youngster!" The man leans back from the car glancing at Juice; he begins to gingerly walk towards the house. He looks back to say, "I'll talk to you when you get inside the house." Manny rolls up his window and begins to speak to Juice like their conversation was never interrupted. "You know how I could stay alive after everything fell with The Perez Brothers? How I built my own after rat niggas made it harder for out of towner's?" Juice stays silent as he looks at his mentor. "Because I don't allow emotions to exist in my decisions. Now I don't give a fuck what your past is with Ken, but it's not your future! So what you're gonna do now is go back to working at the corner store with Sabrina like before! You're gonna stop doing any kind of grimy shit without permission, and so help me, God! I put this on Blue! If I hear about you doing anything besides what I said! I'm gonna turn your ass into a walking billboard! Do we understand each other?" Juice stares back at Manny. His eyes are filled with humility as he says, "I understand." Manny claps his hands, smiles at Juice, and says. "Let's go get something to eat!" Manny and Jalon exit the car. The music coming from the house becomes louder with every step. *"Thoughts Of Old Flames" By* Pleasure, plays as Manny opens the front door. Manny and Juice walk through the front hallway of the Fort Washington home filled with Barbecue's smell. The walls are painted gray, pictures throughout the decades hang in frames along the hallway. Manny and Juice walk through the dining room, greeting his father's friends. They're playing a game of spades. There are three married couples in the dining room. Two couples are playing against each other, while the other couple watches joking and commentating. Beer cans, a half-eaten plate of food, plastic cups, and a bottle of Remy Martin rest on different parts of the table, playing cards, and a note pad and pen. The room temporarily directs its attention to Manny and Juice as they pass through. Manny introduces himself to everyone in the room; he also introduces Juice throwing his arm around him. "This is my little partner Jalon!" Juice turns on his proper camouflage, saying yes sir and yes ma'am as he speaks to the room. Everyone comments on how young Juice looks. "Baby, he said sixteen, but the nigga look twelve." Everyone laughs except Juice. "You swole though there, young brother! I ain't trying hurt ya!" The laughter continues as their focus goes back to the spades game. Manny walks through the kitchen as Juice follows behind. Manny enters the living room. His playful little brother ambushes him, punching and kicking him as he makes sound effects with every strike. Manny laughs as he lifts Adrian Jr. above his head like a dumbbell, kissing his forehead every time he brings him down. Manny gently slams Adrian Jr. on the couch, tickling him and talking with an excited tone. "That's right. I came just for you, Blue! I brought you some Lemon heads, and I brought you some Now-Laters, and you know what else?" Adrian giggles and asks, "What else, Manny?"

"We're gonna go to the movies!"

Adrian smiles widely and says. "Wow, really, Manny?"

"Yep! We're gonna go see *Men in Black*," Manny says with the same smile.

Adrian joyfully gasps and screams, "No way!" "Yes, way!" Manny responds.

"That's so cool! I love you, Manny!" Manny begins to walk outside, and Adrian yells out. "Where are you going?"

Manny shakes his head,"I'm about to go talk to Papi for a second. I'll be right back."

Adrian begins to pout, "I wanna come with you!"

"I'm only gonna be a second Blue." Adrian sits down, he angrily folds his arms, curling his lips and pouting. "No! I wanna come with you!"

"Just wait for me to talk to Papi, and then me, you and Jalon are going to go to the movies." "No!" Manny sits on the couch. He places his arm around Adrian as he gestures towards Juice. "Look, Adrian Jalon's here too." Adrian looks at Jalon, happy to see him, but attempts to remain angry.

"I don't care, Jalon!" Juice walks towards Adrian smiling, but Adrian curls his lips and begins to hold his breath as he gets closer. Manny looks up at Juice. "Ah, shit, here we go!" Manny gets up from the burgundy cloth couch and stands next to Juice as they both commentate. "Aye Yo, how long you think he's gonna be able to go this time?" Juice laughs. "Not too long! Look at him. He's already turning blue!" Manny shouts at Adrian to "ADRIAN LUIS CASTRO JR, YOU BETTER STOP!" Juice taps Manny on the arm. "Aye, I got this! Go ahead and talk to Senior." Juice dashes to the couch. He grabs Adrian laying him to his side, tickling him and speaking in an animated tone. "Boy, you can't go to the movies if you pass out! You can't see Fresh Prince kill aliens if you pass out!" Adrian begins to cry, but his fake tears turn into laughter. Manny smiles as he walks outside, and Juice asks Adrian, "So Blue, do you wanna finish watching power rangers? Or you wanna play Tekken?" Adrian excitingly screams out, "Tekken!"

Manny slides the screen door open; the tan vertical blinds are already pushed to the other end of the door frame. He steps outside, turning his head towards his father, flipping barbeque ribs on the grill. As Manny begins to walk towards his father, he redirects his attention to Willie Banks. Willie is on his way inside the house. Manny shakes Willie's hand and asks him. "Where's Luke? I'm about to take Blue to the movies. I'll take Luke too!"

"That boy got the chicken pocks. I'm about to walk back over there right now before his momma kills me." He responds.

Manny condescendingly says to Willie. "Tell Sadie I said what's up!" Willie paused and was about to respond but kept walking inside instead. The man in the Cowboys jersey stands beside Adrian Sr. telling jokes, drinking out of a beer in his left hand. Adrian Sr. is still laughing from one of the man's jokes. He says to Manny. "I knew you were coming over! You can't say no to your little brother." "Papi, anytime you make Hallaca you know Imma be around!" Adrian Sr. takes Manny's hat off and rubs his head! "Well, I'm glad to see you, mijo. How have you been? You look good."

"I'm just how I look, Papi, I'm gold," Manny talks to his father for thirty minutes. Adrian Sr. and Isabella are getting divorced; although she has forfeited custody of Adrian Jr, Isabella is making the settlement as difficult as possible. After talking with Manny, Adrian Sr. goes inside of the house. Manny sits down in the lawn chair next to the man in the Cowboys jersey. He offers Manny a drink, but he declines his offer. The man looks over at Manny, blandly saying. "You got a problem, son! Whoever in your circle that's been absent for an extended period is rolling on y'all operation, I'm not sure of the cooperator's name yet, but I am certain I heard your café mentioned.

13

The man grabs another beer out the cooler by the grill. He uses his teeth to take the top off the beer bottle. The man begins drinking and telling Manny all the information that he is privy to, at one point, he said to Manny in a passive-aggressive manner. How he should show a little more gratitude for the information that he just provided him with. Manny stands up. He has to look up to the man who stands at six-foot-six. "Look, I think you forget how this works. I don't have to appreciate shit! You're not doing me any favors. This is a business transaction that you're being compensating for in multiple ways. So you're going to continue to do your job and not ever speak to me like that again."

As Manny is talking, Adrian Sr. returns with a Cognac bottle, empty cups, aluminum foil, and steaks. Manny looks at his father, smiling while telling the man, "Your money will be under your car's driver seat. Hey, Papi, you need anything before I leave?"

"Leaving already Mijo?" Manny's father asked.

"Yeah, me and Jalon gonna eat real quick and then head to the movies with Blue. It starts in like forty minutes."

"Okay, Mijo." Adrian Sr. hugs and kisses his son, "Don't buy a bunch of candy for Junior this time." Manny laughs as he makes his way inside, "It's not funny! Last time he didn't go to sleep till three in the morning."

"Don't worry, Papi Blue gonna be knocked out when we get back."

"Three Hours Later" (JULY 3RD 1997)

Manny's Cadillac sits idle in a Bo Jangles Chicken parking lot. Jalon is drinking his root beer as Manny eats his chicken sandwich and talks about his little brother, who is currently sleeping in the back seat. "Look at this boy. He was crying, fainted this time, holding his breath,

Adrian, you did all that just to eat a few fries and fall asleep with one of em your mouth." Juice looks back at Adrian, smiling as the four-year-old snores. "He was funny as shit in the movies." Both men begin to laugh, but out of nowhere, Manny instantly stops. The positive energy that once filled the car is now dark and ominous. Manny quickly presses in the radio-dial, and his hazard light, his stash compartment that is located in the stock radio head unit opens up, but before Manny could reach for his gun. Shots ring out! The first two shots hit the left headlight and the hood of the car. Juice Instantly jumped to shield Adrian Jr, seated in the center of the back seat. The aslant was able to let off the seven more shots. Manny couldn't reach for his gun, he was shot three times. One bullet went into the right side of his neck, another went in his left lung, and the other hit the right side of his lower abdomen. Juice was attempting to shield Adrian and was shot in his right leg and shoulder.

Police cars filled the Bo Jangles parking lot along with other emergency vehicles. People are gathered outside of the yellow tape that now surrounds the scene. Two Prince Georges County Maryland police officers were the first to the scene Juice was taken to George Washington hospital. While Manny was declared dead on the scene, the officer that found Adrian Jr. initially thought he had been shot, Adrian was covered in Jalon's blood. The officers arrived before the ambulances. Manny's lifeless body could still be seen by Adrian, who was in complete shock. Juice managed to exit the car, but he passed out before he could remove Adrian. The graphic scene was burned into the eyes of the innocent child. The officer struggled to remove Adrian from the car as he fought and screamed hysterically. "Manny, get up! Wake up, Manny, wake up now!"

CHAPTER II: WELCOME HOME LUKE PT. 1

"I got my mind up but got my head down, on the crossroads asking where I head now. The thoughts of happiness know that that's a rare sound. I had a child in me once, but he's dead now!"

-Two8G

W ater runs in the guest bathroom sink as Adrian stares at himself in the mirror. His hazel eyes are bloodshot red. Adrian puts both hands together, rubbing water over his cleaned shaven face. He grabs a few paper towels off the roll, drying his face and hands before cutting the sink off and the bathroom light closing the door behind him.

After hearing about what happen to Manny that night after the movies you probably think I'm all kinds of fucked up in the head! Well I am fucked up! That night is only an ingredient, to the walking contradiction, convoluted, indecisive, insecure, impulsive being that makes up Adrian Luis Castro Jr. But we don't have time for all that shit! I have to pick up Luke from the airport and finish pregaming for this party with my boy Caden. The hallway was painted brick red. I ran my knuckles across the wall as I entered the living room, my black Nike ankle socks sunk into the cream colored carpet with every step. Caden just finished rolling up a Dutch Master Cigar with Marijuana. He sat on the couch singing along with a MTV classic music video. The Foo Fighters- *Learn to Fly* played on the flat screen T.V. as I sat on the couch next to Caden singing along with him. Caden has been one of my best friends since the ninth grade. Luke went to a different high school so I spent a lot of time hanging with Caden. We hit it off at a baseball camp our freshman year and have been tight ever since. I ended up attending The University of Maryland while Caden attended Towson University. We still managed to hang out and party on the regular. I had so many of my first experiences with Caden mostly drug related but never the less Caden and I have a plethora of stories and good times in our history. Caden is about to move to Minneapolis next month for a new job. We kind of had a falling off a couple years ago, but we wouldn't let what happen between us be the end to our friendship. Caden rubs his hand through his dirty blond hair after passing me the blunt. I was in a mental health rehab facility six months ago and maintained my sobriety for about two months. Now I'm all the way back to where I was before. Bombay Gin is in my system along with a triple stack E-pill! I think it was a blue dolphin. This is the third time we've smoked in the two hours since I've been here. I think Caden might have sprinkled some molly powder that he had leftover into this blunt we're smoking now! He asks me am I going to finally have sex with Jackie Flowers tonight. Jackie and I have had a will they, won't they thing going on since we were in high school! It's was always something preventing us from hooking up. Either she had a boyfriend or I had a girlfriend, and I have never cheated on a girlfriend in my life. Even though I've been cheated on several times. I don't know why I always choose girls who take advantage of me and treat me like shit, but I wasn't looking for a relationship with Jackie. I was just trying to do something that we both have been wanting to do for years! Plus I haven't had sex in like four months, so at the party she's throwing for her little brother tonight I'm gonna try to seal the deal. Little does Caden know but I've been texting back and forth with Jackie all day. I won't tell him though it's me and Jackie's business. I just played it off nonchalant like I just wanted to party and had no ulterior motives. Off course Caden didn't buy that. He got up from couch laughing as he called bullshit, he walked into the kitchen grabbing us a couple beers out the refrigerator. He came back handing me a cold one, I ashed the blunt into a red solo cup that sat next to an empty bottle of orange juice, and an empty bottle of Bombay Gin. I drank another beer and continued to watch MTV classic videos with Caden until he reminded me that I had to pick up Luke. Shit I almost completely forgot about him! I did our patented goodbye handshake before I left Caden's Northern Virginia apartment to pick up Luke from Dulles International Airport. The sky looked amazing as I drove on the 495 interstate. It was orange and purple as the summer sun begin to set. The late June humidity began to damper down as I cruised in my 2016 Ford Fusion. The car still kind of had a new car smell buried underneath the Newport Cigarette smoke. I was bumping some Mixtape Weezy as I approached the airport arrivals looking for Luke's airline, he texted me about fourteen-minutes ago that he was ready, so he should be outside. Now I've known Luke for twenty years, and I have never seen him smoke a cigarette, but there he was puffing a cancer stick as he spoke with a middle aged woman. I never saw him with that much facial hair either, he looked like he lost weight since the last time I seen him, but his clothes was still fresh though. Luke had on some weird shoes, black cargo shorts, and a shirt on called "Givenchy" that I had never heard of before. It looked clean though.

The same goes for his shoes. You could tell he had been getting plenty of that California sunshine because he was a few shades darker, but I don't know. Something seemed different about him! I hopped out the car and gave Luke a gigantic hug. I really missed this dude even though when he left our friendship was on bad terms. The worst part was he wasn't there for me when I really needed him. I was so happy to see him again though. Luke was like a twin brother to me, and I was glad to have him back around. We put his bags in the trunk and then proceeded to ride towards the interstate. Luke notices the smell of chicken and French fries as we drive. I stopped by a carry-out spot that was close to Caden's apartment and grabbed Luke some chicken, French fries, and mumbo sauce before I picked him up. I knew he hadn't had any since he moved to Cali. He thanked me as I finally got him to actually sound happy. I know he wants to smoke after that six hour flight. I just gotta find what the hell I did with that blunt I rolled. Fuck! I must have dropped that bitch when I hopped out the car at the airport to give him a hug. No biggie I needed to get some more bud anyway. Now I just have to convince Luke to go this party, and right about now it's probably fifty-fifty. I could just drop him off at the crib because he's gonna be living with me anyhow, but I really wanna hang out with him tonight. Luke is head strong I'm probably the only one who can slightly manipulate him. I really hate to do this but I really wanna go this party. I used him not being there for me when I went through my situation to guilt trip him into going to the party. I know that actually wasn't the reason he said "yes." Luke seems like he has a lot on his mind! Deep down inside he probably wants an escape. That's why he said yes. That's definitely why he came back! Luke told me how Juice was the one who helped him get back home with money to his name. I couldn't help but tell Luke how much Juice had been getting on my nerves since I got out of the hospital. Jalon means well but he comes at me with the wrong approach. I drove to my house so Luke could drop his bags off and shower up. That man has definitely been wasting money on clothes. I give it to him though he's clean! Luke takes forever to get ready so after like ninety minutes of waiting around we ride over to grab some bud from this guy I met a couple of months ago. I didn't think son stayed in a trailer park! I always would meet him somewhere like a gas station, or a fast food joint. Now that E-pill I took before I got Luke has already kicked in, and I was not on the same level as him. When I cut the car off Luke said, "Man! Adrian what the fuck? Where the fuck we at?" I know I probably had a goofy smug expression on my face when I told him, "This Pico's house!" He glared at me, "Adrian this ain't no fucking house!" I clutched the back of my neck with my left hand and bust out laughing! I made it worse by speaking in a Cali accent.

"Well homie! A home that is mobile! A home with an engine! Stop acting like a mark ass buster!" He didn't find that shit funny at all! It took some convincing to even get him out of the car. When we got to the door I was trying my best to stop snickering. My high ass probably knocked hard as shit, Pico slung the door open. "Why the fuck you knocking so hard!" Pico saw that it was me and instantly went from aggressive to friendly. It was always weird that Pico acted like we were the best of friends but I've only known him for like two months. The way he greeted Luke I thought I was going to have to defuse something, but Pico ended up laughing and telling us to come in with his raspy voice that sounded like he smoked twenty Black & Mild cigars a day. Pico was a light skin dude with freckles, red and brown hair and cornrows that look like they've been in for eight months. I'm 5'10 so he's probably about 5'5. He's wearing gray sweatpants and a stained white tank top. He probably needs to wear a bigger size because his pudgy stomach was sticking out. Pico is in his late thirties I think, but he could easily pass for forty-seven. The inside of the trailer looked just as shitty as the outside. I was rolling hard as fuck off of that pill, and I was in a really goofy immature mood for some reason. I sensed how pissed Luke was as we made our way through the dirty trailer. The best way to describe the smell would be garbage, baby powder, shit, and cigarettes. The living room set looked like it was straight out of the eighties. I'm OCD as shit when it comes to my house being clean, so I know I had to be high to be able sit down on the dirty ass mustard colored couch. Pico walked over to his CD player that probably was hooked up to his old ass Jamaican dancehall speakers. The flat screen eight-teen inch TV and the Xbox were the only modern technology that I saw in the living room. Luke was smoking a blunt that Pico passed him so I couldn't tell how mad he was. Honestly I was feeling too good to care! I knew once we got to the party he would mellow out around all of those women. We just had to get there first! And Luke might be about five minutes away from telling me to drop him back off. Pico must have put an eighties mix in because a New Edition song came on. I got up and started dancing as Pico asked me. "Boy what you know about this?" Pico did the "Kid and Play" dance with me, as we were laughing Luke spoke up in a serious tone, "Yo Adrian! Grab that so we can bounce!" Pico gave me the what's up with your man's look before he walked to the backroom to retrieve the quarter ounce of weed. Here we go! I knew it! As soon as Pico left the room I knew it was coming! Blah Blah Blah! "Adrian you're always doing dumb shit! Putting yourself in dumb situations! I'm complaining even though I'm going to still get high with you!" Luke blabbered as the front door burst opened like the person was trying to make a grand entrance. An overweight woman entered like she was expecting to find someone. It felt like the trailer dipped as she walked up the three steps at the door and then through the trailer. She threw the cloth grocery bag she was carrying down to the brown carpet. It's no telling if that's the actually color that the carpet is supposed to be. The lady gave me and Luke a dismissive look before asking, "Where's Pico at?"

"Oh how you doing miss. He's in the back room." She waddled to the room brushing off my polite response to her attitude. I'm going to try my best to describe her without being mean, but I can't! Like it's no reason you should be that fat! She can't be any older than thirty. You could see pimples on her double decker neck. I know she probably had them all over her back. Nasty! I'm not gonna lie. I would watch her and Pico have sex for the shear entertainment value. An obese white woman and a short, fat, light-skin ginger going at it. Even the thought is making me laugh. Luke asked for keys to my car as the woman and Pico begin to argue in the back room. "Pico I told you about having all kinds of people in my house!" She yelled. "Bitch shut up this my house!" I looked over at Luke giggling. "This ain't no damn house!" Luke laughed for a second and then went right back to asking for my car keys. I wouldn't give him the keys though. I told him he was so irritated he might leave me! He went to the car as the couple argued on and I sat on the couch laughing. The car door was open so he'd be cool. This shit was starting to get really entertaining. From what the fat woman is screaming. Apparently she a found text messages between

Pico and the trailer park hoe. It was all fun in games until I heard Pico shout. "Bitch keep slapping me and watch what happen!" That's when the domestic dispute evolved into domestic violence. They started to fight like shit in the backroom! You could barely here the music it was Alphaville – "Forever Young" playing at that point. Pico walked out of the room I could tell the big girl held her own. She had to be taller than him by six inches and outweighed him by a hundred plus pounds. Pico limped over to the couch sitting down next to me. He handed me the weed and just started talking like he didn't have a bloody lip, scratches on his face, and a torn tank top. I handed him the money shook his hand, and told him I was out. The quarter ounce of weed cost seventy bucks, and I gave Pico a hundred dollar bill, so he had to go to the back room to get my change. Big girl was talking to herself the whole time she was in the room. Pico told her to "shut the fuck up," as he got up from the couch. Now I hate to say Luke was right, but he was right! I should have just left earlier. Plus I just remembered that I had a couple of grams in the center console of my car that Caden gave to me. We could have just smoked that and got weed at the party. Well that's what I should have done. Because shortly after Pico went back to get my change. I heard a loud screeching scream, followed by what was definitely a shotgun! Pico sprinted out of the room tears running down his face yelling stop! I was out of the trailer as soon as Pico ran out of that room. Another shot rang out as I leaped into the driver side car door! Luke had already opened it up for me. I locked and slammed the car door shut as I scrambled to get my keys out of my front pocket. I dropped the keys on the floor like I was a white woman in a scary movie. Luke is shouting come on let's go! I finally got the keys in the ignition. At that point Pico ran to the back car door trying to get inside but it was locked. I sped off as Pico screamed let me in, he even ran after the car. I could see the fat woman in my rearview mirror standing at the front door of the trailer cocking back a shotgun, and then shooting into the sky as Pico ran for his life. When me and Luke first got to the trailer we were listening to a 50 Cent song titled "I'm supposed to die tonight!" The song continued playing as we drove away from the trailer park making our way towards the Maryland "Two-Ten Highway". I cut the music off because it didn't seem appropriate under the current circumstances. We rode in silence for about five minutes before Luke said, "Blue I haven't been back home

22

for four hours. And I'm already getting shot at!" Why did I have to say, "Well technically she wasn't shooting at you. She was shooting at Pico!" Luke banged on the dash board!

"I haven't been back for four fucking hours! And I'm already getting fucking shot at!" I allowed Luke to vent and berate me for a while before I realized, "Oh shit!"

"Oh shit what Blue? What is it now?" Luke asked with his hands in the air.

"Luke you're gonna be pissed when I tell you this!" I said trying not to laugh.

"How in the fuck can I get more pissed than I already am?" He asked.

I whipped the sides of my mouth and told Luke. "Well! I think I dropped the bud outside of Pico's trailer when I was running!" Luke looked at me like I was the dumbest man on the plant, "BLUE WHAT THE!"

CHAPTER III: GOOD BYE LUKE/ GOOD LUCK LOOT

"A man without loyalty is a man who travels solo upstream in a four-oared rowboat."

-Misfit Z

Y ou ever love someone but wanna smack the shit out of them when you have to look at their faces. Right about now, I want to smack the shit out of Luke! He is the smartest dumbest nigga I know! This idiot just graduated from college, and instead of using connections he has to get a job in his field, he's moving to California with his girlfriend Paige and is going to sell weed to support himself and start a clothing company as a legitimate front. Luke had the nerve to tell me that jobs will always be there, but certain opportunities won't. He's always been a little hard-headed ass nigga, both him and Adrian. Neither one of them listens to me, but when something happens to one of them, everybody is looking at me like Terence, why do you let them do it, or Terence, why didn't tell me something? Even to this day! Like I've been away overseas for damn near four years, my mother asked me why Luke is moving to California? You should talk to him! Like this nigga's a grown-ass man now! Let him fuck up his life if that's what he wants to do. I hear Adrian's high ass coming outside right now! Blue needs to slow the fuck down! "What are you all doing, T.T.?"

"What I tell you about that T.T. shit Blue! You're going to make me punch you in your chest and make your ass go flying back through your kitchen door. What is this an eighties action movie?" Adrian said only half joking.

"Hey, Luke, Terence thinks the Marines gave him superpowers," Adrian condescendingly responded.

"Nah, Blue, the Marines ain't give me superpowers! But if you call me T.T. again and Imma show you what I learned!" Adrian approaches the patio table staged in the center of the concert patio. Terence and Luke are horizontally seated across from each other, and a mosquito candle burns in the center, a new October moon reflects off the corner of the patio table's glass surface. Luke passes Adrian a blunt that he just lit as he sits down at the table. "Well, stop calling me Blue, Terence!"

"Adrian, we're always going to call you Blue!" Luke said.

Adrian turned, "Shut up Luke!"

"Adrian, since when did you start caring about us calling you Blue?" Terrence asked.

"I don't. That was just my excuse for calling you T.T. OUCH BITCH WHAT THE FUCK!" Adrian yelled after Terence jabbed him in the arm.

"I told you! That shit hurt, didn't it?" Adrian rubbed his arm laughing.

"Hell yeah, I can't feel the lower half of my left arm!" Adrian passes Luke the blunt with his limp arm as the three friends laugh together. "Y'all ready to crack this Hennessy Privilege?" Terence asks as he gets up from the patio table walking inside the house. Luke and Adrian remain out back, smoking under the orange moon. The mild early October temperatures begin to drop as the eleven-pm hour approaches. "So Luke, you going to tell me the real reason you're moving?"

"Adrian, let's not do this right now! We had this conversation for three hours on Thursday," Luke replied.

"Yeah, and I still think you're not telling me the whole story!" Adrian uses his fingers to make air quotations, "You're supposed to be brother. What the fuck is going on!"

Luke sighed as he answered, "What's going on is I'm getting pounds of high-grade weed for the low, and I'm selling them for three to six stacks."

Adrian looks at Luke in eye, "Yeah, but you were doing that for almost the past year, all while living in Maryland. You have all your connections out here besides your Cali connect, of course. Floyd and Hunter have been helping you move the shit. Even though you know, I don't fuck around. I plugged you with plenty of clientele. And I meant to ask you this. What was the point of busting your ass to get through these last four years?" Luke's demeanor becomes more agitated. He begins to roll another blunt as he passes Adrian, the one that continues to burn. "Like bruh. I know how hard it was for you to be broke at Morgan State, but we graduated now! You got your Bachelor's

Degree. You don't have to sell weed anymore! Like bruh, we got a house!"

Luke raised his voice, "No mothafucka, you got a house! My daddy ain't buy me no house! Unlike you, Adrian, I have done everything for myself since I turned eighteen. All you've had is mothafuckas give you shit your whole life!"

"Luke, Juice got your ass a job after we graduated just like he did for me. The only difference is I kept mines, and I'll be making six-figures in the next two years. On the other hand, you quit the job that Jalon got you after only two months because Paige got your head fucked up, and you want to be Nino Brown!"

"At least my girlfriend ain't leave me two weeks before graduation and have me all depressed and drugged out like a weak ass bitch," Luke responded

"You're so fucking narcissistic. You think you got some dick control "Iceberg Slim" shit going on with Paige. If you weren't selling pounds at the time, that girl would never have looked your way," Adrian muttered.

Luke looked him in the eye, "And if I didn't introduce you to your ex and give your insecure ass the motivation you needed, you would have never got her. By the way, how is Whitney doing?"

"Okay, Luke! Next time Paige cheats on you, I'm not saying shit!" Adrian promised.

"Blue, we weren't even together at the time, unlike you and your lady. You actually cried over that bitch!" Luke said while shaking his head.

Adrian pointed, "Get the fuck out of my house Luke!"

"Make me!" Luke and Adrian stand up from their chairs, looking at each other as if they are about to go to blows. Terence slides open the back door carrying four red solo cups and a fifth of Hennessy Privilege. Terence comes outside, rapping along with the "Project Pat" song that played from inside the house. Terence instantly senses the tension between Luke and Adrian and automatically jumps into his role-playing peacemaker like he's been doing for over a decade. "Hey!

Hey! Little brothers, what's going on?" Luke breaks his intense stare-down with Adrian looking over at Terence. "Nothing! Everything's cool! Adrian and I are just having a heart to heart!"

"Don't look like it to me. Matter a fact. Imma hit that blunt with y'all." Both Adrian and Luke excitingly say, "For real?" Terence laughs as he sits the cups and bottle of Hennessy Privilege on the table. "Fuck, No!"

"We were about to say!" Terence seems to have brought the tension down, as Adrian and Luke feed into the possibility of smoking with him for the first time in eight years. Terence separates the cups using the top cup filled with Ice to put cubes in the other three cups. He passes the bottle around the table so everyone can tap its bottom before he cracks it open. Terence pours three drinks giving Luke a little more in his cup. He lifts his cup to make a toast. "Now before I make, this toast I need both of y'all to do something for me! I need y'all to hug each other. Don't look at me like that! I'm dead serious!" Luke and Adrian both look at Terence like he's crazy. "But Nah off the no-bullshit for real, Blue, Luke…Look, I know I've been gone for a minute. I couldn't be at either one of you guys' graduations high school or college, but I'm here now! And I refuse to let my little brothers be beefing over some little shit."

"We aren't beefing!" Luke exclaimed.

"Luke, you can say what you want, but at the end of the day, we're family, at least that's how I look at you little niggas! When I was over in the Middle East doing my tours," Terence takes a big sip out of his cup. "When I was over in the desert, all I had were my brothers in arms. If it weren't for the Marines, I wouldn't have messed with most of them dudes. But the only thing you have in the trenches is your brothers. And whether you see it or not! We're in the trenches! You might be able to pass for European Adrian, but you're not!"

"Fuck you, T.T." Terence hits Adrian with a quick jab to the arm! "Ouch Bitch!"

"But in all seriousness, you all are my brothers, and we're at war living in this new Babylon! United we stand, divided we fall!"

"Is that your toast?"

"I know, right; Blue is he toasting or being pastor T!"

Terence smiles as he raises his cup to make his toast! "Luke, none of your brothers, agree with your move, but we all wish you luck! Goodbye Luke! Good luck, Loot! Everyone has their solo cups of Privilege raised as the three-man repeat. "Goodbye, Luke! Good luck, Loot!" The three-man all toast and drink while they begin to reminisce about past events. Caden makes his way outside. "Hey, what up, Caden? I was wondering when you were coming out. Are you trying to hit this blunt with us?"

"Nah, Luke, I'm cool. I have to take a piss test next week for this new job," Caden shook his head.

"Oh yeah, that's right. You did say that!" Luke recalled.

"I will take some of that Henny!" Caden said eyeing the bottle.

"Well, bring your ass over here then." Caden approaches the table and pours a drink into the cup he was already carrying. "You want some Ice Caden. Indeed I do, Terence. I might not be able to smoke, but I got some shrooms if you guys are down"

"Hell Nah! I'm cool; I'll leave that for you three," Terence said quickly.

"What about you, Luke?" Caden asked.

"Nope, I'm good I'll pass." Luke answered.

"Adrian, are you passing too?" Adrian remains quiet and begins to smile.

"Okay, I know that look. Boy, I swear y'all some fucking hippies." I said shaking my head.

"Don't hate T.T.!" Luke bust out laughing as Terence gets up from his chair and puts Adrian in a headlock. The four-man all joke around before Luke lifts his cup and says. "Once again, Caden, I want to give my condolences to your mother. She was a good woman." Caden takes a big gulp out of his cup, and he then hugs and then emotionally thanks everyone for being supportive. Caden takes a moment to gather himself before he returns to his happy energy, telling Adrian. "Oh yeah, Adrian, Sadie said come play the piano before she and Benny roll out!"

"You see how quick he moved to play the piano for Sadie but wouldn't play shit for us when we asked him."

"Fuck you whores! I'll play a couple of songs for my big sister, but not for you two bitches!" Adrian defended.

"But we love you, Blue!" Luke laughed.

"Fuck you, Luke, or I guess it's back to Loot since you're 'Frank Lucas' now!" Terence sarcastically instigates! "Shots fired!" Adrian passes the fresh blunt back to Luke and walks in the house, along with Caden. "Yeah, whatever bitch!" Luke and Terence toast cups again, looking eye to eye. "Yo, Loot, what the fuck was just about to happen?"

"Ain't nothing T! As you said, we're brothers! And by the way, I've meant to ask you this. Why did you buy Adrian a gun?"

"Because he has a clean record and has every right to exercise his second amendment privileges. He lives out here by himself. Anybody can run-up in this crib. You're supposed to be so astute, Mr. Political Science major, but you act like we don't have the family connections we do."

Flush green grass surrounds the front yard. Bright colored flowers surround the orange plastic mailbox. The freshly paved driveway has four cars parked. Luke's Plum 1999 Impala with twenty-two-inch rims sits next to Adrian's maroon 2000 Mazda. Parked behind Adrian is Caden's 2004 white Nissan Altima. Luke's friend, Curtis's Green Maserati, is parked securely behind his Impala. Curtis is a true official blue-blood WASP. One may ask how someone like Luke could be associated with someone like Curtis. The two men have only known each other for eight months and have only hung out a handful of times. That all changed after a recent event. The two men are somewhat bonded together for better or worse! Parked in front of the mailbox is a gray pick-up truck driven by Juice, and a 2009 black Honda Accord driven by Hunter sits parked behind Juice's truck. The house's exterior has oxford blue vinyl siding, and birchwood architectural shingles line the three-bedroom, single-story house roof. Juice stands out front on his cellphone, smiling as he walks towards the black pick-up truck he's driving. "Put him on the phone. I want to talk to him! Hanna, I know he's asleep, wake him up. I want to hear my son's baby gibberish! Plus, he needs to hear his daddy's voice as much as possible!" Inside the house, Sadie smiles as Benny holds her listening to Adrian play his black oak grand piano. His ability to play makes up for his bad singing. Caden sits on the sofa watching Adrian play. Floyd and Hunter are in the dining room, discussing Luke and his sudden move to California. That took both of them by surprise. Terence and Luke remain out back, finishing up a conversation as the men speak to one another, Luke's friend Curtis walks outside. "Remember, at the end of the day, nobody has your back like Blue does!" Terence gets up from the table and begins to walk in the house. "Hey man, what's your name again?"

"Oh, it's Curtis!"

"Oh yeah, that's right, Curtis!" Terence and Curtis chit chat for a second before Terence goes inside, and Curtis sits down at the patio table across from Luke. The mosquito candle still burns in the center of the table. The bottle of Hennessy Privilege is in front of Luke. He pours more Hennessy into his cup as he offers Curtis a drink. Curtis goes back into the house he comes out about a minute later, sitting back down across from Luke, putting a cup and a tray of Ice on the table. Luke slides him the bottle of Henny. "Hey, Luke, your boy Adrian is fucking great on the piano dude! That Elton John cover he just did, was pretty impressive. Listen to him inside. He's killing in there right now. How long has he been playing?"

Luke thought before answering, "Since we were five or six, I think."

"Is he doing anything with it besides playing in his living-room?"

"Nah, he barely even plays for me when I ask. He's only doing it because my sister asked him to do it."

"Well, he's gifted. He should be utilizing it somehow." Curtis lights an American Spirit cigarette, Luke lights up a blunt out of the ashtray. "I appreciate you having me over, though, bro. Your families cool. You're lucky to have people that care about you in your life. That's why I'm perplexed as to why you're moving to California all of a sudden. Last time we spoke when you were up at the cabin, You were adamant about letting your girl Paige live in California while you stayed here, so I don't see why you're leaving? Not to be haughty, but you don't understand how lucky you are to know me! Luke, I authentically like you. In my life, people such as yourself are rare, and from being here tonight, I see you have a lot of people in your life that are authentic, which is the complete polar opposite of my life. That's why I can't wrap my head around why you're leaving?" Luke has his eyes on the fall sky. He downs the remainder of the drink in his cup. "Like I know you're not leaving because of your girlfriend! Let's stop pussyfooting around the truth and verbalize the real reason that you're leaving!" The two men sit in silence for almost ninety seconds. Luke silently stares and blows smoke in Curtis's direction. "Okay, then Luke, since you won't say it, I'll say it for you. You're spooked about what happened! That's why you're leaving. Just say it!" Luke passes the blunt to Curtis but remains silent. Curtis calms his tone and says. "Maybe letting you handle it was my fault. All you people know how to do is talk a good game!" Luke is no longer playing passive-aggressive; he stares Curtis in the eyes.

"What the fuck you say to me?" Luke asks staring Curtis down.

Curtis claps his hand with a Machiavellian smile on his face! "That's what I'm talking about just a little spark to get you out your shell. Now Luke, should I be concerned?" Smirking at Curtis, Luke gets up from the table. "No, Curt. You have nothing to worry about! And I am leaving because of Paige. I'm afraid I'll lose her if I let her go!" Curtis tries to hold in his laughter but can't contain it.

"Bro, that was so gay that you have to be telling the truth!" Curtis snobbishly mocks Luke. "I'm afraid I'll lose her if I let her go! Wow! I'm just playing, dude, let's go inside!" As Curtis and Luke begin to go inside, Curtis stops Luke to ask him? "Is your brother the one who you called for help?"

"Who Benny?"

"Nah, the other one! The only one who didn't speak to me and only stayed for a little while!" Curtis snaps his fingers, trying to recall the name. "Jay him! Is he the one that helped us!" Without blinking or flinching, Luke convincingly says, "No!"

"END OF THE NIGHT"

Music plays again through the Bluetooth speaker, Benny and Sadie caught a cab home. Juice left after only staying for thirty-minutes, Curtis left not too long after talking to Luke, and Hunter left in his baby mother's car with Floyd ten minutes ago. Adrian, Caden, Luke, and Terence are in the living room drinking out of another bottle of Hennessy Privilege everyone except for Terence has an individual blunt. The Ikea coffee table sits a bowl of nacho cheese, a plate of chips beside a pizza box. The conversations they were having were fun and light-hearted until Caden inadvertently mentioned Paige. Terence tried to change the topic once Paige came up, but Adrian took the opportunity presented and went right in on Paige. Luke tried to keep calm with Adrian and his insults towards his girlfriend, but once Terence started laughing, Luke got in his feeling and decided to take his shots at Adrian. Luke talked about Adrian's inability to maintain a woman; he mocked Adrian for being suicidal after his girlfriend dumped him five months ago!

Luke even joked about Adrian possibly being molested as a kid. That's when it became no longer words and evolved into a physical altercation. Luke and Adrian were sitting on separate couches, but they were close enough for Adrian to lunge at Luke. Initially, Luke laughed at Adrian's drunken attempt to assault him. That is until he landed a punch to his left ear. Terence tried to intervene, but by that point, it was too late. Luke landed a body-shot and then threw Adrian behind the couch. Terence dashed over to Luke, grabbing him in frustration, Adrian rose from behind the sofa, hurling an Adidas flip-flop at Luke's nose. Caden attempted to coral Adrian and accidentally caught an elbow to his eye in the process.

Meanwhile, after being pinged in the nose by Adrian's flip-flop, Luke is livid and begins to rush Adrian screaming. "BLUE IMMA FUCKING KILL YOU!" Terence grabbed at Luke and inadvertently pushed him forward, making him tumble towards the coffee table. Luke crashed into the table onto the floor, spilling nacho cheese, pizza, and soda on his hair, face, and black and gray "Sobioto" shirt. Everyone in the room anticipated Luke getting up off the floor and attacking Adrian, but instead, he picked himself up off the ground and stared at Adrian for a minute straight. Luke left out of the house as the room sat silently with nothing but music from the Bluetooth speaker playing until Terence said. "Hold up! That nigga's my ride." Terence darts out the door, chasing after Luke, only to return moments later. Terence closes the front behind him, shaking his head, looking at Adrian, telling him.

"Blue, you're a fucking idiot. You can stay here, or I can drop you off where you need to go." Bitch I don't want to stay here, and I don't want you dropping me off nowhere. Caden!" Caden stands in the corner of the room, holding a bag of frozen broccoli to his left eye as he answers back. "Yeah, what's up dude!"

"Can you drop me off in Oxon Hill?" Terence asks.

"Yeah, I got you, dude."

"Yo, Castro, I'll be back after I drop Terence off." Adrian doesn't answer back, continuing to clean the living room as Terence and Caden exit the house. Luke left for California three days later; he went eight months without speaking to Adrian. By that point, Luke lived in a luxury beachside apartment with Paige and had a safe inside of his closet containing six-figures.

CHAPTER IV: CALIFORNIA DREAMING

"Ambition from an unrighteous man will lead him, and those he travels with on a bloody road where the survivors will stay lost in the wilderness."

-Unknown

FEBRUARY 20TH 2016

L uke gets a three-AM phone call from Hunter that wakes him up out of a drunken stupor. Floyd was gun downed in front of his mother's house earlier that evening. The shooter pulled up in a white minivan that was driven by another masked individual. Nine-inch bullets ripped apart Floyd's flesh. Simultaneously, bullets riddled his car along with his mother's Bowie Maryland home. Floyd had just picked up thirty pounds for Luke that afternoon. In the news that Hunter received, he heard nothing about the pounds of Marijuana. The police had been watching Floyd for a few weeks based on the informant's information. The Prince Georges County Maryland Police would rule Floyd's murder a drug-related robbery-homicide.

Suspects were never apprehended. One eye witness account described the masked shooter as a short black male with purple-tipped dreadlocks. Luke hung up the phone and broke down, crying like he never imagined he could. Paige left him two weeks ago, and he has shed his fair share of tears but nothing like this. It takes Luke forty-minuets to call Hunter back. They would spend over an hour on the phone trying to make sense out of the confusion. The only thing both men thought it could be was that it was a robbery. Hunter was just beaten up and robbed for ten pounds two weeks earlier. A long pause went on in between the last robbery theory before Hunter stolidly says. "Maybe it was over a bitch! Luke sits in confusion for a moment. "Over a bitch, which one?" Hunter takes a long pause before replying, "Fresh said he beat up some little nigga with purple dreadlocks and a scar on his chin over some bitch a couple of weeks ago! I had forgotten all about that shit because it was a few days after I got stuck up for those pounds." Luke sits on the side of his bed, drinking Champagne and smoking a cigarette as Hunter goes on. "Fresh did say the nigga with the purple dreads man's who was with him when they fought lived in his mother's neighborhood." A puzzled Luke asks. "How the fuck did they know about the P's?" Hunter became distracted by a large number of alert notifications on his phone. "My

36

Facebook is blowing up right now!" Luke is an extremely agitated state and lashes out. "Hunter, Fuck your Facebook! This why your dumb ass got robbed for my ten pounds. Because you don't, fucking pay attention! I told you to get rid of your Facebook over a fucking year ago! I got rid of all my social media the day I left for Cali!" Luke is screaming at the top of his lungs, and has broken his flat-screen T.V. from heaving a remote control at it! "Y'all never listened! Neither one of you niggas! EVER FUCKING LISTEN!"

 Two minutes of complete silence go by before Hunter says. "I have to drop Roxy and Tommy off at the doctor's office in an hour. I'll call you after twelve 'o clock east coast time. Aye Loot, before I get off this phone, do remember that conversation me, you and Fresh had when we were at Adrian's house that weekend before you moved to California?

WHAT'S THE PLAN LOOT? (OCTOBER 4TH 2014)

Floyd, Luke, and Hunter sit at the patio table in Adrian's back yard a mosquito candle still burns; most of the wax has melted. The bottle of Hennessy Privilege that Terence opened with Adrian and Luke is almost empty. Floyd removes his Gucci hat, placing it in front of him on top of the table, his dreadlocks rest on his Gucci shirt that coordinates with his shorts, shoes, and watch. Floyd sarcastically asks Luke. "So how much longer till you get married to Paige?" Hunter co-signs. "That's a good question, Fresh I was thinking the same thing. Hunter, you see how he switched up the subject to them strippers that were over here Thursday. He thought we forgot about that whole conversation we were having." Luke gives both Floyd and Hunter the middle finger. First off, y'all are fucking retarded if you think me and Paige are getting married anytime soon, and Fresh, Hunter, is the one who changed the subject to the strippers." Hunter lights up a blunt that rested behind his left ear." "I mean, that shit was wild. I can't believe what Adrian's boy did!"

"What did he do, I forgot?" Floyd responds

"Oh yeah, Fresh, that happen before you got here that night. What was Adrian's man's name again, Luke?"

"It's Liam! Okay, I remember him that was that chubby white boy, right?" Luke

"Yeah him," Luke pours the remainder of the bottle of Hennessy Privilege in everyone's cup before Hunter returns to his story. "So the short light skin chick that danced before you showed up did this trick with a water bottle." Hunter burst out in laughter, and Luke does as well, Floyd smiles sitting in anticipation for the punch line. This bitch did her trick where she puts a bottle of water in her pussy." Floyd begins to laugh as Hunter passes him the blunt. "Oh shit, I know where this is going." Hunter rubs face that is red from laughter!" The bitch started squirting water out of her coochie, and the nigga Liam stuck his head under that bitch like he was in the shower." The table erupts in even more laughter. "So look mo the water got mainly in his hair, and this nigga was letting the water drops hit his tongue, and he rubbed it into his hair and face!" laughter surrounds the table for the next ten minutes as they talk more about the strippers from two nights ago. Luke eventually brings the subject back to business. "So Fresh, we're going to go to Ms. V's house on Monday, and I'm going to introduce y'all, and after that, I'll let you know when you're picking up from her spot. Hunter, all you have to do is keep networking and tone it down. You over there smirking, but I'm dead ass serious."

"Luke, how you gonna tell me to tone down it with Cartier watch on your wrist."

"First of all, Hunter, I got this shit for a deal. Secondly, that's beside the point. We all need to start moving differently! I'm erasing all my social media, and y'all should be too. Mothafuckas don't need to know how we are moving in any way, shape, or form. Once this weight starts going up, that hate will too." Luke ashes the blunt Floyd just passed him. He looks Floyd directly in the eyes. "Fresh, you know I'm not trying to tell you what to do on some boss type shit, but you can't be out here fighting and beefing with niggas over little shit. It's going to be times when you are going to have fifty pounds and on you. We got too much money on the line for the small potatoes!"

"The rains only starting" (March 12th, 2016)

The Southern California night club is festive as people stand outside waiting to get in. It's been damp every weekend for almost a month, which was quite out of the ordinary for a usually dry Southern California. People were excited to have a rain-free Saturday night. Bottle service girls walk to a V.I.P. table that Luke is seated at with two other men. Kanye West – "Fade" radiates through the multi-million dollar sound system. Seated to Luke's right was Derek Roland, AKA D-Ro. Luke met D-Ro within his first month living in California. While Paige stayed with a high school friend in the Bay Area, Luke looked for a place in SoCal.

Jalon has connections of all kinds, all around the country, and he convinced one of the women he deals with, a thirty-year-old paralegal from Compton, California to allow his little brother in law stay with her until he could find a place to live for him and his girlfriend. One day Luke was getting something to eat at Tam's Burgers in Compton. While Luke was pulling out of the parking lot, a car crashed into his car. Luke left his Plum Impala with the twenty-two-inch rims at his parent's house back in Maryland, and he just purchased a silver 1998 used Toyota Corolla a few days earlier. Luke had insured the car and was more than ready to report the accident. He was prepared to make an insurance claim, but D-Ro convinced a reluctant Luke to follow him back to his home, which was a little more than ten minutes away. Luke has a gift in judging people's character. He's almost like a human lie detector. He inherited this trait from his mother, Anna. Luke sensed something in the thirty-six-year-old D-Ro that made him follow D-Ro back to his house. D-Ro kind of reminded Luke of Boogie's country ass, but instead of dark skin country fat dude from Newport News, Virginia, D-Ro was light skin, buff, bald-headed, and from L.A. Luke and D-Ro went back to D-Ro's house they smoked, drink, and chop it up for seven hours. D-Ro loved the fact that Luke didn't call the police about the fender bender, and the fact that Luke was twenty-four but had an old soul. Add to the fact that Luke was from Maryland, like D-Ro's father.

D-Ro would eventually take Luke under his wing. D-Ro used some of his connections in the Midwest and throughout California to help Luke expand his operation. Within four months of living in California, Luke was moving more weight than he ever had, and he would use people he met through Paige to dabble in selling MDMA and Cocaine. Luke also started a clothing company as a front and used some of his music in the fashion industry connects that he made to move Promethazine and Prescription pills.

Seated to Luke's left was D-Ro's younger cousin Vinnie. At first, Luke and Vinnie didn't connect. Vinnie's wild, loud, outgoing personality didn't vibe well with Luke, and Luke's socially cautious nature made Vinnie weary of him, but one night Vinnie got Luke to try Cocaine for a second time. His first time was with Paige at one of her first industry fashion parties. That night that Vinnie got Luke to do coke was utterly nuts and culminated with Luke snatching Vinnie's gun and shooting at three men. Luckily for inebriated Luke, his terrible aim missed the group of men. This stupid crazy show of testosterone impressed Vinnie and made him respect Luke, who he saw as an out of town suburban transplant.

It was after midnight, D-Ro, Vinnie, and Luke have been using bottle service all night at their V.I.P. table, which gained plenty of attention from females. A few of Vinnie's associates would come and go as they sat in the V.I.P. section accompanied by six gorgeous women. Ever since Paige left Luke, he has been on a sex binge having a minimum of two different women a day. Many times in this span, he had sex with two women at the same time. Luke has been taking Cocaine almost every day. It is beginning to become costly and is only adding to his financial instability. Luke lost several packages in the air with that, and the money he previously was putting towards his wedding put him in a cash strapped position. Floyd getting killed and losing those thirty pounds was almost the preverbal nail in his coffin. However, Luke made both D-Ro and Vinnie money collectively, and they just made a move that will help Luke bounce back. Both men are attempting to get Luke out of his depressed state.

Tonight is the first time that either man could get Luke outside of the house for anything besides business. That night at the club was supposed to be a celebratory night. Vinnie's left arm hung over Luke's shoulder. Vinnie's tatted left hand glowed under the club's lights, and his fifty thousand dollar blue and yellow diamond watch shined on his wrist. Vinnie speaks close to Luke's ear to be heard over the music Y.G. "My Nigga" and the loud group of drunken women in their section. "Aye, Luke, let me borrow the Jag!"

"What?"

I said, let me borrow the Jag!" Vinnie repeated.

"What?" Vinnie excuses himself, signaling for a reluctant Luke to follow him.

Inside the man's bathroom, Vinnie and Luke do bumps of Cocaine in the Accessible stall as Vinnie tries to convince Luke to let him borrow his 2015 Jaguar. "C'mon cuz I have the Jag back to you tomorrow!" Luke takes a key bump.

"Man, why can't you take that bitch in her car or an Uber?" Luke asked.

"She ain't got no car cuz," Vinnie shrugged his shoulders.

"Yeah, that figures!" Luke replied laughing.

"C'mon cuz I ain't ever fuck no Asian bitch this bad!" Luke co-signs Vinnie's high praise of the Asian woman he's trying to take home. "Yeah, that bitch is bad as shit! Eating Asian pussy, all I need is sweet and sour sauce!" Both men laugh at Luke's Kanye West reference. After additional minutes of Vinnie pleading his case, he almost begs. Luke finally frustratingly concedes, slamming his car keys in Vinnie's hand. "Here Nigga! I knew I should have made your ass drive one of your cars!" Vinnie smiles at Luke as he does a shimmy causing Luke to laugh at his dance. A man in a wheelchair bangs on the bathroom stall, yelling out! "Hey, could you guys hurry up! You're not even fucking Handicap!" Vinnie meanly yells back! "Shut the fuck up before I come out of this stall, flip that chair and have you face first in some piss." Luke dies laughing at Vinnie's cruel insult as he tries to do another bump of Cocaine.

Luke leaves out of the club with D-Ro and two women an hour and twenty-two minutes after Vinnie took the sexy Asian woman in Luke's Jaguar. D-Ro, Luke, and the two women wait at valet while the attendant retrieves D-Ro's Old School 1980's Cutlass Low Rider. While waiting for the valet, Luke overhears a group of people talking about a shooting that occurred right up the street. Luke doesn't pay it any mind and chalks it up as typical L.A. shit. The group leaves out of the parking lot playing Nipsey Hussle "Crenshaw" album as D-Ro hits his switches in his Low Rider to impress the drunken horny woman. Luke started to roll up a blunt when they left the parking lot and tried his best effort not to ruin their last cigar in his intoxicated state. Luke couldn't hear the women's conversations in the back seat over D-Ro's expensive sound system. However, there was a break in the music. Luke listened to what the women were saying in the back seat. "Oh my God, poor car!" The other woman in the backseat laughs at her friend and responds. "Meeka girl, you ain't shit! Someone got murdered in that car!"

"Bitch please, I'm from South Central! Nigga's die every day! And that's a pretty ass Jaguar! So like I said! Poor car!" Luke and D-Ro both looked at each other at the same time. A total of five shots landed, killing Vinnie, who died en route to the hospital. The Asian woman Vinnie was with survived unscathed. Vinnie accumulated his fair share of enemies, but Vinnie wasn't in his car, he was in Luke's car! So did one Vinnie's enemies spot him at the club? Or maybe one of his homies that came through the V.I.P. that night set him up. Are maybe those shots were meant for Luke? These questions would haunt Luke's mind over the next several months.

Luke sits inside of a house on the outskirts of Fresno, California. Allen tries to cheer up a depressed paranoid, Luke. Allen has been Luke's California connection for over three years. Luke met Allen in the fall of 2012, which was his junior year of college. They met while attending a bachelor party for a Marine buddy of Terence's. Luke and Allen were the only non-service men in attendance for the weekend celebration. Everyone who was there was friendly to Luke except for Allen. When Luke introduced himself, Allen didn't even respond. It didn't bother Luke, though. It was his first time in Las Vegas, and he hadn't seen Terence in a while. Some random amigos rudeness he thought he would never see again once the weekend was over wasn't going to bother him. On Luke's second day in Vegas, he stayed behind in the Casino while the other guys walked the Las Vegas strip. He thought he was the only one who stayed, but while sitting at the bar, he overhears a man passionately singing along with Tears for Fears – "Everybody Wants to Rule the World" Luke felt the man's passion and started singing along with him. It turns out it was Allen! The man who had slighted him the previous day, the two would end up drinking and talking at the bar for hours. Allen and Luke became like best friends that Vegas weekend. Luke hung out with Allen more than he did Terence. It turns out that Allen was the groom's first cousin, but more importantly, Allen was a Marijuana grower who had zero East Coast connections at the time they met. Luke worked two jobs for two years, all while attending a community college. He was supposed to use the cash to get him through the school year, but he saw an opportunity and took a risk that paid off. Currently, Luke has never taken anything on consignment from Allen in their almost four-year business relationship, but now he was in a position that had too. Luke went up to Fresno to pick up ten pounds. Allen had a massive sale that he had to make in Vegas. He was going to give Luke fifty additional pounds once he returned. Luke's time with Allen in Fresno made him forget about all the accruing chaos in his life. At least for the moment! Luke would end up staying with a woman in Clovis, California, that night instead of heading back to Long Beach, where he lived. Luke didn't hear anything from Allen for a week. Becoming ever so paranoid that

Allen got arrested transporting the heavy load of Marijuana to Las Vegas. On the 8th day, Luke got a call from Allen's wife telling him that Allen had died in a car accident on the Grapevine freeway en route to Las Vegas. His wife was a grower too. She didn't have any idea through her grief when the operation would be up and running again. Even though Luke could have kept the money, he made sure Allen's wife got paid for what Allen gave on consignment and then some.

"IT'S RAINING HARD IN SOUTHERN CALIFORNIA" (JUNE 2016)

Luke drives a rental car to a warehouse where he is attending a huge party. He was reluctant to go to initially but went because it was D-Ro's birthday weekend. Luke would find out from D-Ro that he was the intended target the night Vinnie that died. Luke had been having sex with a woman who was the girlfriend of one of Vinnie's homies. D-Ro told Luke how the man came in the V.I.P. the night of the shooting to make sure he was there. The man knew that he drove a cherry red Jaguar. Luke never liked the car's color but got it because cherry red is Paige's favorite color. The man thought that Luke was in the car when he shot it up. The streets found out what happened, and it was taken care of, D-Ro thought this news would put Luke at ease, and it did. Well, that plus the MDMA and Cocaine. The party was epic that summer night. Luke had never been to a party where the female to male ratio was so high. For every one guy at the party, there were four women. It was crackin that night! Real Cali vibes. Luke had been dancing for a while when he decided to go to the bathroom. He saw D-Ro posted at the make-shift bar with a woman who had an ass like a stallion. D-Ro handed Luke a drink and smiled at his little homie. Luke stood in front of him, sweating from head to toe.

D-Ro was happy to see Luke having fun. He managed to convince his little homie to stay in California. Luke planned to move back to Maryland after Allen's death; he did a massive Cocaine line in the bathroom, downed his drink, and headed back to the bar to get another. While Luke is drinking and dancing by the bar, he notices a large group of men enter the party. Luke instantly felt a dark overcast in the once festive atmosphere. Twenty minutes after the group of men entered the warehouse. Luke continued to drink and dance with a different woman and chalked up what he felt to paranoia and too much Cocaine. Two more drinks later, a song by the D.M.V. artist Wale comes on entitled "One-eyed kitten." Luke is dancing with the woman with the ass like a stallion that stood next to D-Ro earlier.

While D-Ro was dancing with a woman who has an equally lovely figure, they all danced about twenty yards away from one of the doors, mid-way through the Wale song, everything goes silent. Luke feels like the world is moving in slow motion, and then three gunshots ring out! D-Ro pushes Luke towards the door as the shooting has caused complete pandemonium in the warehouse; music continues to play over the speakers. The D.J. caught a stray bullet, a group of people has fallen in a pile as they tried to flee the warehouse. Shots continue to ring as Luke composes himself and proceeds to rush out of the door. Luke notices the woman he was dancing with down on the ground. Luke doesn't help the woman up; instead, he just keeps running. Luke was able to spot D-Ro in the massive crowd of fleeing people. Luke is running full speed towards D-Ro. He notices a man in dark clothing approaching D-Ro extending his arm. The man shot D-Ro in the head in the middle of the massive fleeing crowd of people, causing even more chaos. Luke escapes to his rental car. They must have sent the entire police force; Luke had never seen many cops at once. He was able to flee the scene before the police prevented people from leaving. D-Ro's funeral was a couple of weeks after that chaotic June night. Luke moved back to Maryland shortly after burying his big homie.

CHAPTER V: CHRONICLES OF THE JUICEMAN VOL. I

"As far back as I can remember, I've always wanted to be a millionaire."

-Jalon Knight

T he stairwell door burst open as they sprint down towards the fifth-floor footsteps rapidly, loudly, ascending from the ground level. They have no choice but to now run towards the building's roof. The access door almost flies off of the hinges, an alarm rings as three teenagers sprint through the threshold onto the flat rooftop gravel surface. They have to think quickly. They don't have much time. "Isaac grab that metal rod and prop it in-between the front of the door and the corner of the rooftop wall! Chris, hurry up and try to find the fire escape." After instructing Chris and Isaac, he looks over at the roof of the building across from them. Chris yells out, "Yo ain't no fire escape up here!" Banging on the rooftop access door thuds as Isaac runs over, "Jalon, what the fuck are we gonna do?" Jalon looks back at the metal rod that is progressively losing its grip, slipping away from the door and brick wall. Jalon looks at Isaac as Isaac pulls his twenty-five-millimeter pistol from the back of his jeans. Chris holds onto the bookbag's straps around his shoulders as he looks back at the rooftop door, his eyes begin to fill with tears. Jalon looks over to the roof that's about fifteen to twenty feet across from them, the building across from them is also one story lower. Jalon looks back at the metal rod that can give way at any moment. He looks at both Isaac and Chris before he back peddles and then runs full speed jumping off the ten-story building roof where they stood over to the building across from them. Isaac watches as Jalon lands on the other rooftop. Isaac immediately puts his gun in the back of his jeans, back peddles, and then attempts the same jump that Jalon just made. He almost slips off the other roof; he hangs from the edge. Jalon pulls Isaac up almost instantly. Chris looks over at the other rooftop with tears streaming down his face. Jalon anxiously screams over to Chris, "Chris, you have jump now! Throw the bag over first and then jump! BUT YOU HAVE TO HURRY UP NOW!" Chris takes the bookbag from over his shoulder, he shuffles backward, builds momentum, and tosses the bookbag. It lands on the edge of the roof to the building across from him. Isaac picks up the bag, puts it over his shoulder. He and Jalon both frantically wave over to a petrified Chris to jump. There's no longer time! Chris finally builds up the courage and begins to backpedal; as Chris back peddles, the rod propped in-between the door, and the brick wall finally gives way. Two men in dark clothing spill onto the rooftop carrying flashlights and pistols. Isaac pulls his twenty-five out and begins to shoot at the man on the other rooftop as they move towards Chris. Isaac shot, and they shot back. Chris jumps over the edge of the roof, attempting to make it to Jalon and Isaac. Chris got shot in the back as he leaped towards the other roof, his head bounces off the side of the building where he is attempting to land. Jalon watches Chris's body fall towards the concrete of the alley below. Isaac shoots at the man on the other building, he grabs Jalon's shoulder to retreat. Jalon and Isaac run full speed down the stairwell of the other building. One man has leaped across and pursues Jalon and Isaac, while the other remains on the rooftop. Jalon and Isaac exit the building's back door and run down the alley, the man who remained on the roof begins to shoot at them. Jalon and Isaac exit the alley unscathed, they run for their lives, both Jalon and Isaac are in unfamiliar territory. Chris was the driver and set up the whole capper! She screams, "Please don't kill me!" as Isaac snatches her out of her 1994 Volkswagen Jetta. Isaac speeds away from the red-light as the man who was pursuing them appears from the alley, standing thirty feet away from the woman who traumatically cries as she picks herself up off the street. Jalon counts the money from the bookbag as Isaac drives. "I know where we're at! We're right by the "Key-bridge" slim we about to be right back in the city. How much did we get? Jalon, how much did we get?" Jalon ignores Isaac as he counts and recounts the money in the red Jan-Sport backpack. After crossing the Potomac River into Northwest D.C., Jalon finally tells Isaac. "Twenty-nine-thousand, seven-hundred, and thirty-two-dollars."

"How much is that after we pay that Spanish nigga?" Isaac asks. "We owe him sixteen-thousand. After we pay him and pay Janet her two thousand, now that it's just the two of us. We both get five-thousand-eight-hundred and sixty-sixty-dollars apiece." Jalon responds. Isaac shifts the gears of the Jetta as he reacts pleased to what Jalon just said. "Nigga how the fuck is you happy right now? Chris just died, and we almost died over five rolls?" Isaac inconspicuously parks the car, he looks over to Jalon. "Slim the metro like five blocks up. Let's get low before they start looking for this joint." Jalon zips up the book bag, he and Isaac wipe down the car with the black bandanas that hung from around their necks. They exit the car leaving it in front of a laundry mat. Jalon carries the red bookbag as they walk to the metro station. Isaac laughs and shakes his head. "I can't believe that nigga was crying. That was your mans! Did he bounce when he hit the ground?"

As I looked over at Isaac, all I could think about is how my mother used to tell me that I would become the first black president one day. Instead, I'm going to become one of the biggest criminals this country has ever seen!

1981

My auntie Delilah once told me that my mom and dad never were in love. Two people like that could never love anything outside of themselves. They were just addicted to one other. I was born in "UASM Medical Center" in Little Rock, Arkansas, on January 7th, 1981. My father, Barratt, was from Hampton, Virginia, and my mother Oliva was from Pine Bluff, Arkansas. Delilah told me that she remembers the first time that my mother brought Barratt around. She said that Barratt looked precisely like the last man my mother had. Auntie Delilah is eight years younger than her sister Olivia.

Olivia's father only had two kids with my grandmother. My grandfather had another family, and my grandmother was only his mistress. Barratt's father died in the Korean War at the age of twenty in 1953. He had two sons that were eleven months apart: the oldest Chester and the youngest Barratt. Delilah told me that during my mother's sophomore year at Hampton University, she started dating a Basketball player who went to school with her, my uncle Chester. A year later, she was pregnant with Chester's younger brother Barratt's baby, my older brother Benjamin. Barratt and Chester hated each other once Olivia became pregnant with Benji. One of my earliest memories took place in the winter of eighty-five when I witnessed Barratt beat Chester to death. We were living in D.C. at the time, and Chester was visiting.

My aunt depended on Olivia at that point in her life, so she co-signed Olivia's and Barratt's story that it was self-defense. The family thought that I was Chester's kid and not Barratt's. Chester lost his life for that reason! Delilah said Olivia and Barratt were always beefing with one another. The only reason they stayed together was because of Benji after I was born, and Olivia started her new career working in the office of a United States Senator. Barratt became more disillusioned with her after he killed his brother over what turned out to be about money and not me. They split up. Olivia and Barratt were never married; they just went their separate ways. Barratt stayed in Northeast

D.C. with Benji while Olivia and I moved to Northwest D.C. in the summer of nineteen-eighty-five.

<u>CHINA TOWN</u>

As far back as I can remember, I've always wanted to be a millionaire! I came up in D.C. during a golden age. I saw kids Benji's age who were driving BMWs and carrying thousands of dollars on them. Some kids that went to the same boxing gym as Benji's stopped boxing to hustle. Benji was too focused to allow himself to succumb to the game. It's nothing in this world that he loved more than boxing and his baby brother. Benji would come to spend as much time with me as he could, but at that time, he was too determined on making the eighty-eight Olympics that was only a couple of years away. Even though Olivia wasn't living with Benji anymore, she tried to make sure that he would be a high school graduate. I don't have a lot of positive things to say about my mother. One thing I can say is she made sure that I was highly educated. I could read on a middle school level by the age of four, and I was doing multiplication, fractions, and percentages by the age of six. Olivia sent me to "an Elite private school" in Northwest, D.C. It's an upper-class private school that usually only rich people and politicians kids attended. At the time, I was too young to understand how Olivia was able to make so many things happen, but as I got older, I found out how the world works and how intelligent and beautiful women usually can get what they want. Especially if they're willing to use their bodies to get it. Olivia would make me ride the bus to her job after school to keep a close watch on me. Adults don't think kids understand things, but I caught so much from ear hustling in that Senator's office. After a while, the Press Secretary forbid my mom from having me I the office, but apparently, she knew how to work her mouth to get what she wanted, and eventually, he came to his senses. The real thugs weren't on the street corners. They were in the Capitol buildings instead. After I finished my homework, the only thing I had to do to pass the time was reading magazines and newspapers. I would read Forbes, Time Magazine, The Wall Street

Journal, and many others. Olivia thought she was keeping me out of trouble, but all she did was enhance my game. After Olivia left Barratt, she ended up finding us an apartment above a Chinese restaurant, located in Northwest D.C. On the days that I wasn't at the office with her or Benji, I would stay with the landlord's elderly mother. The landlord also owned the restaurant downstairs; I guess Olivia's mouth worked magic. The old Chinese lady didn't like my mother, but she loved me. She watched me for six years and treated me like her grandson every single day of those six years. Her son lost his wife to cancer, and he never had kids or remarried. I guest Ms. Zhao saw me as a surrogate grandson. Many of my experiences showed me that Chinese immigrants tend to be prejudice towards Black people. Ms. Zhao wasn't, though! At least not towards me. Ms. Zhao taught me her language, Mandarin Chinese every day that I was with her. It's a shame that I have to say this, but Ms. Zhao was the closest thing that I had to a grandmother for a long time. Ms. Zhao wouldn't let me out much, but I hung out with my best friend, Isaac when I could get away. His father owned a deli right outside of China Town, and they didn't live too far away from us. Isaac and I were partners in crime out of the gate. We worked well together. I was the brains, and he had no fear. When I wasn't with Olivia, Ms. Zhao, or Benji. I was out stealing shit with Isaac. We used Isaac's fair complexion to our advantage. Isaac's father was Italian, and his mother was a light skin Jamaican woman. People would act like Isaac was white instead of mixed, and we would use that to our advantage to do dirt when we could. Life was good those first three years living in China Town. I didn't like my school because they saw me as their black mascot, the token negro, but I was smarter than them and held no reservations about being my authentic self. I had the highest marks in my whole grade. I was getting better and better in Mandarin every day. Life was good at that point. That is until everything changed in the winter of eighty-eight. Benji was going to be in the summer Olympics. I couldn't wait to hear the announcers say the name, Benjamin Knight. He was known as Benny The Brawler in Northeast, but he would be known worldwide as an Olympic gold medalist by the summer. That's what we all thought until he accidentally killed someone.

Benny was out celebrating at this Go-Go spot with a few friends when they got into it with a group of men. One of the men head hit the concrete and died from bleeding to the brain. Benny was only seventeen at the time, but they still gave him twelve to fifteen for manslaughter. Benji's trail was the last time I would ever see Barratt, and the last time I saw my mother not be a junkie. Delilah told me that Olivia did coke with the white folks at her job, but after Benji got locked up in Lorton, she started smoking crack, and she progressively got worse and worse. By the age of nine, I was out of that Private school and no longer living in the China Town apartment. Ms. Zhao agreed to watch me still even after we got evicted, but we ended up moving to the other side of town to Southeast D.C. That's when I met Kenny Watson, aka K Dub, aka Killa Ken, aka GoldWatch. By the age of ten, I skipped school with K Dub to hustle and do delinquent shit. We used to hang around this diner off of Georgia Avenue. This old Jewish man ran it, but the streets thought its real owner was the owner of the diner, OG named Jimmy Brooks. Now they say Jimmy Brooks was a Heroin selling mothafucka back in the '70s. He was young, rich, and fly, and then he just disappeared one day out of the blue, and so did his product. He became a mythical legend. Some people said Jimmy Brooks was dead, he was in the Feds, or he got plastic surgery and is still around. The theory that made the most sense to me was that he owned some businesses and was laying low. So I would eat at the diner rumored to be owned by him, hoping to run into him one day. I didn't know what the fuck he looked like! Nobody did! But I knew if I was lucky enough to run into him. I would know!

Over the next two years, things became progressively worse with Olivia so much that my auntie Delilah moved back to the DMV (D.C. Maryland, Virginia to be closer to Olivia and try to help her get better. I was a lost cause at that point. I started to become more like K Dub. Kenny became my best friend just like Isaac, but unlike Isaac, who had a two-parent household. Kenny was the definition of a product of the system. He was in and out of foster homes until his aunt took custody of him at the age of nine years old around the time we first met. K Dub's aunt was a heroin addict who kept him around the lowest of the low lives. His aunt's old man died in a work accident, and she has lived off his life insurance settlement since. One day in the spring, when Kenny and I were eleven years old, we played his Nintendo that he would hide from his aunt. (He would only play it when I came over, so she couldn't sell it because she thought I brought it over). One day one of the scum bags K Dub's aunt kept around was high on "The Love Boat," "Dipper," or more commonly known as PCP. Ken and I were making fun of his aunt's high ass boyfriend, which turned out to be the wrong thing to do. Ken and I were shooting shit up on Contra when I paused the game and got up to use the bathroom. I was having a rare good day. Out of nowhere Kenny's aunt's boyfriend caught me in a headlock in the hallway. He choked me out and threw me down on the floor onto the mattress in Ken's aunt's room. I lost conciseness and when I came to he had my pants and underwear down. The sound of an overweight man breathing heavy and a belt-buckle unfastening rang in my groggy ears. He pressed my face in the bed to the point I could barely breathe. I fought as hard as possible, but I was an eleven-year-old seventy pound boy while he was two hundred plus pounds and forty-years-old. I heard him spit twice. The first time he spits and wipes it in my ass as I swarmed. I struggled for my life! "Shut your little ass up!" I heard him spit a second time and a gunshot not too long after that. I turned my head to the left and seen the scum bag with a hole in his head. I quickly hopped up and pulled my underwear up and my pants around my waist. Killa Ken stood with the gun in his hands; the barrel still smoky. His aunt was so high she didn't even get up until hours after the gunshot. When she came into the room hysterically screaming about her dead boyfriend in her bedroom. Ken and I were playing Nintendo as if nothing had happened. Child protective services put Ken back into foster care until his ninety-year-old grandmother took custody a year later. Delilah temporarily got Olivia to be a mother to me again after I almost got raped by that dipper head. Delilah convinced Olivia to move back to Arkansas with their uncle and aunt to get clean and get me away from the city, becoming the murder capital.

That year in Arkansas opened my eyes to how big the world was and how to move better as a man. My cousins made me grow up that year. Olivia would move us back to D.C. and stayed clean for a little while. I was thirteen years old. It was nineteen-ninety-four, and a lot had changed in a year and a half. Delilah told me that my mother Olivia, tried to stay sober as long as she could but ended up dying of a drug overdose on December 16th of 1994. It was twenty-one days before my fourteenth birthday. Not too long after Barratt killed his older brother Chester in eighty-five, my aunt Delilah moved away from Olivia and Barratt and got married two times in five years. Her first husband was this cat named Melvin, who was twenty years older than her. Melvin use to cheat on her and mentally abuse her constantly, they ended up getting divorced in Eighty-Seven, and she got married a year later to this white jewish man named Jude from Manhattan. Jude used to beat the shit out of my aunt and left scars that stayed on her for the rest of her life. Jude was older than my aunt Delilah just like Melvin was, and he ended up having a massive stroke in his Forties while beating on my aunt. Jude didn't have any kids from his first marriage,, and Delilah got everything he had. Delilah is a lesbian, and she has known so since she was younger, but she came up in a much different world from the one that Adrian and Luke live in. Back then being openly gay could mean you could lose your employment or, even worse your life. My aunt didn't finally start accepting who she wanted to be until after my mother died. That's also when I started living with her. Barratts whose name was on my birth certificate, was my only legal living guardian, but he still wanted nothing to do with me and forfeited custody to my aunt after Olivia died. I was back living in Northwest D.C., but this time, I was with my aunt, who I adored instead of Olivia, the woman that gave birth to me but never truly loved anyone but herself. I was able to reconnect with Isaac when I moved in with my aunt. Isaac told me a story about this kid who used to say his uncle was connected to Rayful Edmond's old crew. The kid would try to pick on Isaac all the time. One day while I was living in Pine Bluff, Isaac caught that kid who tried to bully him in an alley, beat him with a bat, and used a pocket knife to crave an "I" in his face. His older brother came back at Isaac a week later, but Isaac knew it was coming. The boy's older brother planned to catch Isaac walking home and intended to stab him up. Isaac waited for him to post up at the spot he planned for his ambush. Once he heard sirens, he walked up and shot the older brother in the back of the head. Isaac used a gun that he stole out of his father's collection. After that, people thought twice about fucking with Isaac! I got a job at the Chinese restaurant I used to live above, shortly after moving in with my aunt. With everything that went on in my life, I still somehow managed to contact Mrs. Zhao and take Mandarin lessons over the phone whenever I could afford the call. When I moved back, Ms. Zhao kept giving me lessons, and she got her reluctant son to give me a job working at the restaurant. I worked at the "China Hut" part-time and went to High School part-time. School was another hustle I mastered early. From D.C. to Arkansas, I felt that I had seen the American educational system in all of its forms, and knew how to work the fucked up system. Early on, I realized that the teachers were people just like the people on the block. I know I could always find an angle to use. By the time I got to high school, my skills were phenomenal. My teacher Mrs. Carson use to have it where I was covered even though I was rarely there. I lost my virginity to Mrs. Carson when I was eleven, and she was teaching at my Junior High School in Southeast. She was in her Mid Forties, but she looked good for a white woman that age. She ended up getting promoted. She definitely was still having sex with underaged black males. Mrs. Carson had it set up sweet for me to the point where I was barely in school during my freshman year. Isaac's father became a degenerate alcoholic, but he worked hard, and he was able to keep the business afloat that his father passed down to him. Isaac's father's rowhouse used to be the spot. Isaac's mother died while I was living down south, and his parent's crib became our hub while his father was out numbing himself. Isaac's father would catch us with some shorties and would be too drunk to do anything but go to his room. Isaac and I use to fuck a lot of women in that rowhouse. I mean bitches in their thirties and forties. It was a month before Issac's fifteenth birthday, and he wanted to celebrate. He wanted to go up to New York and do it big, but neither one us had the bread. Isaac and I weren't corner boys. We were working bamas. Nigga's ain't look at us like that. There were kids our age who were on their way to becoming millionaires or already millionaires. Isaac and I made sure that we stayed out the way and kept our heads down. We made our money from being stick up boys. At fourteen-years-old, Isaac and I were making paper from robbing rich white folks. We almost got caught by an undercover, and we have been chilling ever since, but then one day, I ended up making a delivery for the Chinese restaurant that I worked at that changed it all. I delivered an order of Lo Mein and Chicken and Mumbo sauce to a Colombian restaurant a couple of miles away from "The China Hut." I had to use the bathroom really bad and convinced the cook to let me use theirs. While I was in the restaurant's back leaving out the bathroom, I saw a woman pushing a tray of meat into the back office. I could see money in between the slabs of raw pork. The chef spotted me as soon as I came out of the bathroom, and I acted like I didn't see shit. But in actuality, I found the capper that was going to get set me right. The restaurant was next to a laundry mat. But dig this! I use to fuck the girl whose father owned the laundry mat, so I know that building in and out. The room we use to have sex in is connected to the Colombian restaurant. All you have to do is crawl through the ceiling, and it puts you in? That's right! Right in that office with the slabs of meat. Now I just had to figure out where they were keeping the money. After weeks of hiding in the ceiling, I finally saw where kept the cash. I planned everything out to the T. I knew they were out of the restaurant by usually two or three in the morning at the latest. I just needed someone I could trust to be lookout and someone else to be in the ceiling. I could use Isaac to be in the ceiling to take the money and help me back up. I wanted to use Killa Ken, but he was up at "Boys Village" (a juvenile detention center) for six months. So I just wasn't sure who I would use to be lookout. Let me tell you about the third member of this capper, Muhammad! Muhammad was Isaac peoples. He was from a family of killers from Philadelphia. His father has been on the run since the early eighties. Muhammad was a short dark skin nigga with a temper! He was 5'3 but not to be fucked with! Muhammad saw what I was made of when he did his first robbery with Isaac and me. We've been solid since that day. I got everything planned out. Now we just have to execute! I have to break into the electrical room through the back door of the laundry mat. Muhammad was out front, keeping look-out from the other side of the street. While Isaac was by the back door. I was able to get into the office and I was able to open the hidden safe from memorizing the code. Muhammad hit us on the walkie talkie, he shouted, "CODE RED ABORT!" I was in the process of handing Isaac the bag of money. Lucky for us the person must of forgot something and went back to their car leaving. We came off with seventy five thousand dollars each. Isaac's birthday was about to be off the chain. I wanted to go crazy after the robbery that we just did but I didn't. I was about to ball the fuck out on the low out of town in New York with Isaac and Muhammad. I had the money hidden in a spot I knew was safe from Delilah who would lose her mind if she found all the money that I had. I would give my aunt money every month after I started working at the carry out when I moved in with her because I felt like that was my responsibility even though she didn't need, nor want my money. On the day of Isaac's birthday I was hype. I was gonna go to work and then met Isaac once he got off. Muhammad and Isaac were doing too much flashing with their money after the robbery. This nigga Muhammad brought a truck and he couldn't see over the steering wheel. This motherfucker Isaac got the whole bottom row of his mouth in 14 carat gold. Isaac pops was mad because he wanted a cut to support his new heroin habit that he developed after his mother died. Isaac and Muhammad was moving out of control and I had to get these nigga's under control before they got us caught up by the nigga's we robbed or by the law. One day I was ease dropping on the moves conversation from the ceiling, I could tell whoever we were about rob was serious. A couple of days after, Isaac, Muhammad, and I robbed that Café. I was making delivery's like any other day that I had to work, as I rode my bike to the delivery address everything suddenly went black! I woke up in a daze seeing nothing but darkness. A bag was over my head and my hands were tied behind my back. I could hear someone cursing to the far right of me I could tell it was Isaac's voice. "Yo I got to take a fucking piss!" I heard a man threaten Isaac, he told him if he doesn't shut up, he's going to let off two gun shots right next to his ear. Another man's voice appears in the room. The two of them have a conversation in Spanish. I had an elementary level of understanding Spanish. English was my first language of course, and Mandarin was almost fluent to me at that point. I really wish I spoke Spanish! The two man who held me and Isaac hostage had a conversation for about four minutes before one of them left the room. After that I heard footsteps slowly approaching me. He rips the bag off my head. The sudden bright light blinds me. That was the first time I saw him. That was the first time I met Manny Castro. I wasn't sure if he gonna kill me or not because he showed me his face, but I knew for sure he wanted his money back. I finally got my vision in order. I looked over and saw that Isaac was tied up. With a bag over his head, and piss under his feet, the gun shots by his ear made him urinate himself. Isaac cursed with his mouth gaged as Manny talked to me. Manny's blue, red, and yellow diamonds shines as he spoke to me. He asked me if I wanted some water. I nodded yes and then Manny slowly poured water into my mouth. "So where is my money Jalon? I'm gonna spare you from asking who your other friend is! But I don't have time to play games! Where's my money at?" I asked how Manny found out it was them.

Apparently a girl who had a crush on Isaac noticed his new gold teeth. This girl just happened to be the chef's daughter. Isaac just so happened to be mean to the girl one day. And that particular day just so happen to be the day after he got his gold teeth, and a couple of days after the robbery. They watched Isaac and I, snatched us up five days after we hit the capper. "Now Jalon I'm gonna ask you three more times for my money!" Manny told the man something in Spanish and he put his gun against Isaac temple. Isaac curses and struggles in the chair. "Where is my money?" He asked. "Let him go and I'll tell you!" I yelled. Manny's henchman cocks the gun back. "This is the second time that I'm asking! Where is my money Jalon?" I pleaded with Manny not to kill Isaac. Manny says something to his henchman in Spanish. The henchman knocks Isaac out with his gun, and then carries him out of the room. "I promise you Jalon this is the last time I'm asking!" If you don't tell me where my money's at, I'm going to yell to my friend Ernesto and he's gonna shoot Isaac in the head. And after he's shoots Isaac, we're gonna cut something off of your body until you tell me where my money is at! Do you understand?" I slowly nodded and then told Manny how we executed the whole robbery. I told Manny how I stayed in the ceiling for hours at a time some days, and pissed in a bottle. At the end of my explanation I told Manny that I had $69,375 dollars left, but he wasn't sure how much his crew had spent. Manny sat in a chair seated across from me as I explained to him what went down. Manny finally broke his scowl and laughed when I got to the end of my story. "That's pretty impressive for someone your age Jalon. But you let your man's end your life because he couldn't be nice to some girl! Manny pulled a gun from the back of his waist band, cocked it back and then put it directly to Jalon's forehead.

"Wait! Wait! Please don't kill me!" I begged.

"Well I know where most of my money is now! And we'll find your little friend! So tell me again why I should let you live?" Manny asked.

"Because I'm special!" I said.

"What'd you just say?" Manny asked surprised.

I repeated, "I said I'm special. If you kill me! You're killing the next John D Rockefeller!" Manny laughs at Jalon's enthusiasm he tells Jalon, "You know Rockefeller hated negro's right?" "Don't they all?" I asked. Manny laughs at me again and then decides to let me and Isaac live, as long as we brought all his money back in three days. If we didn't have his money back we already knew what was gonna happen. Isaac had 65,000 left after buying jewelry, and feeding dad's habit. Now we just had to find Muhammad and hope he hasn't spent more than we can recoup. We ended up finding Muhammad outside this chick house, this idiot had the money with him. When we found him he was waiting on this girl to come outside. Muhammad tried to play like his money was stashed somewhere but Isaac ended up finding it in the back of the truck. I couldn't believe that this nigga had the money on him. We told Muhammad to drive to Isaac's girl house to get his cut of the money. Muhammad was the first person I ever killed in my life! That feeling of being a murderer was the feeling of being murdered. I knew I was gonna have to be the one to pull the trigger when I talked to Isaac on the train. Isaac never said it directly, but he said! "I did that Wilson boy! I can do this!" In my life time I've had deep conversations, and the deepest ones have come from the eyes. I had to be the one to do it! I was sitting in the backseat seat when I shot him. I made sure I called out his name so I could look him in his eyes. Not to see the fear in his eyes. Not to be tough! I wanted him to know why I'm doing it, and my eyes will say it all. We made sure he pulled into a car port were he wouldn't be found for at least a couple of days. They questioned both me and Isaac, but our stories were the same and both checked out. I made it to the drop off the spot that Manny told me to be at with forty five minutes to spare. I dribbled a partially inflated basketball that was left on the court like I was practicing to make it seem like I was doing something besides what I was doing. Ten minutes after Manny said I had to be at the spot. A Hispanic bama around my age pulled up on a dirt bike, he didn't speak English well, but I understood when he asked for the money. Manny didn't say shit about sending nobody. I knocked the dude off his bike before he could pull a blade or a strap, by the time he got some shots off I was out of dodge. My heart was racing! I had a book bag full of cash in a neighborhood that I had never been in. I finally started to calm down and a black Lexus pulled up on me. Manny rolled down the window and told me to get in the car. It's not like I became his protégé overnight. I had to pay him back the sixteen thousand that was spent out of the two hundred and ten thousand dollars that we stole. I had two days after I gave him the money back out of what we spent or me and Isaac were gonna die!

"A generation that's been left behind, four years of college yet a job is hard to find, accumulated debt just to work minimum wage, working just to pay the bills, generation new slaves."

-Two8G

Luke finally mellowed out after the fiasco at Pico's trailer. I ended up finding those seven grams of weed that I thought I lost as I ran for my life. Luke even took one of the E pills that Caden gave to me. We're bumping "Gucci Mane" while I'm driving trying to find my turn on these dark ass backcountry roads. I finally find the turn that gets to Jackie's party. The green and white road sign reads Flowers Drive. There was a big field that spanned about three hundred yards. The road leading up to the house was unpaved, not too narrow, but if you're driving too fast, you're going to fuck up your whip. There were cars parked to the side of the country dirt road as we pulled up to the house, so I knew the party was about to be poppin. Caden said he held the space behind his car in the driveway for me before my phone lost service. I hope he's still there. When I pulled up to the paved inverted U shaped driveway, Caden was leaning against the trunk of his orange 2011 Mustang; he stopped the conversation he was having with this decent looking blonde chick and approached my car. "Hey, bro, you can't park here! Oh shit, what's good Adrian? I didn't realize that was you!" How didn't you know it was me?" I asked. He shrugged "I don't know, bro, you've only had this car for a few months." Caden leans down into Adrian's window. "Holy shit, is that my man Luke fucking Beck?" Yeah, it's me, Caden, could you stop shining that light in my face?" Luke responds frustrated. From the sound of Caden's voice, I could tell he's feeling good. Well, at least I assume so because I AM ROLLING FUCKING FACE! Like it's no question in my mind that I'm fucking Jackie tonight! I just gotta play it cool and not let her sense how horny I am. This party is looking lit as fuck! Jackie's family has a two-story farmhouse in southern Maryland that looks straight out of an old horror flick. It's dirty, off-white with faded red window shutters, and the house most definitely needs to be power washed. Without question, it sits on more than a few acres of land. On the surface, people were having the time of their lives. In reality, we all were numbing our pain! There's a group of Jackie's little brother's friends smoking on the front porch. All four rocking chairs swing occupied with younger generations of fellow "Misfits." Three of their other peers stand around engaging in the decadents. A group of wasted chicks plays on the tire swing that hangs from the huge oak tree out in the front yard. A little closer towards us were a few guys who looked like they were still in high school, smoking and freestyling over the music from inside the house. Without question, they need to keep practicing! Luke and Caden were talking outside of the back of my car. I sat inside my Ford people watching and rolling up a few doobies. When I finally got out, I overheard Luke telling Caden about what happened at Pico's house. I took a big ass pull off the doobie that I twisted. I walked up to Luke and Caden, feeling authentically happy for the first time since visiting California. Luke and Caden were drinking straight out of Luke's bottle of Jamison Whisky and chasing it with Ginger Ale. I knew Caden was about to ask me about what happened at Pico's house. "Yo, Castro, what the fuck happen?" While I'm telling Caden my perspective, I hear a loud, obnoxious voice approaching, rapping to the music playing from inside the party. "Every time I fuck, I gotta hit me least bout two bitches!" It's my boy Liam's drunk ass. Liam is a few years younger than Caden and me, but he was still on the varsity baseball team with us. Liam is one of those. How can I say this? A dumb asshole! But Liam's a good dude if that makes any sense. Liam's about six-two or so, I would say about Luke's height. Liam isn't quite fat yet, but he definitely will be in three or four years if he doesn't constantly work out. Liam is wearing tan khaki shorts, a white and black shirt that says titty inspector; on top of his head, Liam has a red Washington Nationals hat with a white team logo leaning backward on his black hair with Pomade thrown in it. Liam has white and black Vans sneakers on his feet and a bottle of Captain Morgan in his hand. Liam lifts his iPhone flashlight light. "Liam, get that fucking light out my face like you, the God damn police!" Luke yelled. Liam smiled and hugged Luke. This idiot dropped his bottle off Captain Morgan in the process of his hug. Next to Terence, Liam is one man that I can always say will remain the same. He's lucky that bottle ain't break on the concrete. Like the smart ass, I am. I told him. "Liam. You dropped your bottle." To which he replied. "Go fuck yourself, Castro!" We passed the Jamison bottle and doobie around and talked outside for a little while before Luke interjected. "Aight fellas I'm bout to go book something. I'll catch y'all inside!" I stayed outside with Caden and Liam and kept chopping it up. Liam drunk ass finally realized that I had a new car and wanted to examine the inside. I let him into the back car door just so he could shut the fuck up, and then maybe I could hear what Jackie told Caden about me. Yet and still, Liam wouldn't shut his drunk ass up. "Castro, when did you get this?" "He got it a few months ago." Caden answered. "Shut up Caden, I didn't ask you! I asked Castro!" Liam yelled. "I got it three months ago, Liam," I repeated. Liam got comfortable in the back seat of my car, commenting as usual. "Hey, bro! This car is a little more spacious than I thought it would be." Liam lays stretched out in the car's back seat with his Van sneakers' soles on the driveway. Caden and I finished our cigarettes and then started to go inside of the party. I told Liam chunky ass we were going inside the party, and that he needed to get out my car! "Give me one second, Castro." "Nah, for real, Liam, get out my car! I'm going inside!" I said. "Just give me five minutes, Castro." Caden started laughing like it was funny. I didn't have time for this shit! I hit my car alarm and kept it moving. These pills got me ready to fuck, and from what Caden just confirmed, Jackie is too. I told Liam he better not throw up in my shit, his drunk ass yelled back! "I'm going to throw up in your shit!" "Liam, dude, I'm not playing with you! You better not throw up in my shit are else you're going to be cleaning it up." Caden patronizingly repeated what I said, and Liam told him to. "Shut the fuck up!"

I chopped it up with some of Jackie's little brother's friends before I walked through the front door. "*Santeria* by the group Sublime played as people throughout the house drunkenly sung along. I wasn't able to take a headcount, but there had to be well over a hundred people spread throughout the house inside and out. There was an office directly to your right when you enter the house. People were in the office playing "Mario Kart." Entering the party, so many faces were familiar. A group was seated on the first couple of stairs, but Jackie put up a child gate so no one would go upstairs. Like mothafuckas can't just step over the gate. Caden disappeared when we entered the house. I wasn't worried about him or Luke. It was only one person I was concerned about, and that was Jackie Flowers. I haven't seen many people at the party in years, so it took me a minute to make it through the front hallway. I finally made my way into a full kitchen as I attempted to get myself a drink. I know I'm going to run into Jackie soon. One of Jackie's friends was in the kitchen, making shots for everyone. At this point, I can smell Jackie. I ended up spotting her in the living room adjacent to the kitchen. She was standing on the couch dancing with my homegirl Sarah. Jackie's eyes lit up when she saw my face. I thought she would just hug me, but she French kissed me too. I know it's about to go down! Sarah hugged me as she gushed over Luke. Sarah talked about how Luke looked even cuter than he did before. I feel Luke and Sarah hooked up before, and they probably will again. Sarah's looking sexy tonight too. Sarah is a short tan, white girl with long dark hair, and a decent body not outstanding in one area, but she is a pretty girl. Jackie turns down the music that played as she tried to get everyone's attention. I hopped on the couch with Jackie and yelled out! "Hey, y'all be quite Jackie's trying to say something!" " Fuck you, Cockstro, eat a dick!" It had to be somebody that I use to play baseball with. Jackie is finally able to get the Birthday Boy, Cody in the living room. He hopped on the couch were Jackie, Sarah, and two other girls were standing with me. The girl who was handing out shots made her way to the couch gave all us a shot. Everyone drunkenly sings Happy Birthday; a few people sang the Stevie Wonder version of Happy Birthday. Everyone in the area rose whatever drink they have in their hand as we toasted happy birthday to Cody. Jackie kissed Cody, and then she yelled out on in a drunkenly unrhythmic manner. "All I want for my birthday is a big booty hoe!" Someone turned the music back on. Everyone started rapping along. One of the girls on the couch with us sat Cody down in a chair nearby and began to give him a lap dance. Jackie got up off the couch and started dancing with me. I'm going to enjoy this and see how long it takes for her to invite me upstairs. We danced with one another for at least three songs before she whispered in my ear, "Meet me upstairs in twenty minutes!" I was like Bet! I swear I was just about to ask her if she wanted to go upstairs. I looked down at my phone, and it was twelve-forty-seven AM. I went looking for Luke to see what he was doing while I waited for those twenty-minutes to pass by. I found Luke playing beer pong with Caden against a goofy looking dude and a douche in a Tom Brady jersey. When I got close to the table, I could tell Luke was serious by his expression. I heard him tell the douche bag in the Tom Brady jersey, "Ain't gon be too many more Nigga's coming out your mouth, homie! I already asked you nicely before. I ain't gon keep asking!" The goofy-looking dude played the token roll as he tried to vouch for his friend. I wonder what happened with Luke in California? He never really cared about non-black people using the N-word. That was always like a Terence type of stance. Something must have gone down to change his attitude. Eventually, the tension subsided, and Caden and Luke were one cup away from winning the game. Caden took his shot and made it. When it was Luke's turn, he took the shot with his left hand over his eye, ignoring Caden's pleas to shoot it normal. Luke made the shot in the red solo cup as beer splashed from the ping ball. Everyone in the garage watching cheered Luke's shot, as he and Caden celebrated. I looked down at my phone, and it was one-zero-five-am, time to meet Jackie in the master bedroom. There are four bedrooms upstairs, and my high ass walked into three out of the four bedrooms before I found the right one. In one of the bedrooms, two girls were sniffing pills. I got to the master bedroom, and Jackie was lying on the bed in nothing but a T-shirt. She had a bottle of Vodka in her hand as she seductively smiled at me, slowly waving me over to the bed with her index finger. She ain't have to tell me twice. In record time, I was out of my shoes in nothing but my underwear. We took a few drinks out of the bottle of Vodka before we started making out. We both were wasted and knocked shit off of the nightstand in the heat of passion. The room went dark as the candle got knocked off the nightstand with a few other things. Jackie nor I paused to pick up anything off the ground that fell. We were caught up too much in the moment. So much so that I didn't use a condom, and I've only done that with my ex-girlfriend. Not to brag on myself, but I knew I did my thing! Jackie almost decapitated my head with her legs when I was eating her out. I know for a fact that I have an average size dick according to the internet, but Jackie was screaming like I was king ding-a-ling. She is either an outstanding actress or these two triple stack E-pills I had taken are like a performance enhancer. We were in bed looking up at the ceiling as we reflected on that intense sex session. She said we could do another round after the party, but we should head downstairs soon. I went to take a piss in the master bathroom before I got dressed and headed back downstairs. I thought I heard someone in the bathroom, but no one else was up there but us, at least that what I thought. This drunk dude was sitting on the toilet, shirtless, with his pants completely on. There is vomit on the man's shirt, the toilet base, and the bathroom wall's bottom left side. "Aww, dude, what the fuck! Gross!" Jackie dashed to the doorway standing next to me, dressed back into her peach Valentino shift dress; she was angry as fuck! I'm glad I waited to use the bathroom because his drunks ass would have ruined the whole moment. The dude was one of Jackie's little brother's best buddies. I prevented Jackie from murdering him. I told her that I would help clean the bathroom after the party. Jackie turned on the "Halogen Torchieres" lamp that stood next to the Transom style bedroom window. Jackie hit the bong as she vented to me; her little brother Cody made his way in the room. Jackie started arguing with Cody, that's when I decided to ease my way downstairs. I went out to the back deck to smoke a victory cigarette! After what we just went through, I was tired of jacking off into a rag. I'm feeling like a million bucks right now, and this brew and this cancer-stick is just what I needed. Luke was standing out on the deck with Floyd's little brother when I got outside. It was nice to see Fish. He looks exactly like his older brother. Fish did fuck up, though, by telling Luke that me and Hunter almost got into a fight last week at this bar called "Hard Times." Luke downplayed it, he said. "Well, that's odd cause when I talked to Hunter early this week to tell him I was moving back, he said he hadn't spoken to you since you all came to visit me, and Blue earlier, you said the same thing. I wonder what that's about?" Luke changed the subject and then lit up a blunt we were still smoking when Caden came out to the deck and told Luke that those dudes were begging for a rematch. After smoking with Fish and me, Caden and Luke headed to the garage to give those dudes a rematch. I went back inside to grab another beer and some jungle juice. Jackie's little brother Cody and his friends were in the living room getting rowdier by the minute, those little dudes where on liquor, weed, and all kinds of other shit! It's only a matter of time before something happens. I went back outside to finish rapping with Fish and smoke another cigarette. Fish and I were chopping it up for a minute and then *Faneto* by the hip-hop artist, Chief Keef came on. A few of Cody's friend who was outside on the deck, rushed in the house to join the mosh pit forming in the living room. I was going to join, but I wanted to hit the blunt a few more times before I knew it, one of Cody's friends darted out the deck door. "Hey, Castro, your brother's fighting!" I hopped out of the chair I sitting was in and rushed in the house. Fish followed right behind me. It took me a lot of effort to make my way through the crowd of drunken party-goers to fight that was ensuing. I was able to push my way into the garage. Caden was the closest person to the fight as he repeats. "One on one, one on one!" A girl screamed, "stop, he's out already!" Jackie pushed her way through the crowd screaming. "IF YOU WANNA FIGHT! FIGHT OUTSIDE!" Luke walked away from the guy who curled up in the corner; blood dripped on his Tom Brady jersey as his goofy friend tried to help him off the ground. Luke aggressively snatches his shirt from Caden, who was standing nearby, laughing, and drinking. Jackie was pissed! She was screaming a bunch of shit at me, but I focused on getting Luke's attention as he stormed out of the double-deck doors. Outside, Luke paced back and forth as he smoked a cigarette. I was confused, and I asked Luke. "What the Fuck happened?" Caden came out, interrupting, laughing as he tried to shake Luke's hand. I was still confused about what happen and asked Luke again. "Aye bruh, what the fuck happened?" Before Luke could respond, the house's fire alarms started going off. The sight of smoke and all the people who started to party after the fight was now panicking! Screaming, yelling, and the music were the only things I could hear as people were fleeing the farmhouse.

Fish and Luke were the first to react. Caden ran behind them, and my dumb ass was the last to make it off the deck. I grabbed Luke's bottle of Jamison and a random woman's purse off the table by us before I hopped off the deck. The scene is complete pandemonium! I saw Sarah trying to calm down a hysterical Jackie, but she just screamed at the top of her lungs in agony. Flames begin to engulf the upper level of the farmhouse. People scurry to their cars frantically, attempting to flee the scene. Cars start to jam up on the country dirt road. As others drive through the country field, some vehicles get stuck, attempting to reach the main road.

Luke frantically grabbed at my car door, looking towards the back of the house. Caden got to his car first. I got to mines shortly after. Both Caden and Luke were screaming at me to hurry the fuck up! I backed out of the driveway like I was a Nascar driver. I was able to ride through the field without getting stuck. I got on the main back road and screamed out in adrenaline. "That party was lit! LITERALLY!" This time Luke was asking me, "Yo, what the fuck just happen?" "Bruh, I don't fucking know! I think that shit started in the basement." I said. "Nah, that shit came from upstairs." Luke responded shaking his head. "Fuck man! Is this why you left home?" "Yeah, Blue, this exactly why I left," He said agreeing. "How the fuck did you get into that fight, though? That's what I wanna know." Luke started to tell me what happened when suddenly, my heart skipped ten beats when I heard a groggy voice appear from the backseat of my car. "You got into a fight Luke?"

CHAPTER VII: DEEP CREEK LAKE

"They say if you're born a Black man in America, then you're born probation, born a white man in America. Then you're born on vacation!"

- Aaron The Misfit"

Labor Day weekend is at hand as Luke contemplates what he wants to do for the night. Adrian lays on the couch feverish, with two pillows and several blankets. Luke has stopped by dropping off a care package specially made by his mother, Anna. Luke and Adrian are in the living room playing Call of Duty 3 Zombies! The *Master Mind* album By Rick Ross plays over Adrian's Bluetooth speaker. Adrian has been working his new job nonstop since he graduated with a bachelor's degree in Computer Science three months prior. Adrian has been working six days a week, sixty hours a week, and was looking forward to this weekend. Instead, he's sitting with three blankets wrapped around him, playing video games. Adrian is delighted that Ms. Anna made him that care package; his mother certainly wouldn't have! The guys stopped playing the game. Adrian was curled up on the couch, flipping through "Netflix," as Luke texted on his phone. Adrian blows his nose and asks Luke. "Who are you over there texting. Paige?" Adrian asked. "Nah, Curtis." Luke responded. Adrian frowns, "Who?" Luke snaps back, "Curtis!" Adrian gathers his thoughts for a second and replies with his mucus-filled chest, "Oh, that Dude that threw that party a couple of months ago?" "Yeah him!" Luke answers. Adrian shrugs, "What he want some bud?" "Of course," Luke laughs still texting. Adrian sees the intensity on Luke's face, "How much?" "Two Ps! And he's asking if I can get an ounce of coke too." Luke says smiling. "He knows you don't sell coke, right?" Adrian asked seriously. "Yeah, but he's asking, and he said he'd look out for me if I can make it happen." Luke puts his phone down. Adrian lies on the couch, sweating and taking sips of a bottle of Gatorade, "Yo Blue, you know where I can get some yayo?" "Not an ounce, I don't think. I did meet this Dude Giovanni through my job. We did an account for his company, and we went out one night, and he had some terrific blow." Adrian coughs up mucus. Luke covers his has face with his forearm. "But I don't know him like that yet," Adrian continued. "Then what was the fucking of the point of telling me that?" Luke responded irritated. Adrian shrugged again, "I don't know. You asked! I don't know why your acting like you can't find coke. Just use who we both know." Luke pauses, "Yeah, I don't want too though."

Luke sits on the other couch, looking through his phone. Adrian asks Luke. "You gonna have to go over Ms. V's house to grab your pounds?" Luke nods, "Yep!" "Where would you have to go to meet Curtis? Would you have to go to that big ass Mansion in VA?" Adrian asks as he props himself up. Shaking his head Luke responds, "Nah, he said he at some spot called Deep Creek Lake." Where the fuck is that?" Adrian asks. "I don't know. I don't really feel like going. I'm only considering it because he said he'd give me a five hundred dollars just for the drive," Luke says. Adrian grabs his phone off the floor as Luke is talking, "Damn! I see why! That fuckers like three, four hours away." "Yeah, but I can make almost ten G's for this trip," Luke shares. "Sounds like you going out there to me!" Luke shakes in frustration for a second, blurting out like he has Tourette syndrome, "Fuck!" Luke takes a deep breath, gets up from the couch, gives Adrian a fist pound! "Aight, bruh, I'm bout make this journey." Luke rubs his face thinking about all the driving he's about to have to do. Adrian asks Luke. "Are you coming back tonight?" "Nah, I probably won't get over there till after seven and Imma chill. I already know I'm gonna be drinking, and Curtis said I could crash up there." Adrian nods, "Okay, bruh, be safe driving, hit me when you touch down!" Luke begins to leave out of the house; he tells Adrian as he walks out. "Feel better bitch!" Adrian raises his middle finger as Luke closes the front door.

"WELCOME TO DEEP CREEK LAKE

"Sometimes we look for a burning bush, not recognizing the little voice in the back of our head is enough of a sign. That ounce of doubt could keep you from a world of trouble".

-Misfit Z"

The wind blows a cool lake breeze into Luke's car window as he turns off "Deep Creek Drive" onto the road that approaches the six-bedroom, two-story log cabin. A Northern Red Oak tree stands in the Cabin's front yard; cherry blossoms line the outside from the front door to the end of the front exterior. Four cars sit parked in the driveway. A 1989 Red Lamborghini Countach, a 2012 Black H2 Hummer, a 2010 Benz Jeep, and Curtis's green Maserati fill the driveway. Parked off to the side, away from the luxury cars, is a sliver 2002 Toyota Corolla. Luke parks on the opposite side of the Toyota he pops the trunk before he gets out of the vehicle. Luke opens the back car door grabbing a drill and an empty book bag. He lifts the trunk of the car and begins to unscrew the speaker box. He unscrews the twelve-inch speaker then pulls out two tightly sealed black plastic bags, dusting off coffee grounds before stuffing the plastic bags into the empty book bag. Luke also grabs a coffee-can out of the speaker box. Luke screws the box back up, closes the trunk, and makes his way inside the Cabin.

As Luke walks toward the front door, two blond haired women leave out making their way towards the burgundy Honda. One of the women flirtatiously greets Luke, he turns from the blond woman, and three other women leave out the Cabin, one of the women excitingly greets Luke, "Oh my God, Luke!" "Oh, shit, what's up, Sarah!" Sarah runs over to Luke as he bends down to hug the 5'4 petite woman. Her scented black hair rubs against Luke's cheek. "What the fuck are you doing up here?" She asked. "I'm meeting my boy, Curtis." "Oh, you know Curtis?" Sarah asks in a disappointed manner. Luke tells her. "Well, I'm getting to know him…" "Well Okay! How the hell are you doing though? I can't believe you're a college graduate now." As Luke talks to Sarah, a red-headed woman with keys in her hands, angrily walks over. "Come on, Sarah, let's go! I need to get the fuck away from here before I murder Joshy!" "Hey, Amber, do you remember Luke?" Sarah asks. Amber snidely looks at Luke. "Oh, hi, Luke! Come on. Let's go, Sarah, before one of them comes out here." On cue, two frat boy looking guys stand at the door frame with beers in their hands, laughing as they loudly talk. One of the men shouts! "Hey, ladies, don't leave. The party just got here. Come on in Dude!" The man shouts to Luke as he waves him to come in the Cabin with his beer hand. Smiling, Sarah tells Luke. "Alright, Luke, we need to go!" Sarah hugs and kisses Luke and remarks. "Be careful around those guys." Luke confidently looks at Sarah. "I'm always careful! Okay, bye. Those are some really nice shoes, by the way." "Oh, thank you, pudding! And Luke, you smell like Starbucks. Jesus!" Luke laughs as he and Sarah part ways. Luke realizes he left his phone in the car. He doubles back to grab it and overhears some of Sarah's and Amber's conversation. "Amber, I told you we shouldn't have come up here!" "Sarah whatever! I don't care! Joshy can jerk his friends off, or get hookers, or whatever they're going to do!" Amber complained. "Amber, I told you about him. They'll probably get those slutty looking girls that tried to hit on them at the lake." Sarah said. "Oh my God, those girls looked like they were fourteen." Amber replied shocked. "They said they were twenty," Sarah shrugged. "Yeah, right in like four or six years!" Amber raised her voice. When Luke gets to the doorstep after grabbing his phone, he is greeted by the two men as he walks inside the Cabin, one of the man remarks. "Fuck, bro, I'm so glad you're here! I'm ready to rail a line!

$SKULL \ \& \ BONGS$

This Cabin is fucking dope! I mean, it smells like pizza, beer, smoke, sweat, and cologne, but other than that, it's really nice. There's a painting of "Teddy Roosevelt and The Rough Riders" on the front hallway wall. The two guys that opened the door for me made their way into the living room as Curtis greeted me. "What's good, Luke, my man!" Curtis hugged me and threw his right arm around my shoulder as he walked me into the living room area. "I appreciate you coming up, bro! I'm going to make it worth your while." Curtis shook my hand, handing me five-hundred-dollars. "Here's the cash for the trip as promised." Curtis took his arm from around me, walked ahead, looking back, saying. "Come on in and meet the fellas. You ever drink "High Land Park" Luke?" "Nah, I haven't! I know what it is. I just never tried it though," I said. Curtis white teeth and dimples appeared on his face as he told me. "Well, I think you'll like it! This is the expensive Shit!" "Are these two pounds and this ounce of yayo just for this weekend?" I asked. "Yeah, for the most part. The guys are going to a wedding tomorrow, and half of the pot is for the groom," he said "Are you going to the wedding?" Curtis smiled as he told me. "Fuck no. I don't have to, so I'm not going. It will probably end up just being a few of the other guys and us here tonight. It would be cool if you stayed for the whole holiday weekend. Sunday, I'll have some people over, and Monday, we're taking the boats out again. Alright, come on. I want you to meet the guys before we get down to business." I first met Curtis Gethermire the 3rd the winter of my senior year of college while I was at this chick's Tiffany's dinner party that I was fucking with. Before Paige and I started to get serious with one another, I met this girl Tiffany from going up to Columbia University with Hunter to sell weed to his friend. I met Curtis at Tiffany's dinner party, and even though Curtis and I were from completely different backgrounds, we connected for some cosmic reason. It's almost like we knew each other in a past life. Curtis is probably about Adrian's height. He has his sandy brown hair cut short on the back and sides. Curtis isn't one of those wealthy people who are above showing it. He flaunts like a rapper who just got a record deal. When we got into the living room, I saw that it was one of those situations where I was the only one. Curtis introduced me to his buddies as we stood in the center of the room behind the Maple Wood table. It was lightly littered with trash, staged in front of the unlit fireplace. Curtis introduced me to all eight of his friends, but only three stood out to me. Firstly it was his college buddy Joshy, he had a goofy unique personality, plus he was one of the bama's to greet me at the door. Secondly, I remember Bradley. For one, he was tall as shit he was at least six-six, or six-seven. Bradley was real skinny though you could tell the summer sun had been taking a toll on his pale ginger skin. He was wearing a bright colored tank top, jean shorts that are cut at the bottom, and flip flops with the thong string between your big toe. Bradley is Curtis's first cousin and is cool compared to the other guys. Especially the third of the stand-outs Connor, as I introduced myself, I walked over to everyone shaking their hands when I shook Connor's hand. He instantly gave me bad vibes. I sensed a level of hostility when I shook his hand, he said. "What's up, LeBron?" Now I don't know if you can tell yet, but I'm the only Black man in this Cabin. I'm on my guard anywhere I go. My pops, Benny and Juice, taught me that, but my pops would empathize, especially around white people. He would say, "They're the greatest liars ever. You always better be on guard. I don't feel like that, but I do feel like living in Waldorf and playing a predominantly white sport like Lacrosse in high school gave me a better understanding than my pops. He grew up in Chicago till his thirties and probably only interacted with white people because of work. I feel like I sensed racist vibes very well, but fuck all that, let's get back to this fuck boy Connor! I ignored that first petty comment and just tried to brush it off as just drunk white boy shit. After the initial introductions, Curtis and I got down to business.

We made our exchange, then we all started to parlay. We smoked, drank, and chopped it up. They were talking about all kinds of crazy Shit. For the most part, I just sat back and laughed. I didn't talk too much, but I noticed Connor would say little slick racial Shit. Like we were all talking about women, and he commented. "I know Luke's an expert in getting Jungle booty!" And then this asshole had the nerve to ask me if I would drink Watermelon flavored Hennessy if it came out. I'm not going to lie; some of the Shit that Connor said was kind of funny, and yes, I definitely would try Watermelon flavored Hennessy if it came out. Then the subject of colleges they attended got brought up, and that's when everything went left.

Most of us migrated to the basement; the stairs are adjacent to the living room. The basement compliments the rest of the Cabin. The bar is stocked with a flat-screen TV on the wall, sits in-between autographed Yankees jerseys, and a pool table with blue felt and oak wood. Joshy and one of the guys were up-stairs talking in the living room. Two of the guys were out back in the hot tub. Bradley and this short dude with a red shirt drink beer at the bar, a plate of cocaine, and a pizza box sits in between them. Curtis was on my team against Connor and his flunky. I can't remember his name; I just remember that he had an incredibly punchable face; he racked the balls on the table as he laughed at Bradley and the red shirt guy as they argued back and forth. "Bradley, for someone who went to Dartmouth, you sure are fucking stupid!" He said. "Fuck you, at least I went to Dartmouth. Didn't you go to Arizona State?" Bradley accused. "Fuck no dude. I went to Columbia that's Joshy's cousin that went to Arizona State!" He responded. Bradley yells up-stairs for Joshy's cousin to come down to the basement. After yelling his name five times, Joshy's cousin came running downstairs. Bradley points at Joshy's cousin with his beer. "Dude, did you go to Arizona State? Yeah, I did. Why?" He asked. The guy in the red shirt slaps Bradley on the leg. "See, I told you it wasn't me! Well, it makes sense he is trailer trash!" "Fuck you! You shit dick ass pirate!" The cousin yelled. The guys laugh for a moment before Bradley says. "Shit, I bet Luke went to a better college then Arizona State. Even if he only went to ITT TEC, it would still be pretty close to graduating from Arizona State." Curtis chalks up his pool cue and breaks the rack knocking three balls in, two solids and one stripped. The guys all laugh as blunts, and a plate of cocaine makes its way around the room. Joshy strolls down the stairs as Bradley asks Luke, "So where did you go to school? I know it wasn't ITT TEC." I smoke, laugh, and reply to Bradley. "Hell, Nah!" "So, what school did you graduate from?" The guy in the red shirt asked me as I took and missed my shot. "I graduated from Morgan State!" I proudly declared, taking a sip of my glass of Scotch.

Connor obnoxiously started singing *The Ghetto* by Elvis Presley, after I said that I graduated from Morgan State. Connor followed up, saying. "Luke, you would have been better off saying you went to Arizona State with B Rabbit over there standing behind you." "Hey guys, not everyone was smart enough to get into Ivy League." I finally got fed up with Connors' slick comments and snobbish disposition, so I told him. "Well, not all of us could ride daddy's dick to Yale!" Curtis made sure he reiterated the fact that Connor didn't go to Yale. "Joshy and I went to Yale! Connor went to Dartmouth with Bradley," he said. Bradley was behind the bar pouring shots. I was in my impressionist bag because I started to perfectly imitate Connor's voice as the guys in the room laughed harder the more I spoke, "I'm about to be a lawyer because my dad is going to get me in a big firm just like he got me into college. I get drunk and do too much yayo. It makes it hard for me to get an erection sometimes. My Ex Tiffany would fuck me in the ass with a dildo. At least one of us had a hard dick!" Everyone in the room was in tears from laughter at this point. Joshy hunched forward in laughter. I could tell Connor was mad the way he looked at Curtis as if he had betrayed his trust. At that moment, I realized that Connor was in the dark about his ex-girlfriend and me. "Oh, shit Connor, you don't know about Tiffany and me!" I started laughing hard because I could tell I struck a nerve. "How do think I met Curtis, Connor? I was smashing Tiffany for like three months after you all broke up. I started snapping my fingers as I tried to recall a girl's names. "Curtis, what was her friend's name you was smashing?" Curtis has a big amused smile on his face as he swirls his glass of Scotch. "Her name is Rachael Lawson." Joshy was sitting at the bar next to his cousin; he was still laughing at my impression. Bradley brought the tray of shots around the room as I knocked in the two-ball in the side pocket. Joshy stands up from his stool, animatedly asking? "Holy Fuck, Curtis! Was

Luke nailing Tiffany Lynch?" Curtis nods, laughing, sipping his drink. Connor aggressively looked at me Joshy walked over to me as I missed my shot and shook my hand. "I gotta give your props, Luke. You fucked Republican ass Senators Lynches daughter." Joshy laughed and pointed the blunt at Connor. "Luke. Connor was so in love with that girl. I thought he was going to jump off a bridge for sure when she left him," Curtis interrupted Joshy to make a toast as he quieted down the room; he raised his shot glass. "To being young and rich in Obama's America!" Bradley jokingly told Joshy's cousin and me not to raise our glasses. Everyone took their shots of Tequila, and Joshy went back into talking about his disbelief in the fact that I had sex with Connor's Ex-girlfriend. Connor interjected as Joshy laughed. "Hey, Joshy, how about you go sit back down at the bar before I smack you and make you cry like your dad did at your birthday last year!" The laughter in the room has now begun to be directed at Joshy as Connor verbally humiliates him. Connor made his way behind the bar getting two beers and doing a quick coke line before redirecting his energy towards me. "Now back to you, LeBron! Bravo buddy, you fucked my Ex! You're not the only guy, so you can feel accomplished all you want, but at the end of the day, she was slumming!" Connor laughed as he asked me, "What kind of degree did you get from that Affirmative Action college?" I lit up a blunt, and Curtis slide me the ashtray, Joshy cousin tried to pass me the plate of cocaine, but I turned it down once again. I took a sip out of my glass of Scotch on the rocks as Connor's flunky took his shot after Curtis and missed his shot. "Connor, I don't have to worry about working at Boost Mobile when there are coke heads like you in this world! I knocked in another shot as Connor asked me. "So you went to college to become a drug dealer? Congratulations on that one, buddy! So, Luke, let me get this straight. You made Yo momma spend all her welfare checks for you to go to 'Hillman College' just to become a drug dealer?" I had to give Connor bitch ass his props. That was funny. "Hillman College!? I didn't think you would know something like that, props. But I hold my own nuts, unlike you, Connor buddy boy. I don't need my daddy to help me make it. I'm a businessman! No different from Joe Kennedy. I wasn't born into millions, but I'm going to make them on my own. You said some slick shit about Affirmative Action earlier, but in reality, white women like Tiffany benefit more from affirmative action than I do. Gay men like Bradley over there benefit more from affirmative action then I do. No offense Bradley." Bradley ate a slice of pizza and replied, "None taken, Dude. I like what I like. Bye the way, how would it sound if I said no offense after I said Luke is Black!" I couldn't say much to Bradley's point but agree with it. I knocked in another shot in the corner pocket, and then went back to flaming Connor's bitch ass! "So Connor, you can talk all slick White Supremacist bullshit, but you envy someone like me at the end of the day! A man who fucked your Ex-girlfriend better than you ever could!" Curtis blurts out, "Luke's on a roll!" The guys all laugh and instigate even more. "I'm a man who has more swag and charisma than you. Tiffany liked to pillow talk, and she would tell me all about you. She would tell me how much you used to dick ride Rappers. It's funny how you say all this Shit about the Black man, but you love everything we do and create." Connor snobbishly tried to come back at me. "Luke, you guys, don't create Shit! If it weren't for us, you would still be in Africa with bones in your hammocks. Every immigrant group has surpassed and outperformed African Americans. You guys are too busy killing each other while you complain about 'The White Man.' You'll end up in jail or making thirty thousand a year eating chitin plates for dinner!" I ended up missing my next shot. Conner hit the eleven ball directly in the pocket in front of me. "Connor, I'm not gonna lie. You're pretty fucking funny. Hammock! Wow! You said all that Shit just to show how fucking ignorant you are. There wouldn't be the United States of America if it weren't for Black people." Conner missed his next shot. "And not all of us came from Africa. Many of us were already here, but a smart Dartmouth boy like you wouldn't know something like that. And for your information, Black Americans have fought in every war in this country. Not to mention if it weren't for us, European settlers would have starved to death or kept eating each other. So you should learn more about your history before you try to use your 'Third Reich,' talk radio talking points on me!" Even though my words landed on my intended target, I could tell some of the other guys felt some type of way about what I was saying. Which made me feel even better. The whole situation amused Curtis. Connor tapped his flunky that has the punching bag face on his shoulder. "This nigga really thinks he's smart?" Now, normally I don't get offended by the N-word. It's just that a word, but the way he said that Shit rubbed me

80

the wrong way! "You like saying nigga a lot, don't you, Connor?" I said. "What are offended now, Luke? We've been saying nigga this entire time. Pretty much everyone but you and cock gobbles over there." Conner pointed his pool-cue towards the bar as Bradley laughed and ate another slice of pizza. "What are you going to do? Beat me up now?" He asked. "Yeah, maybe I will!" Now I said, "maybe I will" in a completely playful manner, but Connor postured up like he was ready to fight! "Government cheese, I would wreck your ass! I'm not some pussy ass white boy. I'd put your black ass in the hospital!" Everyone in the room yelled out "Oh," as Curtis grabbed my shoulder and started to talk like a reporter in a press conference. "It seems like we have a challenge," Curtis holds his pool cue in front of my face like it's a microphone. I just smiled and kept lining up my shot. "Luke, are you gonna let Connor talk to you like that?" I looked both Connor and his flunky in the eyes when I called out my shot. I knocked the eight-ball into the right corner pocket. Curtis cheered as Conner and his flunky shook their heads. I grabbed Curtis's pool cue and talked into it like I was doing an interview. "Nah Curtis, I ain't worried about Connie over there. She's just hurt because Tiffany got dick from me!" Curtis goes over to the other side of the table he puts his pool cue in front of Connor's face. "How about this Luke, I bet anybody a thousand dollars you'd beat Connie's ass in a fight! Does anybody want to take that wager?" Connor's flunky interjects, as he emphatically praises Connor. "Curtis, I'd bet you five thousand." Curtis steps directly in front of Connor's flunky. "Okay, I'll take that bet!" The flunky pointed at me, saying. "No offense Luke! You don't seem like a bitch or anything, but Connor's like really legit. He does Muay Thai, and Ju Jit Su, he's trained with real freaking UFC fighters!" Connor stepped forward and took his shirt off, looking at Curtis. "Fuck that, Dude. I'd bet you ten thousand dollars I'd knocked du-rag over there the fuck out!" Curtis shockingly laughed and looked back and forth between Connor and me. "Holy Shit, you know I love to gamble now we're talking!" Connor, you guys, just lost two hundred apiece in Pool!" The other guys in the room began to yell out wagers. Curtis leans over to me, whispering in my ear. "You hear how much these dudes are betting against you? Look, bro, if you win. I'll give you forty percent!" I looked Curtis in the eyes, then looked around the room, and then at Connor, who was behind the bar pouring a drink with his shirt around his neck, staring at me like he's ready to go. I took a few puffs off the blunt looked at Curtis with a big smile on my face. The two dudes out in the hot tube came downstairs with towels around their shoulders, slightly still dripping water. I downed my Scotch and put my arm around Curtis, whispering back in his ear, "Make it fifty percent, and we can shake on it!" We looked at each other in the eyes, and then I told Curtis as we shook hands. "I would have fought this Dude for free, Curt!"

"BECK VS.ATWATER"

"We all stood in the Cabin's back yard next to a path that leads to the river. There is a Bluetooth speaker in the gazebo playing music from Joshy's phone. The guys have formed a circle; Curtis, Connor, and I are in the middle of the circle. Curtis plays the role of announcer and referee. Curtis holds up two papers as he begins to talk in a lively, exacerbated manner. "Alright, gentleman, are you all ready for tonight's entertainment?" Joshy yells back. "I thought the escorts were tonight's entertainment." Curtis looks down at his Rolex. "They're the main event, Joshy, and they'll be here within the next hour. Curtis holds up two pieces of paper. "Here, we have the contracts that were agreed upon by the two fighters. Bradley wrote the contracts. Thank you, Bradley! Conner's contract explicitly states. That under no circumstances will you Mr. Atwater press charges of any kind, or involve law enforcement of any kind in any shape, way, or form! Luke's contract explicitly states. That under no circumstance will you, Mr. Beck file a lawsuit or seek litigation of any kind, for damages, received, as a result of this agreed-upon friendly sparring session." Curtis waved Bradley over, "Bring the money box over here!

Bradley walked over to Curtis, handing him the shoebox full of money and checks. "Alright, fellas, this is tonight's purse. There's a lot of money on the line. It's going to be some upset people out here. No reneging or canceling checks. You're over there laughing, but so help me God, if Luke wins and you don't pay me and Joshy our money!" Curtis just stared at the Dude in the red shirt with a blank expression. It gets awkwardly quiet for a moment before Curtis snapped back into character. "In the left corner, we have Connor "The Carnivore" Atwater! Connor comes in at 6'2" one hundred and ninety-one pounds. Connor started to showboat and stare at me as I calmly chilled, standing on the opposite side of the circle with my head down. I was chewing on several pieces of gum to keep my jaw loose just in case he landed a lucky one. I periodically looked up at Connor and Curtis. Curtis went on with his spill as the guys all drunkenly listen along. "Connor is proficient in Muay Thai, Ju Jit Su, and Taekwondo, Connor also claims he has never lost a fight to a Black guy, and he wants me to emphasize the ever! In the right corner, we have Luke, and he told me to state this verbatim. "Fuck all this play shit let's go!" (P.S. everyone but Joshy and Curtis are retarded as Shit for betting against me. Thank you for the money!) The guys all booed me. Joshy threw his hands up and down, chanting, "let's go, Luke!" Curtis looks at both Connor and me as he hands Bradley the money box. Bradley was the only one who didn't place a bet. "Alright, gentleman, we went over the rules. I'm going to step out the way, count to ten, then you guys can go at it. Remember no sissy fighting, biting, scratching all that crap. No stumping on a man's head if he's down on the ground. In the case of submission, if a man begins to tap out, you must release him. If a man goes limp, you do not continue to beat on him. Alright, gentleman, those are the rules. Protect yourself at all times. Everyone else spread the circle out. Let's give them plenty of room. Let's touch fist fighters." Curtis attempted to get me and Connor to touch fist. I reached into bump fist, but Connor just looks at me while he smacked his knees is his palms. "Well, it looks like Connor is ready to brawl Luke. So I'm just going to step back and let you fellas go! Remember, at the count of ten." The fight starts! Curtis begins to step back as the guys around the circle all drunkenly comment Curtis tells Joshy to put on some music for us to fight to; Curtis stepped back by Bradley and then started to count aloud, "One, Two, Three…" Damn, I didn't think I was going to end up in a fistfight when I decided to come up here. I do know this. I'm about to walk away with like thirty grand. This mothafucka thinks I'm about to be intimidated by his martial arts. He doesn't know that my boy Terence knows all that martial arts shit too, and he hips me to a lot of techniques, especially defensively. Not to mention the fact my brother in law Benny trained me in boxing from the ages of eight to fifteen. I know Connor's about to come out fast and aggressive, so I gotta be ready. Joshy walked over to Curtis and put his arm around him, drinking out of his beer, as Curtis continued to count, "Six, seven…" the guys all do their own thing as the count gets closer. "Eight, nine," Curtis asked Joshy, "What the fuck kind of fight music is this?" Fleet Wood Mac – *Dreams* plays through the Bluetooth speakers in the gazebo.

Alright, Luke, always remember Technique can't be beat! Pace yourself, be patient. HOLY SHIT! Was that just Connor's foot? Fuck, this boy is fast. Aight! I can't lose this! Fuck! Fleetwood Mac continued to play over the Bluetooth speaker as the fight commenced. Joshy spilled his beer on Curtis's Armani shirt while cheering in excitement. The dude in the red shirt and Bradley sing along with the music while they spectate, exhilarated by the fight. Connor's flunky drinks a beer while he looks on confidently. Joshy's cousin does bumps of cocaine as he cheers along with two of the other guys. Connor has come out with a flurry of kicks going for the kill shot immediately. I was able to dodge the initial onslaught by the most minute measure of inches. Connor threw an unorthodox punch that landed, making the inside of my mouth bleed. As I back stepped, I created enough space that allowed Connor to attempt a flying knee. Showtime Baby, I knew he was going to try some fancy shit! While you try to recover your balance, buddy boy, take this quick jab to the stomach! Now that I have you opened up with that stomach jab. I bet you think I'm about to go up top, don't you, Connor? But nope! Oh, my God! I got perfect spacing too. I'm about to break something. Eat this rib shot, you pussy ass, racist, bitch! I landed a left hook that landed directly on Connor's rib cage. Connor immediately falls to the ground and begins moaning in agony; he gasps for air in between his cries. Curtis dashed over to me. I was about to go in for a few additional punches. Curtis hugged on me and cheered enthusiastically. Connor's flunky sprinted over to aid him. Joshy's cousin is laughing as he walks over yelling "Worldstar" recording Connor lying on the ground. The guys who bet against me all had looks of shock and distress on their faces. One of the dudes was pulling his hair up while Joshy danced in his face! Joshy's cousin walked over to Connor; he speaks loudly as he bends over to talk to Connor, "Damn bro, what the fuck! I just lost two hundred bucks on you. You showed me videos of you sparing in the gym on your phone!" Connor's flunky shoved Joshy's cousin away from Connor. "Back the fuck up dude! Give him some space to breathe!" As Joshy's cousin recovered from getting shoved, he notices something on Connor's leg, and he points with his finger and the light on his cell phone." Hey, bro, is his leg bleeding? Wait, that's not blood! That's Shit! Connor pooped his pants!" All the guys laughed except for Connor's flunky. He just lost seventy-five-hundred dollars and is attempting to tend to his best friend. Car headlights begin illuminating from the front of the Cabin; Curtis composes himself from laughter and yells out. "I think the escorts are here guys, Bradley do you have the money box?" Joshy happily dances over to Curtis. "Joshy, I don't know why you're so happy. You know you're paying for this shirt."

CHAPTER VIII: CHRONICLES OF THE JUICEMAN VOL. 2

"How can you be something if you don't know what you want!"

-Millie Mac

THE PREACHERS SON

Isaac kept floating the idea of us robbing this stash house that he heard about from one of the old bitches that we were fucking. We didn't need any more enemies, we thought about robbing this liquor store, but the possibility for failure was too high. I needed to figure something out because I was about sixty percent sure that Manny would kill me, but I was ninety-nine percent sure that Manny would kill Isaac if we didn't get the rest of his money. I had to figure something out fast, and that's when it hit me like a bolt of lightning. One of Delilah's few requirements was that I attend Church with her at least once a month. The Church that we went to was a joke. The preacher was pimping the congregation, even my aunt. I think Delilah gave money to the Church because she felt that God would forgive her for being gay. The preacher was gaming everybody in that Church I kind of found enjoyment in watching that snake work. Other than that, those three hours in that Church was worse than a whole school day. Delilah and I sat in the same spot every time, and the preacher's son would always find a way to sit around me. Pastor Stewarts's son Chris wanted to be street so bad; his daddy had a big house outside of the city in the suburbs, he went to an excellent school, but this nigga wanted to be Tupac. Chris didn't know how I got down, but I could tell I was what he wanted to be. I had to check him more than a few times. If I didn't know any better, I would think this nigga was the police as many questions that he asks. One day he told and showed me something that caught my attention. Delilah asked him to take me home one Sunday after the service. She stayed after until into the late evening to help set up for an upcoming event. Chris drove his 1992 Pontiac Grand Am on the 395 highway leaving out of Washington D.C.. He turned down the "Strictly 4 My N.I.G.G.A.Z" tape that played and started to tell me how I could make thirty grand. Chris said that his dad kept some of the Church's money in this office building outside of the city.

Pastor Stewart couldn't have all the money he was running through the Church going into the banking system, so he kept it in an inconspicuous spot, and people wouldn't ask too many questions. The office sat in plain sight, disguised as a charity. Chris showed me a grand that he said he took from the stash. Chris said they didn't even keep the money in a safe. They kept it in different boxes in a padlocked closet. Chris said there were cameras in the building, but they didn't work most of the time. The building had a few security guards, but they were unarmed. The only thing we would have to worry about was the security guard that stayed inside the office overnight. Chris said that was where I could help. I could handle the security guard while he broke into the closet with the money. That nigga felt he was thug after he told me about the capper and his plan. I couldn't help but clown Christopher's bama ass! This nigga wanted to be a criminal so bad! I have never seen a nigga who had such a good life, work so hard to fuck it up. I didn't even consider what Chris told me. I kept going to Church with Delilah, my required one time a month, and Chris kept trying to be cool with me and front like he was a bad boy.

SIXTEEN THOUSAND

Isaac and I had two days left to get Manny's money. I never thought I would be reaching out to Chris, but I was running out of time and couldn't think of any ideas. I figured I might as well scope out the spot that Chris talked about, I paged Chris, and he called me back on the pay-phone outside of the diner. Chris was delighted that I beeped him. He met Isaac and me up at the diner spot that I continued to go to after all these years. I still haven't run into Jimmy Brooks yet, but I still think he's alive. Chris showed up and was more reserved than usual, which was good because the last thing I wanted was for him to say something wrong to Isaac. Chris explained how all we had to do was subdue the one security guard that stayed overnight in the office; he said we didn't have to worry about the building security guards because they didn't secure the building. Chris told us that we wouldn't have trouble getting inside because a few offices in the building ran overnight, and people were in and out. This nigga was trying to do some strong-arm shit that he saw in a movie. Chris told us that unlike the building security, the guard that worked overnight carried a firearm. Chris expected me and Isaac to knock on the office door, and when the guard answered, we could rush him, and while Isaac and I were handling the security guard, he would hit the closet where the money was and start grabbing cash out of the boxes. There were so many flaws in his plan that I just wasted my time. This nigga was going to get me, and Isaac killed, he expected us to go at a full-sized grown-ass man, and it's no telling what kind of training he has, or who he has connections with.

I decided to get Chris to take us to the building to scope it out for myself. From the outside, the building looked like it might be able to work. I hopped out of Chris's car, leaving him with Isaac while I inspected the building's outside. When I looked around, I saw two other exits, other than the front door. One of the exits wouldn't work because it's fenced in, but the alley's side exit might work. It shared the same passage with the building next to it, and the path didn't lead to any main streets, so if we had to, we could park where the alleys ended and run to the car after we pulled the move. At that point, I was about at ten percent on leaning towards pulling the move. The only way I would do it was to get to a high enough percentage where I felt comfortable was to see the inside, but I wasn't sure how to get inside without raising any suspicion. Chris was probably telling the truth about people going out of the building overnight, but I was sure none of those people were a fourteen-year-old Black kid with a babyface. I had to figure a way to get in the building, and that's when I thought about the pizza spot we passed that was a few blocks away from the building. We posted outside of the pizza spot for like an hour. Chris and Isaac were bugging the hell out of me, but I was concentrating, and my intentness through all the noise paid off. I found this middle-aged white man leaving out of the building wearing the pizzerias uniform. Cigarette smoke sprouted from his direction. I approached him in the most non-threatening manner that I could present.

My mother was someone I still dislike to this day, but she was the smartest person I've ever come across. Not only did she have an academic mind, but Olivia also posed the ability to read and control people like no other, and that's one thing she passed down to me. I knew Jerry was on that shit before I even introduced myself. He had the same fiend energy that Olivia fell victim to as she progressively withered away. I didn't have to front with Jerry. I gave him fifty dollars that I got from Chris to buy his shirt and hat. I brought some pizza from the spot, and as we drove back to the building, Isaac grabbed my shoulder, telling me. "Slim, I see what you're trying to do. You're about act like the pizza boy, right?" He asked. I responded saying, "Nah, you are!" "Why can't you do it?" Isaac asked. "Because you look older and they'll recognize Chris!"

MONEY BY ANY MEANS

I planned to use this old head Isaac, and I used to fuck with as a decoy and our way into the office. The night that Isaac went in dressed as a pizza boy, he told me the guard in the lobby was watching his portable T.V. and just waved him in as he walked towards the desk. On the other hand. The guard in the fifth-floor office was different. He told Isaac nobody order no fucking pizza and to bounce before he beat his little ass. Isaac described the guard and knew that Janet could distract him long enough for us to do what I planned. On the night of the capper, Janet walked me through the lobby of the building. The guard was sleep this time. I stopped the elevator on the second floor to get off, run down the stairwell that leads to the alley, and let Isaac and Chris inside. Janet left the office door unlocked like I asked while she kept the guard busy in another room. Isaac watched the front door, and Chris went into the room with the money closet. I stayed in the center watching everything, but I missed Isaac not locking the door behind us. A burly man walked through the door carrying Chinese food; Isaac pulled out his twenty-five caliber handgun and shot the muscular man in the knee once he spotted him. The security guard with Janet in the room on the opposite end came out with his gun drawn. Lucky for us, he burst out the room with Janet so fast that he didn't have time to pull his pants up all the way, and he fell and dropped his gun as Janet ran past him. I felt like I was close enough to grab it, but instead, I used my adrenaline to get out of dodge. Chris was the first one out of the door I kicked by old boy Isaac shot. He tried to grasp Isaac as he ran out of the office, using his reach to grab Isaac's ankle and trip him up. I kicked him in his knee, Isaac got up from the ground, and we pushed it full speed through the hallway towards the stairs. Chris's slow ass didn't get too far ahead of us; we caught up to him. The last thing Chris said to me before we went into that stairwell was. "Jalon, don't let me die. I don't want to go to hell."

JEFE'S APPRENTICE

There was a backlash after Chris's death. The cops tried to figure out why, this straight "A" student, son of a beloved preacher, was in an alley with his head bashed in, a gunshot to his back sixty-thousand-dollars stuffed in his pants. That snake ass nigga Chris was trying to keep the sixty grand for himself and still split the thirty thousand with Isaac and me. That shot to Chris's back saved Isaac or me from putting one in his head; he definitely would have become a problem. It didn't take long for the police to stop looking for the other two culprits of the break-in; they were more intrigued by the fact that the office of Charity had armed over-night security. Pastor Stewart cooperated with the police immediately. He was laundering money through his Church and charity. Pastor Satan. I mean, Pastor Stewart gave up a crew out of Southwest D.C. to stay out of prison and keep his house and assets. I told myself that was the last time that I would be that reckless. I let Olivia's death have more of an effect on my mental then I allowed myself to recognize.

I created a problem for myself that could have got me, and Delilah killed, and then I attempted to alleviate the quandary by pulling a capper with a nigga who I knew wasn't built for it, all the while potentially creating more enemies who probably wouldn't have been like Manny. After that capper, I wasn't sure what my next move would be once I gave Manny the rest of his money. I had grown weary of the direction that I was taking, but I wasn't sure what my new path needed to be. The next afternoon following the capper with Isaac and Chris. I met Manny at the Café that we robbed. Manny was seated at a table to the very back of the cafe; he placed the book down that he was reading "The Prince" and waved me over. Only a few people were seated two elder women eating grapefruit and the other two people. There was a woman and a man that mean mugged me as I walked towards the back. Manny didn't say anything for at least twenty seconds when I first sat down; he just sat there and stared at me, then out of nowhere, a big smile came across his face; he laughed for a moment before he started the conversation.

"Jalon, I bet you get a lot of girls wearing that shirt!" Manny pointed to my shirt. I was wearing my China Hut work shirt and blue-jeans, I told Manny, "I have to go to work soon." "So let me ask you this, Mr. 'I have to go to work soon.' Is the "China Hut" or robbing people your part-time job because I'm confused," Manny asked. A woman with an apron around her waist came out of the kitchen. Manny called her name. She walked over, and he whispered something in her ear. She looked over at me and then walked away; as soon as she left, Manny continued.

"So Jalon, which one are you?" I responded, "I'm the one who is apologizing! I meant no disrespect. I got twenty thousand in the doggie bag next to me. I'm hoping this means that Isaac and me a squared away." Manny placed the doggie bag that I handed to him under the table on the seat; he looked through the bag and then asked, " How did you get the money?" "I robbed a liquor store!" I said quickly. Manny laughed, "Well, they must have been having a good night." The woman Manny whispered to came over, placed a plate of food and a drink in front of me; Manny handed her the doggie bag. Manny shrugged, "Since you don't know which one you are, Jalon, I'll tell you. You're neither of them. You're nothing! You don't even seem like you know what you want. How can't you be something if you don't know what you want!" "I know what I want!" I said. "And what is that China Hut?" he asked. "I want to own a piece of the world." I said slowly. Looking at me in the eyes he asked, "Why not the whole world?" "Because I'm not greedy, overeating can kill you," I answered. "I guess this taught you not to bite off more than you can chew, huh kid!" Manny smiled.

Manny talked to me for a little bit as I ate my food. Before I finished, he got up told me to quit my job and meet him back at the café in four days. When I got to the café, I had the expectations that I would actually be doing and learning something, but instead, Manny wasn't even there. The girl who served me my food four days ago told me that Manny said to help out around the café and he'll talk to me when he gets time. They had me scrubbing dishes from nine in the morning until eight at night. I was pissed! The girl told me that Manny said he should have time tomorrow. I went through the same routine of going to the café expecting to meet Manny, but instead, she said that he said to help and he'll talk to me when he gets time. On the fourth day, I had finally had enough. I just told the girl that I was done. I wasn't washing another plate, emptying another trash-can, or cleaning another toilet. I was passionate about what I was saying without being loud are aggressive. The girl looked me up and down and just left out. I talked to myself in disbelief! I was frustrated at my core. I threw my apron to the floor and left out. I walked out of the kitchen I saw Manny sitting in the same spot from five days before. He got up, walked over looking at me. I was wearing my frustrations on my sleeve. Manny just smiled and nodded towards the front door. My Timberland boots submerged into the mid-January snow that lined the sidewalk. We hopped in Manny's Purple Lexus GS, and from that point on, class was in session. Manny was like other street dudes that I had come across, but he had the perfect mix of the street side of the game and the mentality of a cooperate CEO. Everything was just business to him. Manny rarely took things personally. Manny had three other business partners, and together they called themselves "The South American Baron's, there was "Jalapeño Juan" from Uruguay, they called him that because he put Jalapeno's on practically everything, and he had a very flamboyant, spicy personality. I've seen Juan put Jalapeno's in Ice cream. And then there was "Aruban Alejandro", there was "Stone Face Ernesto." They called him that because no one has ever seen him smile, even growing up as a child in Ecuador it was said that Ernesto never smiled. Probably because he was the muscle and a heartless killer with no empathy, and last but not least you have the head of the "S.A.B." Manny Castro aka "Millie Mac." Manny had an extremely magnetizing personality. It's like no matter what room he entered people were drawn to him in some capacity. Manny was a natural born leader if his world would have been different he could have been the head of the "United Nations." Over those next twelve months from January 1994 to January 1995 I quickly learned the game and rose in the organization. At first I was just an errand boy, but Manny use to have me ride around everywhere with him. The other dudes in the commission Juan and Alejandro didn't really care for me. They were prejudice against blacks and would often let me know that fact. Ernesto didn't care though. One day Manny told me that Ernesto said that he liked the Negro kid that was always around, Manny was Venezuelan but took on the mentality of a Black American man. Manny knew so much about Black history that I never was taught or heard of in my life. Manny use to educate me about so much when it came to the history of my people. I eventually saw why Manny was like he was when I first met his father Adrian Sr. in the spring of 95'. Manny was just like him, personable, funny, honest, and very intellectual. Adrian Sr. told me about the Haitian revolution and how their rebellion inspired Simon Bolivar to help Venezuela gain there independence. While I was learning from Adrian Sr., Manny was upstairs with his little brother Adrian Jr. The happiest that I would ever see Manny is when he was with his little brother Adrian Jr. Manny's father and step mother were constantly at odds, and on more than a few occasions Manny would take care of Adrian Jr. while his father was out chasing his step mother who would always run off to Florida to be with her family, and probably dude on the side that she had out there. I'll will never forget what Manny said to me when we got in the car after leaving his father house. "Hermanito I'm going to stop just calling you Jalon. You need a name to match who you are now." Manny looked in the rear view mirror running his hands through his jet black curly hair, "From now on your not just Jalon. You're Juice!" "Why Juice?" I asked. "Because your pure Hermanito! And you have the ability to mix in anything," he said. The name and the explanation didn't really make sense to me but I just accepted it and followed Manny's lead as always. I became like Manny's little brother, he told me that I reminded him of a younger version of himself, we were like a family. Especially after Manny helped get Benji out of jail. Benji was up for parole and Manny used his connections with this capitol hill lawyer to get Benji an early release. It turns out the Judge and District attorney in Benji's case were dirty as fuck, and the lawyer was able to get Benji an early release, he only served seven years on his fifteen year sentence. Benny knew what it was with me before he even got out of Lorton. Nigga's in jail ain't got shit to do but talk about what's going on with nigga's on the outside, and Benji heard that his little brother was running with some Spanish cats who were slinging in the city with the blessing from the locals that ran the scene. Back then D.C. nigga's wasn't fucking with out of towners doing business in the city especially nigga's from New York. "The Rat" got niggas locked up and so many others in the city killed. That if you came from out of town you better come with respect and honor or you was getting sent back home in a body bag. Even though Manny got Benji out on an early release I could tell that he had reservations about Manny, but Millie Mac being the man he is threw Benji a welcome home party where the both of them had a one on one talk for over an hour. After their talk a drunken Benji pulled me outside, he told me that he knew I was too far gone and he knew that I was gonna be in the game no matter what, but Benji said that he trusted Manny to be the Lion to navigate me through the jungles. "Benji Tigers are in the jungle not Lions! Jalee shut the hell up, I'm drunk! You know what I meant. Regardless either way little brother I love you and I'm happy to be home. Now let me get back up in here so I can holla at this big booty bitch from "Trenton Park." From 1995 going into 1996. I was happy like I was before Benji got locked up. Delilah had grown to accept that she couldn't do anything about me being in the game. She knew that's what I was going to do no matter what. If she wants me to be in her life she was just going to have to accept it. Delilah was happy at that point in her life too, she was dating a cool woman from West Baltimore, she had a second successful business up and running. Delilah was in a good place but was concerned about her nephew that had dropped out of high school, and she thought that I knew something about what happen to Chris but only hinted towards it. Manny sat down and had a one on one with Delilah. It almost felt like a college coach going to meet a five star recruits parents the way Manny had conversations with Benny and Delilah. Manny is a one of a kind person, not only was he able to get my aunts blessing but she agreed to sign for an apartment on the contingency that I get my GED before I turned seventeen. They both agreed and I had my own apartment three months before my sixteenth birthday. Manny taught me so much and made both me and my family's life better. We had a make shift tribe that we had developed. Manny's father treated me like his son and Adrian Jr. loved me like I was his brother. That little dude was so sweet and happy, he was always laughing expect for when he didn't get his way. Adrian the little manipulator would hold his breathe when he didn't get his way. One day I called him Blue and it kind of just stuck after that. Adrian Sr. ended up becoming really tight with this cat that stayed in his neighborhood Willie Banks and his wife Anna Banks. Willie had a teenaged daughter named Sadie. Eventually Sadie was babysitting Blue along with her little brother Luke. Sadie was fine, smart, and slim, she was cool like she was one of the fellas. I was confident in my game at that point and had been fucking bitches since I was eleven, but Sadie wouldn't give me the time of day. I was kind of taken back by her not going for me. At that point no females that I pursued was turning me down no matter what age. I already had game before I met Manny, but after I became his little man's my game went to five thousand. Any time I tried to get a shorty I got her, but not Sadie. Manny never told me but from being around him all the time. I ended up discovering that him and Sadie had a fling, and Manny took her virginity, but it ended up being Sadie who called off the fling, leaving Manny who never gave a fuck about a chick ended up being the one who in his feelings. One day at my apartment in 97' Benny and Sadie crossed paths and they have been connected ever since. Shit was moving at that point. I was far from an errand boy. I was able to have my own crew. It was Isaac, and one of Ernesto little man's Diego. We would drop off packages sometimes, or we would scope targets for Ernesto on some stake out shit. I wanted Ken to be with the crew but Manny wasn't having it. Manny told me straight up that I couldn't rock with Kenny because of who he ran with since his release from Juvie. I always kept it solid with Manny. I did everything I was told and more, but I could never just cut off Ken. I remember the first time I killed someone for Manny it was the winter of 97' just a couple of weeks after my sixteenth birthday. My second body was this twenty two year old, pretty ass redbone named Yolanda. Manny had a stable of woman and Yolanda was just one of many. At first she accepted there situation but that didn't last very long and she started to become extremely jealous, she started talking crazy to Manny about how she knew he was a drug dealer, and maybe other people should know too. This is the most responsibility that Manny had ever entrusted to me. I haven't killed anybody since Muhammad and I still see his face in my dreams, but this is the life I chose and what has to be done has to be done! Yolanda use to flirt with me all the time so he felt it would be perfect to send me because she liked me and wouldn't be suspicious of anything. I went over to her apartment with blue tulips and a bag of sour patch kids which were her favorite candy. Yolanda had just gotten out of the shower her hair was dripping wet when she answered the door, she was wearing a robe the top of her voluptuous titties glisten. She looked at me as I stood with the blue tulips and sour patch kids in my hand. Yolanda contemplated for a second and then finally let me into her apartment. She offered me a drink but I turned it down and just asked if I could use her bathroom. I asked her was she getting freshen up for someone or was someone already here, she snidely told me no, and the continued to complain to me about Manny. I went in the bathroom, closed the door behind me, took a water bottle out of my backpack and poured it into the toilet. I flushed the toilet and then cut on the sink. I took my backpack from around my shoulders and put the empty water bottle in it, and then I pulled out a "Beretta M9A3" that had a suppressor attached to it. I already had on gloves because of the winter weather. Yolanda's bedroom door was cracked, when I completely opened the door Yolanda was butt naked putting lotion onto her body, at first she didn't see the gun in my hand and turned to me and said. "BOY GET OUT! I'M GETTING DRESSED"! I shot her twice from where I was standing by the door frame and then I walked up to her body and shot her twice up close. I took the flowers and candy that laid on top of her bed put them in my bookbag. I looked for and found the pager that Manny gifted to Yolanda so they could communicate. I put the pager in my bag and then rolled out. I was driving at that point and all I could think to myself was that unlike Muhammad this time I didn't feel shit. It was just something that had to be done. Manny was pleased with the way I handled myself. His connection in the department told him that they didn't have any witnesses, evidence, or leads when it came to the homicide of Yolanda Yates. It was the end of January when I took care of that problem for Manny. The next five months felt like a year, so much would transpire. Barrett died of a heart attack at the age for forty six. Ms. Zhao was diagnosed stomach cancer. I was making a lot of money at that point and could afford to pay for her medical expenses, as often as I could. I would spend time with Ms. Zhao and we would only speak in Mandarin to one another during my visits. I ended up developing a romantic relationship with one of Sadie's friends Rose Jenkins. Rose came from a family that was known for their criminality, she was a ghetto princess so to speak, and Rose one of the finest women I've ever seen. She got an academic scholarship to George Town University, but she decided to choose Howard University instead. Niggas were on Rose heavy but she chose me and that came with a lot a hate and bullshit, but I had developed a reputation and nigga's would seldom try me. The crew that I formed had dissolved. Isaac got sent away to military school. Diego was serving time for breaking a cops jaw, and I was still keeping my distance from Kenny. Manny started to having problems within his organization in the spring of ninety-seven. "Stone Face Ernesto" was killed outside of a bar in Quito Ecuador. Ernesto was back in Ecuador visiting his son who was celebrating his 9th birthday. Manny never told me who killed Ernesto, he just kept me focused on the moves that he wanted me to make for him. Manny was always composed, and in control, but there were moments that I could tell he was distracted. Either that or he knew something that I didn't. Manny was out town a lot in that five month time span, but when he wasn't out of town we were spending time with his father and little brother. Manny brought a single family house in Indian Head Maryland, he put in the house in his aunt's name and the house would go to Blue if he graduated high school and college. Manny gave me an address and a code to a safe just in case. I was nervous for the first time in a while. I didn't know what was gonna happen. Jalapeno Juan ended up going missing in the middle of June, he sent all the money he was supposed to send from the deal, but never got back to Manny and Alejandro. It was a Friday morning on the last week of June. I was in the living room of Adrian Sr. house, while he was at work. Sadie was babysitting Blue and Luke, she was in the back yard talking to Manny while I sat in the living room. Blue and Luke were watching this show called "Angry Beavers" the commentary that the two of them were having while they looking at the cartoon had me geeking laughing. Those two youngins are something else. Benji tells me all the time that Luke is just like I was as a kid. I kind of see it sometimes when I'm around him. The kid is only four, and he likes trying to make his own money. Luke and Blue always make me smile when I'm around them. Just look at the two of them. They started off laughing with each other and now their arguing. And then their right back to laughing and joking again. Manny came into the living room and told me we had to go. Blue started throwing a fit, but Manny just left Sadie to tend to the boys, while we went and attended to business. I ended up driving Manny up to New Jersey so he could meet with someone, and then from there we flew down to Miami, we got back on the first of July nineteen-ninety-seven. After we landed in Reagan National Airport Manny said he would get in touch with me. I parted ways with Manny and went to my Aunt Delilah's spot instead of going to my own apartment. I was tried after all that running around with Manny. I needed some home cooking and comfort. I slept for a day and a half, Delilah woke me up on the morning of July third, breakfast awaited me in dining room along with Manny who was eating and reading a newspaper. I barely ate as Manny finished his plate and cracked jokes with Delilah and her girlfriend. We left Delilah's spot and I spent another day watching Manny handle business. The way he was able to deal with people was amazing. Manny had the ability to disarm the most anti-social person, he made cold blooded killers laugh. We finished attending all of Manny's meetings and headed to his father's house to pick up Blue so we could go see "Men In Black." When we left out of the movie theater I just remember thinking that this life I chose can be beautiful when you do it right! Two bullets went into my body as Manny gurgled blood from the gunshot to his neck. My last recollection was crawling out of the passenger seat of Manny's Cadillac and attempting to get Blue out of the car. I don't even think I heard the kid crying. I woke up in the hospital. Benny and Delilah were waiting for me but so were two detectives. They tried all the scare tactics but they couldn't get shit out of me. The one thing they said that caught my attention was the name Alejandro Diaz. Aruban Al didn't care for me in first place, so why let me stay around with all that I might know. I got released from the hospital two days after being shot. I had too much on my mind and didn't know what my next move would be. I decided to go to the diner that me and Isaac always went to, I hadn't been in a while and felt like having the meal I use to always eat up there, and I hoped it would help me gain some clarity. My right arm was in a sling. I was walking with a heavy limp from the gunshot to my right leg. I sat down and Ms. Baker the waitress who had been serving since I was in elementary waited on me. Ms. Baker gave me extra's because she felt sorry for me. I sat there eating my food thinking about my world. Manny was dead and that shit had a major effect on me. Isaac was gone to some military academy in the Mid-West, and Killa Ken was back in jail. This time until he twenty-one. I found myself staring at my plate mid-way through my meal. This bummy ass nigga that was always outside of the diner approached me, usually I'm a patient person, but I was about to knock this nigga head off if he asked me for something! This nigga can't be older than fifty but he out here homeless. Fucking bum ass nigga! He said, "Say young blood! Why don't you come and get some better food?" I stared at the man for a minute straight before I said, "But ain't this your restaurant?" He looked at me and said. "You coming or not youngblood?"

CHAPTER IX: SADIE & BENNY

"Honest men make the worst liars"

-Anna Banks

T he smell of fried food fills the second-floor apartment
complex hallway. Sadie knocks on the apartment door two-thirty-six;
she pulls a wallet out of her front pocket, looking in it to make sure all
the money inside when she found it is still there. Jalon answers the
door as he wipes an apple off, smiling at Sadie, knowing she's mad at
him. "Jalon, you think you're slick!" She accused. "What are you
talking about?" He asked. "You know what I'm talking about," Sadie
slams the wallet into Jalon's chest! "Leaving your wallet at my parent's
crib so you can get me over here, I already told you I don't want your
young ass. Plus, I told you, my homegirl, Rose liked you." Sadie
shoves her way into the apartment. "Move boy, I gotta pee!" Jalon
smiles as he closes and locks each lock on the door. "How you just
gonna come in my apartment acting all rude and shit slim?" "Yeah,
this is your apartment until the Law takes it from your little ass!" She
said. "First off, I would have to get knocked, and I would never allow
that to happen. Secondly, you're only four years older than me, and
finally, the apartment ain't in my name. As you said, Sadie, I'm a
minor!" Jalon stands in front of Sadie, blocking her path as she does
the, "I have to take piss shuffle." "Stop playing Juice! Which one is
the bathroom?" Jalon laughs as he steps to the side and points towards
the back hallway. "It's gonna be the first door on your right." Sadie
leaves out of the bathroom, drying her hands with Burger King
napkins. She wasn't paying attention as she bumps into Benny. "Damn
shorty 'excuse me' is the word you're looking for!" He said. Sadie cuts
her eyes at Benny but is instantly attracted to him. The two have a
momentary standoff before they both fall victim to love at first sight.
There is a brief light-hearted back and forth before Benny made Sadie
bust out laughing. The two future soul mates talk in the hallway
uninterrupted for twenty plus minutes before Jalon inserts himself.
Sadie leaves, annoyed by Jalon. Shortly after she left, Benny asks his
little brother on the fly about Sadie. Jalon tells his older brother how
Sadie is the only woman ever to turn down his advances consistently.
Jalon would have thought Sadie was just a pretty ass dike if he would

have never overheard Manny and her talking. Benny nonchalantly asks his little brother, "Is Manny talking to shorty?" "Nah, I don't think so; from what I overheard, it just seemed like a fling!" Jalon responded. Benny and Jalon spent another hour hanging out before Benny exited the apartment. All he could think about after he left was his interaction with Sadie. It took Benny a few months before he arranged a date with Sadie. The two progressively grew to enjoy one another's company after that first date on Valentine's Day of nineteen-ninety-seven. Two and a half years later, Sadie was staying with Benny in his Upper Marlboro Maryland townhome. Sadie was working for an accounting firm, and Benny's janitorial service business was growing, but like any good relationship, they had their fair share of turmoil.

"THE FEAR OF GOD IN HIS SOUL"

"My first instinct was just to cut him off! If he's willing to jeopardize what we have to relive his past, then that's his loss. But this isn't that. This situation happens to be a sneaky bitch trying to tempt a man she doesn't have anymore. My birth mother left my father and me when I was a baby, and my stepmother Anna didn't come into my life until I was a teenager. We just started getting along a year ago when I graduated from Howard University, and our relationship has evolved into mutual love, respect, and admiration. Right now, we're sitting in the living room of my mommy and daddies house. My daddy is out fishing with Benny, Adrian Sr., Luke, and Adrian Jr. I'm asking my step-mommies advice on handling this situation with Benny and this old flame trying to slither her way back into his life. This bitch is trying to use her son as a way to get back in with Benny. Benny trains kids at a boxing gym in Prince Georges County Maryland and this heifer signed her son up at the gym earlier this year and slowly but surely, this bitch has been on the creep. A few months ago, I got a major red flag when Benny and some of the other trainers took Luke and five other boys to a two-day boxing tournament in Philadelphia. Of course, some of the parents went along, and that bitch just happened to be one of them. I would have gone, but I couldn't take off work. Now I didn't have any hard evidence besides my intuition, and something felt different about Benny when he came back from Philadelphia last month. My Mommy was quiet as she listened to what I was saying, drinking from her wine glass. My Momma is in her early forties, but she could pass as my older sister. She's like an Angelia Basset or Tina Turner, a true living example of "black don't crack". We were sitting on opposite ends of the sofa. She put her glass on the coaster, and then she started talking. Anna told me stories about my father that I had never heard before. "Sadie baby, I'm so glad we're at the point where we can talk Woman to Woman instead of Stepmother to Stepdaughter! I want you to understand that I will always love your father regardless of what our future holds, but with that said…I have to value myself and my worth as a woman more. Sadie, you're way more mentally mature than I was at your age, so I know you know your value. Do you feel this current relationship is cheapening your value?" Sadie pours the rest of the wine bottle in her wine glass before locking her stepmother's eyes, "Mommy, honestly, I'm not sure anymore! Ever since I told him I wasn't going to be ready for kids for a long time, I felt a slight distance that has only grown with our work schedules, and the devil is sending this bitch back into his life has only made things more uncertain." Anna smiled at Sadie, getting up from the couch in the living room, going into the kitchen. She returns with a bottle of wine, uncorking it with a wine key before sitting back down on the sofa with Sadie. "Do you remember your Senior year of high school when your father and I spent that weekend in Virginia Beach with the Turner's?" She asked. "Are you talking about when daddy came back with stitches?" Sadie begins to laugh. "How did daddy fall down the stairs again?" "Sadie, he didn't fall down, no damn stairs. That's just what we told you and Luke. I found out that he had been messing what some fast ass tramp from his job," she admitted. "How did you find out, Ma?" Sadie asked in surprise. "Oh, I knew a month before we went to Virginia Beach. Honest men make the worse liars. And I caught Willie up in a lie, so I decided to follow him with Betty," she continued. Sadie is both intrigued and shocked, "What did you and Ms. Betty end up doing?" "Nothing! The hardest part was trying to get Betty, not to kill her and not let your father know that I knew. I know Ms. Betty probably had a brain aneurysm trying to hold it in. Child, you don't know the half of it!" Both women start cracking up laughing.

"Girl Betty was saying so much slick subtle shit to your father he had to know something was up." "What did he do?" Sadie asked. "What could he do but just come out and confess the truth?" she said. Sadie asked quickly, "Did he?" "No, not at first. His male ego was still lying to him." Sadie pours more wine into both of their glasses, tuned into her step mom's story like must-see TV. "So it was Saturday, I think? Yeah, had to because we got back that Sunday night, so Betty and I made sure we got your daddy and Mr. Turner real drunk that night. After we saw Bernie Mac in concert, we hung out in the Turner's hotel room a while before we went back to ours. Now I'm usually not able to get your Daddy to try much, but I got him to do some role-playing. I brought some real sexy lingerie just for that weekend. Your Daddy was hanging out the bottom of his silk boxers." "Eww, Mommy, I don't need to know all that!" Anna has her legs crossed as she smiles and reflects on that evening. "So I got him to let me tie him up like I was a sexy kidnapper. We started getting into it, and I waited until he was comfortable before I got serious. And that's when I put the fear of God in his soul!" Sadie is stunned after Anna tells her what she did to her Father. "The whole point of that story is to tell you that your Father is a good man, a great Father, and has always been there for me. Willie was a ladies man back in the day when we both used to live in Chicago, and even though I had a newborn when we reconnected, he saw past that and still wanted to be with me, but even the greatest of man is bound to fall victim to their male egos. Cheating is no damn mistake! It took me a lot not to leave your father, but deep down inside, I know he was a pure-hearted man who is willing to die for all of us. What I'm trying to convey to you, baby, is how great is Benny really? And does he deserve your forgiveness?" At that moment, the front door was unlocking.

Willie enters first, carrying Luke in his arm as he slept on his shoulder. Adrian Sr. and Adrian Jr. enter the house next. Adrian Jr. let's go of his father's hand, rushing over to greet Sadie. "Adrian, you don't know how to say hi to me?" Anna scolded. "Oh, hello, Ms. Anna!" Adrian Jr. says. Benny enters the living room last, carrying a red cooler with the fish they caught inside. Benny respectfully greets Anna first before he talks to Adrian, who is holding on to Sadie. "Adrian can I have my women back?" Adrian defiantly tells Benny, "No! She's my woman,

and I'm gonna play the piano for her and marry her when I get big!"
Everyone laughs as Benny playfully pulls Adrian off of Sadie before
he hands him over to his father and leans in to kiss Sadie. "What's
wrong with you, baby?" Sadie calmly smiles as she tells Benny
nothing. Anna interjects, saying. "All of y'all need to get out my living
room, y'all smell like the damn Chesapeake. Benny, go and put that
fish in the back yard and grab some newspapers so I can cut the fish
up." Adrian Sr. tells Anna. "No need Ann. You ladies, go back to
whatever you were discussing the men are taking care of dinner this
evening." Both mother and daughter look at each other and then at
Benny for a split second. Benny jokingly asks what he did to which
Sadie replies. "Nothing at all. You can just tell that you've been
fishing!"

WOMAN TO WOMAN (AUGUST 22nd 2001)

"So I spent about a month collecting all info I could on Benny's old
flame, Jasmine. I knew this Bitch's schedule like I was her assistant. I
finally decided to confront her on a Wednesday night as she was
coming out of Bible Study. She and the Pastor were usually the last
ones to leave. That Bitch is probably fucking him too! I had Rose with
me because she is the only person I can trust with some shit like this.
Plus, she had animosity towards that Bitch, Jasmine, like she was
sleeping with Jalon instead of Benny. Rose was driving while I sat on
the passenger side, and fate was on our side that night because the
pastor pulled out of the parking lot before she did, she was all by
herself. Rose drove up behind Jasmine's car, blocking her in as she
tried to leave out. I wore a yellow ski mask over my head. I was
pulling her out of the car before she even knew what was going on.
Now I don't have many regrets in my life, but that night Rose, and I
might have gone too far. I know she was still alive because she was
whimpering and crying when we finally stopped. I had so much
adrenaline pumping I didn't even realize that I had her earring in the
palm of my left hand attached to a piece of her earlobe. Rose wild ass
was way more celebratory than I was. I still had to confront Benny
about the whole situation finally, and I would do it over dinner. I knew

106

Benny wasn't going to get home until a little before Midnight, so I made sure I stayed awake to have our talk. I made beef stew and already had his bowl for him waiting in the microwave, and an ice-cold beer was on the kitchen countertop. I waited about ten minutes before I went into the living room to talk to him. "Oh, what's up, baby, what you still doing up?" Sadie is smiling and calm as she walks over to Benny, kissing his cheek and neck, and then massaging his shoulders. "I just wanted to make sure you enjoyed your dinner, and I wanted to talk to you." Benny eats a spoon full of the stew, "Girl, when do I not like your cooking? And what you wanna talk about?" "Oh, I wanna talk about Jasmine," she replied. Benny avoids eye contact as he continues to eat his stew." "God damn Sadie, not right now! I'm tired as hell. I had a long fucking day. I already told you ain't nothing going on between us. Her son just works out at my gym, and I train him. That's it! I told you! You need to grow the fuck up and stop with this little girl paranoia that you got floating around in your head!" Sadie removes her hands from Benny's shoulder, sitting down in the chair next to Benny so she could look into his eyes. "Benjamin, I want you to look at me in my eyes, and tell me nothing is going on. I'll leave it alone." Benny shakes his head as he continues to avoid eye contact and tries to redirect the conversation, "You see, Sadie. This is why we bump heads. You're so fucking stubborn! I already told you ain't nothing going on between her and me. I don't know why you even coming at me like this." As Benny takes a spoon full of stew and then bits down on something hard, he removes a diamond earring out of his mouth attached to part of a human earlobe. Benny looks down at his palm in shock and then up at Sadie, who tells him, "Since you like being in that bitches ear so much, I figured you might as well have a piece of it." Benny rushes to the toilet to vomit. When Benny got out of the bathroom, Sadie was gone!

MRS. KNIGHT (MAY 25TH 2005)

"I have never been the jealous type of nigga. For one, that's a trait of a weak man, and I have never been that, and finally, I trust my wife! I know my wife is the person I can trust the most in my life besides my little brother, but even a woman as strong as Sadie can fall victim to a predator. I first met Glenn at a company event that I attended with her. From the second I met Glenn, there was something about him rubbed me the wrong way. He was joking too much, and Sadie was laughing too hard. Every time I had any interaction with Glenn after that event, I still had the same feeling. Now I'm a man! So I can smell when another lion is trying to infringe on my territory, and I know Glenn was doing that from the first time I met him. I kept it back in my mind until Sadie took a business trip with Glenn and a few of her other co-workers. I could tell something happen on the trip when she came back. I didn't feel that she cheated, but I know the thought might have crossed her mind, and I know that sucka Glenn tried to move in on my wife. That's when I decided to show this mothafucka who I was! When I was in prison, and my commissary and the money on my books began changing, I already knew Jalon would be too far gone for me to tell him shit. Niggas in the Bing gossip like bitches, so I knew Jalon was running with some Spanish cats a few years before I got out. Once I got out after doing eight years of my 15 year sentence I got myself a legit job as a janitor. I was always a Boxer. That shit kept me out of the game growing up, but when the streets are where you live, that opinion is always there. Especially for a young nigga with potential, the game is full of predators, and the weak prey on the strong before they know their strength. Prison shows you parts of human nature that most are blessed never to see, and I could tell what my little brother was becoming even before he knew it. I could handle this Bama Glenn by myself, but I have too much to lose to do this solo, and this is the type of life my little brother chose, so I might as well use the resources that I have at my disposal. It was a little after nine-thirty-pm. I told Sadie I was leaving to hang out with Jalon. That's one thing about Sadie when I say I'm with Jalon, she never really asks questions. She lets me and my little brother's relationship just be without interfering. That plus, Rose is one of her best friends, so she knows she always can confirm with her. I parked down the street from the address. The spot was inconspicuous. It was a brick front with a two-door garage. Tinted windows line the garage doors. Boogie opened up the back door moments after I knocked. He was smoking a black & mild cigar as he handed me a ski mask to put on before I walked inside. Boogie nodded his head toward the white work van with black tinted windows. A thousand-watt halogen light plugged in the corner of the garage, partially illuminating two-thirds of the garage, leaving a shadow on the rest. A tall slim light skin man was standing by the van's back door wearing a ski mask. He opened the back door pulling Glenn out of the van. He struggled so much that some of the tools fell off the shelf as the van rocked side to side. Boogie put a forty-five caliber hand-gun to Glenn's head to calm him down. He cowers on his knees, both hands tied behind his back and a Sheep mask, with drunk-googles over his head. Boogie whispered in his ear before removing the gag in his mouth. The tall man who was with Boogie walked over to the garage's corner, cutting off the halogen light. Glenn screamed out when the light was cut off and begin whimpering as Boogie told him to shut the fuck up. The tall man cracked a road flare open, and he held the flare extended to the left as he approached; he threw the flare to the side once he got to the van. Boogie spoke for me because Glenn might recognize my voice. "Glenn, shut the fuck up before we pay your son a visit at Hart Middle School. Glenn breathes heavily as he tries to compose himself. Boogie continues to talk to him. "Now look, Glenn, I'm going to allow you to save your life!" Glenn blurts out. "Look, if this is about Kim, I swear to God she told me that you separated!" Boogie pulls off the beer-googles and sheep mask from over his head. Glenn blinks as his eyes adjust to the flare's light and sway as he tries to get his balance. Boogie taps the forty-five on the back of Glenn's head as he gets him to look forward to me. "You see him right there, Glenn?" Glenn nods his head slowly as his sniffles. "Well, look, Glenn, this is how this will go. If you can knock him off his feet or unconscious, you get to stay alive, but if not…" Boogie cocks the forty-five back, "Then I'm going to kill you right here in this garage." Glenn tries to plead with Boogie as he slowly rises from his knees. "Shut fuck up. This is what I'm going to do for you to give you a better chance to live. I'm going to put a bag over his head." Boogie nodded over to his partner; he put a black cloth bag over my head. Glenn tried to build up the courage to fight for his life. Boogie threatens Glenn again before he yelled out a battle cry and attempted to fight me. He probably missed about five to six punches before I put him to sleep. I lifted the bag over my head, looking at Glenn as he lies unconscious snoring. Boogie looked at me, nodding his head as his partner dragged Glenn to the van's back. All I could hear is crickets chirping as we stood outside the back door. I reminded Boogie what to say to Glenn when he woke up before we parted ways. As soon as I got in the car, my phone rang. It was a woman telling me to meet her at a restaurant in Woodbridge, Virginia. I was in Lorton, Virginia, so it's probably only a fifteen-minute ride at this time of night. I know it was Jalon because that's how he moves. I got to the diner, and Jalon was already talking to the waitress as I walked in. He gestured towards me as the young brunet waitress turned around and smiled at me. We waited until she took our orders and poured coffee before we started talking. "Rosette been asking about her uncle. She hasn't seen you in a while. I know every time she's been over the house lately, I've been at work. You see that, Benji. How beautiful that statement is coming out of your mouth. I've been at work lately. I couldn't see my niece!" Jalon adds more sugar to his coffee after he takes a sip. "That's why it's so perplexing to me that you would risk it all because you think some nobody is fucking your wife." "Well, that nigga doesn't know where it came from, and I bet you he won't be meddling on another nigga's territory again!" Jalon looked at me, shaking his head, smirking before he begins snickering. "Damn Benji, all these years of square living made you forget how shit works. You think I would honestly do all this because of you and your fucking wife!" I was confused by what point Jalon was trying to make. "Benji, that nigga had a contract on him for sticking his dick in the wrong cookie jar. It's crazy how the universe works. Out of all the people that get presented, one of them happens to be fucking Sadie. I knew about Glenn before you even reached out to me. A friend of mines was already taking him off the map. I got him to hold off because I wanted to show you something!" A moment of silence goes by before I asked, "And what are you trying to show me, Jalee?" Jalon took a moment to respond. The waitress brought our meals over and asked us in a chipper manner. "Is there anything else I can get for you guys?" Jalon smiles at the young woman and tells her, "No, ma'am, we're good for now, thank you!"

Jalon begins to eat his food without responding to my question, so I asked him again. "What were you trying to show me, Jalee?" Jalon leaned back, looking at me, putting his arms around the booth, sucking his teeth and saying. "I was just reminding you to be satisfied with what you ordered off the menu, and to be happy that it came out the right way." Jalon smiles as he points at my plate. "Now eat your food, big brother, you don't want it to go cold."

CHAPTER X: PAIGE

"The fabulous type the vanity the eyes hold, but her beauty left you blind to her cold soul."

-Two8G

My name is Paige Leeann Logan. I'm a Leo, I have Amber green eyes, a nice shaped ass, and I wear D-Cups. My butterscotch skin is silky smooth, and my curly brown hair that smells like the sweetest berries. I can't stand a weak or broke nigga. Nothing gets me wetter than a tall, strong, sexy man with a backbone and a bankroll. I like all races of men, but I've mostly dated white guys, but when I met Luke, he was the exception. My best friend Kelly convinced me to come up to a party at The University of Maryland in College Park, Maryland. She was a freshman up there at the time, and even though I was seventeen and a senior in high school, my parents allowed me to go. They pretty much let me do whatever I want. It was early spring me and Kelly were with two other girls at this frat party. One of the girls had on a skirt with Ugg Boots! Like a skirt with Ugg Boots! Are fucking kidding me! Yuck! So ghetto and tacky! Anyways guys were hitting on me nonstop as usual. A few of them were cute, but you could tell they didn't have any money. So if I wanted some dick, I would have to settle for a guy without a trust fund. The party was pretty cool. I was dancing with Kelly when I started to feel a little tipsy from the Jungle Juice. I got hot from dancing with Kelly, so I decided to go out back for some fresh air. It took me forever to get outside. The party was packed, and drunk horny guys were harassing us as we tried to go outside. The other girl who was with us, whose name I can't remember for the life of me, came out and lit up some pot. As we were smoking and talking, I could feel the energy outside shift. There was a group of guys in a circle, smoking, drinking, laughing, and talking about guy shit probably. One of the guys was kind of cute, I guess, he had a gorgeous smile, but you could sense his lack of confidence and insecurity, and that shit is so unattractive. Standing next to him was the energy I felt. Luke Lamar Beck! He is a gorgeous Black Man, and his swag was so incredible; he had on Versace and a Cartier wristwatch. Oh my God, I'm getting wet just thinking about it! He was just above six feet one and fit with a body Adonis, the doobie me and the girl were smoking went out, and we didn't have a lighter. I could have asked someone next to us, but I saw it as an opportunity to introduce myself to Luke. You could tell those frat boys were eating up every word he said whatever they were talking about, Luke was the center of attention. When I initially asked for the lighter, he didn't hear me. The guy who was standing next to him let him know I was talking to him. Luke looked me in my eyes, and I've had him on lock ever since. The guy standing beside Luke is a Latino boy named Adrian. It turns out they're best friends, more like brothers. I don't get along with Adrian because he's weak and a distraction to Luke. He thinks he wants what's best for Luke, but he doesn't. I know what's best for him, and lately, Luke has seen that a lot more.

Fast forward from when Luke and I first met in March of 2013 to December 2015. I'm finally spending the holidays with his family. I've been doing everything to avoid this, but Luke purposed with a gorgeous ring, and we're getting married next summer, so I have to spend time with my soon to be in-laws. At Christmas, it was just his parents and us. Luke's sister and her husband were out of town, but she wanted to meet me, so they flew back a few days early. Christmas was on a Friday that year, and his sister, who I hadn't met in person, wanted to throw us a get together to celebrate our engagement on the Saturday that they got back in town. I didn't want to do it and don't know why I agreed to it, but I did. If I didn't, Luke would never say it, but I knew it would make him unhappy. Plus, he brought me a Sapphire, Diamond Necklace, Red bottoms, and an Anna Courter dress. So I thought to myself that I could spend a little more time with his ghetto friends and family, but he's going to owe me a new purse!

"NICE TO MEET YOU"

When we arrived at his sister's house, I have to admit I was quite surprised. Their house was so freaking nice. It was bigger than Luke's parent's house, and it was in a gated community. Luke has been acting funny since we got here. At first, I thought it was Jet-Lag, but it was because of Adrian's weak ass. Like we've been here for almost a freaking week, and we've only had sex once. Once! But he's been acting like his normal self for the first time in a few weeks, so I can tell this is important to him. It's almost as if he cares more about what his sister thinks of me than what his mother thinks, which is weird.

Alright, so here we go! My baby is opening the car door for me, as always. Looking all fine in that Isaia Suit, I brought him for Christmas. Well, he got it, but I picked it out, so I kind of brought it. Oh my God, I think he's about to give me a pep talk. Oh no, he is! I can tell by the way he wiped the side of his mouth. Anytime Luke is about to say something I'm not going to like, he wipes the side of his mouth. Like he's wiping it off for the bullshit that's about to fly out of it. Yep, he sure is here comes some bullshit!

Luke smiles as he grabs his fiancé's hand, helping her out of the luxury rental car. Luke opens the back car door as he grabs several gifts. The couple walks closer to the door. Luke stops to tell Paige. "Hey, Baby look, I appreciate you doing this. You know it means the world to me that we came back this year to spend Christmas with my family. Especially with Blue being in the hospital." Paige forces a big fake smile on her face as she tells Luke. "Babe, they're going to be my family soon. This is important to me too." Luke smiles as he hugs and kisses Paige. "That's what I wanted to talk about, Babe. It's not going to be just Benny and Sadie here." Paige rolls her eyes and insincerely smiles at Luke. "Babe, obviously, there are other cars out here!" As Paige is talking, a drunken man happily opens the door. It's Boogie with a plate of food and an unlit Cuban cigar in the other hand. Boogie joyously answers, hugging and slightly lifting Luke off of the ground. Luke pushes the six-four, two-hundred-forty-pound man off of him as he reciprocates Boogie's enthusiasm and introduces Boogie to his new fiancé. Boogie examines Paige for a second, and then he proudly tells Luke. "Damn little cuz she looked good from the pictures Terence showed me, but she's even finer in person. I see why he is marrying you girl. God Damn," Paige loves all the admiration she is receiving from Boogie, imperiously soaking up every compliment he sends her way. As Luke and Paige enter, the house Boogie tells Luke, who inquires where he's going, "I thought y'all were gonna be here a little earlier mane! My bitch bout to come to pick me up now!" A 2016 Benz Jeep pulls up as Boogie is talking to Luke and Paige. "Here she goes right here, mane! Imma holla at you folk, it was nice to meet you, Miss Lady. Make sure you treat my little cousin right. Paige hugs and kisses Boogie replying. "Oh, don't worry, I have been since I first laid eyes on him. Plus, if I don't, I know Mrs. Banks is going to get me.

Paige does her infamous fake laugh as Boogie walks to the Benz, telling her. "Oh, it's not her you gotta worry about, it's the one you're about to meet!" Boogie turns around, walking back towards Luke and Paige handing Luke a stack of money. "Oh yeah, Merry Christmas, little nigga!" Paige smiles gleefully as Luke casually thumbs through the stack of money Boogie handed him.

When I got inside the house once again, I was surprised. The interior was freaking amazing. From the pictures I've seen of Sadie, she didn't appear to have that much style. She was wearing off the rack Nordstrom clothes like a basic bitch, but I guess looks could be deceiving because the house's décor was fabulous. I mean, like fucking unbelievably fabulous for someone without much taste like her. As we walked through the house, I heard several hoodrat voices, laughing, gossiping. Luke and I got to the dining area where they all were seated, and he began introducing me. He nervously introduced me to his sister's friends. I smiled politely, spoke, and acted like I gave a fuck about being there. Sadie wasn't in the room at the time, but as Luke was introducing me, she entered. Sadie enters the room and immediately started showering her little brother, who she had not seen in over a year, with love.

Luke and Sadie share their moment before he starts to introduce Sadie to Paige…

"WHAT IS MY LITTLE BROTHER THINKING"

"Now my Dad asked me to be on my best behavior, so I'm gonna try, but I've known this girl for two seconds, and she already is rubbing me the wrong way. She gone have the nerve to say, "Oh my God, I love how your house is set up from what I have seen so far. The painting and statues are a little too Afrocentric for my taste, but none the less the house still looks fabulous!" What did this little heifer just say to me? Okay, Sadie, keep smiling and calm down! I'll give her a pass with that one. I told Luke that Benny wanted to see him downstairs because I want to feel her out when Luke wasn't around to get more of an honest read on her. My little brother did look so handsome in his outfit. She does have him dressing better I'll give her that one. Now that Luke is out of the room, I'm going to grab Paige a drink so she can feel more opened and relaxed. I asked Paige what she wanted to drink, and this girl asked me, "Do you have Carbonadi Vodka? It's okay if you don't. I can settle for cheap vodka if that's all you have." What kind of shit is this Boujee Bitch on? Okay, just go and make this girl a drink and get to know her first...

Sadie returns to the dining room as Paige charmingly talks to her friends. She gives Paige her drink as Paige picks up a gift that sat on the floor next to her chair. Paige hugs Sadie, kisses her on the cheek and tells her how excited she is that they will be sisters. Sadie opens it up her gift as Paige looks on, anticipating a positive reaction. Sadie's two friends chatter in astonishment as Sadie pulls out the cherry red Hermes Birkin Bag.

This bitch thought that I was going to be impressed by a fucking Birkin Bag! At least Luke hasn't been that reckless to let this bitch know our family business. What my dad told me was echoing inside my head, but I couldn't be an actress for her. I said thank you and then sat down and put the bag back into the box. I could tell she was offended, but all I kept thinking in my head is, what is my little brother thinking?

"THE TALK"

Luke enters the finished basement. There is a fish tank inside of the wall leading to the bottom of the staircase. Luke looks at the signed Sean Taylor Washington Redskins jersey noticing all the changes that have been made to the basement since he moved to California. Benny and Jalon are seated with a bottle of Louie the 13th, two unlit Cuban cigars are resting in the ashtray. Luke shakes both Benny and Jalon's hand. He then hands them both Christmas gifts. Neither man opens their Christmas present, but they both verbalize their gratitude before Luke sits down on the couch, looking directly at the Benny and Jalon. Luke knows they're about to give him a speech. Benny grabs a glass for Luke and pours him a drink. Jalon starts the conversation asking Luke. "That's a nice suit. How much it cost you?" Luke examines and dusts off his suit, "It cost me a few racks." Both Benny and Jalon stare at each other in disappointment, "It cost you a few racks?" Jalon asks Luke as he relights his Cigar. "Yeah, I got it for a deal out at this spot in Beverly Hills," Luke responds. Benny sips out of his glass, asking Luke, "Oh, you one of them niggas now?" Benny gets up from the couch and begins to walk upstairs, stopping by where Luke is seated to tell him, "Loot, I been trying to cover for you with your sister, but you too fucking stubborn to help me out." Benny leaves as Luke sits back, surprised by what Benny just told him. He picks up his drink as Jalon looks at him with a puzzled expression. "Luke, I have always seen you as a sharp kid. I always have seen you as a youngin who was going to do something! But right now, all I see is an over-privileged little nigga who don't know how in over his head he is right now!" Luke's facial expression changes from passive to serious after that statement. He sits up positioned in the middle of the couch directly across from where Jalon is seated. "What you mean by that big brother?" Luke asks "Loot, I don't wanna hear that big brother bullshit! You think I don't know you went around my back after I told you not to. You think Boogie gonna take a chance if something happens? You think a nigga like Derek will take a chance if something happens with your out of town ass?"

The aggressive demeanor Luke was beginning to conjure up devolved back into one of humility. Jalon blows smoke towards Luke as he puts the Cuban Cigar back into the ashtray, looking him directly in his eyes, "Oh, you didn't think I knew about D-Ro, did you? I can tell by your face that you're shocked that I know that name. Let me guess you're taking some of that weed money you're making and giving it to D-Ro to invest in powder. You're probably also taking some of that powder and selling it to Paige's Hollywood modeling crowd, and oh yeah, I can't forget about the Molly too, but you get that from Vinnie, not D-Ro, right?" Luke looked at Jalon, flabbergasted, oblivious of how to respond. Jalon just smiled at Luke momentarily before asking. "Honestly, Luke, how much money do you have saved up?" Luke swigs out of his glass before looking back up at Jalon, "I got like ninety grand stacked up." Jalon looks at Luke, offended. "Nigga you mean to tell me that from what I know, that you don't know I know. You only got ninety thousand dollars saved up?"

Benny's footsteps can barely be heard with a thud, blending in with the music that played from the living room. Benny walks over to the couch, sitting down next to Jalon, eating a crab cake. He chews his food as he looks over and tells Jalon. "You know this nigga. This little nigga," Benny points his half-eaten crab cake at Luke, "This little nigga Luke brought Sadie a Birkin bag!" Jalon taps his big brother on the shoulder. "Fuck that bag this selfish little bastard ain't visit Adrian in the hospital!" Benny is visibly upset.

"Loot you ain't visit Blue in the hospital?" Benny asks. Luke swallows his spit as he responds with a guilty tone, "Paige thought it would be best that I waited till after we got back. She felt that everybody would have time to respond to the situation in the appropriate manner!" Jalon closed his right hand, lifting it to his mouth, he contemplates his rebuttal, but instead of responding, he walks upstairs. The music plays from upstairs as Luke sits with his hands folded, Benny looks for the remote control for the seventy-two inch flat-screen TV.

"Luke, you trying to watch *Petey Wheatstraw*?" Luke lethargically looks back at Benny. "Come on Luke. Watching Black seventies movies is our Christmas tradition!" Luke tells Benny "Okay" after he takes another sip out of this glass of Louie the Thirteenth. Benny tells Luke in a disappointed manner as he searches for the DVD in the five hundred page disk booklet, "Little brother, I do love you, but you're gonna get what you deserve if you marry Paige. That's all I got to say about that!" Benny pulls the movie out of the booklet and picks up Jalon's unlit Cuban Cigar leaning over the table, handing it to Luke and telling him. "Adrian is gonna be there for you after Paige leaves you, and he shouldn't be!" Luke was searching his pockets for his lighter until Benny tells him, looking directly in his eyes, "Luke, the light is in your hand!" Luke looks into his right palm at his Redskins Zippo lighter. Benny puts his hand on Luke's shoulder, calmly saying, "Pay attention, little brother! Pay attention!"

"THREE WEEKS LATER – WEST HOLLYWOOD

Paige and Luke stand poolside at a West Hollywood mansion arguing, as they try not to make a scene. The young couple has been at odds for the past week and have been bickering even more, particularly today. They're attending a party thrown by a woman who is essential in

Southern California's fashion world, and it is vital to Paige that the couple make a good impression. Everyone attending the party dressed in very high-end formal fashion except for Luke. Luke dressed in a Hilly Hanson black and gray overalls, a black True Religion shirt underneath, and black Nike boots. Luke cuffed a fifth of Hennessy; he's been drinking on it for over the past hour. The bottle is more than halfway finished. Luke purposely dressed in his attire and is drinking out of the Hennessy bottle because he knew it would make Paige upset, as she aspires to impress the pretentious uptight West Hollywood crowd. Paige finally gets fed up with arguing back and forth with Luke, slaps him, and then storms off, going back inside the mansion. Luke just laughs it off and continues to drink as he stands poolside. A German man approaches Luke while he stands alone by the pool, drinking out his Hennessy bottle. The German man is the only one at the party that Luke has been social towards. He comes over talking to Luke as if they have been friends for decades. After minutes of back and forth conversation filled with laughter, the two men go inside the party as a woman jumps off a diving board into the Olympic style swimming pool. When Luke and the German get inside the mansion, the German man speaking with a heavy accent, invites Luke to do some cocaine. Luke and the German do a few lines and converse before Luke returns downstairs, leaving the German man in the bathroom with two other women. Luke stands next to the bar adjacent to the dance floor, sipping out his Hennessy bottle, watching Paige dance excessively erotic with a tall blond-haired male model. Luke looks on as Paige spitefully dances with the man, glancing up at him periodically in a smug, condescending manner.

So this Bitch gonna do this right in my fucking face like I ain't even standing here? All the shit I got going on right now, and this Bitch wanna play fucking games. If shit keeps going like it's been going, we aren't going to be able to afford a wedding in Bali we're gonna have to get hitched at the justice of the peace. If she only fucking knew all the shit I have been through to keep her ass in designer and eating out daily. And she got the nerve to be dancing like this in front of me.

Maybe Juice and Benny were right! I might wanna fall back on this wedding shit. Hold up! Is that mothafucka inching up her thigh! Oh, hell, Nah! This bitch got me fucked up! Does she think she's about to play me like I'm some Bama or some shit like that? Okay! I'm bout show to this uptight low key racist ass West Hollywood mothafuckas how the DMV gets down. I'm about to beat the shit out of this Swedish faggot like he stole something!

Luke takes a big gulp out of his Hennessy bottle, slams it down on the bar, and walks over to Paige and the Swedish man. Luke doesn't say a word, grabs him by his shirt collar, and open hand slaps the man extremely hard. Luke wallops the man, making him stumble diagonal as people on the dance floor now watch the assault. Luke continues to hit the man as Paige tries to stop him. Luke pushes her back to the point that she falls. Luke doesn't even help his fiancé; he just continues to slap the man as he cries and yells to stop. It takes three people to get an infuriated Luke off of the helpless, confused Swedish man. Luke tells Paige, who is being consoled by another woman, as he exits the party, "I hope you understand this shit is all your fucking fault!" Luke angrily leaves, shouting at the onlookers, "What the fuck are y'all looking at?"

CHAPTER XI: PACIFIC OCEAN VIEWS

"I've been affected by the ills of life, gravitating the fascination, admiring the vanities lead to miseducation."

-Two8G

This nigga doesn't seem to appreciate that Floyd and I put his ass in the position that he's in. Luke really thinks he did this shit all by himself like he's Scarface or something. This nigga has really been feeling himself lately; he brought a brand new Cherry Red Jaguar. I guess it's a nice addition to his Oceanfront apartment. It was a beautiful night when Adrian and I landed in L.A.X. This has been one of those few occasions where it's just him and me hanging out. Usually, there's somebody else around, whether it be Floyd, Luke, or Terence, when he is in the country. It's not that I don't like Adrian or that we don't get along. It's more so that we're just too different. If Luke and Adrian didn't grow up together, I don't really think they would be friends. Adrian moves like a corny white boy sometimes, but he acts like Luke or Terence when he's around them. This mothafucka is a chameleon, which makes it hard for me to trust him. Adrian and I stood in the arrival area at L.A.X., smoking jacks, which is cigarettes for those who don't know D.M.V. lingo, and waiting for Luke to pull up. I could hear Luke before I could see him. I could tell Adrian was excited to see Luke. Evidently, they got into a brawl after I left the night of Luke's going away get together, but they've been back cool as of recently. I swear I fill like a kid in between a dysfunctional relationship when they're together. An outsider would think they weren't as close as they are, but one thing I can say for sure is that I've known Luke for ten years, and he has always referred to Adrian as his brother. Luke had someone with him in the passenger side when he pulled up. He hopped out of the car to greet Adrian and me. All I could smell is loud-pack. Luke was fresh from head to toe Prada shoes fourteen karat diamond earrings, a Cartier watch, skinny black jeans, and a Prada shirt. Does this nigga have a nose ring now? Oh, wow, he does. This nigga done really went Hollywood. This nigga probably has a chain wallet. Holy shit, this nigga really does. The car smelled like ganja with a hint of Black Ice air freshener, Luke and Adrian talked to each other like me, and his homie wasn't even there. His man's name was Vinnie, now I'm not from Cali, but I think I know somebody who's gang-affiliated when I see them. Son had a heavy ass Cali accent. This nigga was really energetic and cracked a lot of jokes. He had a short Caesar haircut and was Iced the fuck out. I could tell Luke was fucking with some real niggas out here. That's probably why this nigga has been feeling himself so much. This nigga Luke's apartment is off the fucking chain. I'm not jealous or no shit like that, but fuck! There was a perfect view of the Pacific Ocean as we stood on the balcony, smoking a blunt of this new strain of weed his grower yielded. The stars illuminated the night sky as Luke and I stood outside, talking business and catching up. We really haven't chopped it up much on the phone like we use to. I go through Floyd every time I need to re-up, so this is the most we've spoken since he left for Cali. I was surprised that Luke let Adrian drive his car. He went to pick up some taco's and get some liquor and brews with Vinnie because the only liquor Luke had at the house was champagne. Chilling with Luke made me realize how much I missed kicking it. Even when Luke was up at Morgan State, we would hang out when he had time. It wasn't until after he met Paige that shit really started changing. I never saw a female have an effect on Luke like Paige does. I guess I kind of understand Paige is one of the baddest bitches that I have ever seen in my life. My baby mother is definitely fine as shit, but I must admit Paige is a different type of fine. Even with that said, I couldn't believe what Luke did next. He passed the blunt looked me in my eyes and said, "Hunter, I got to tell you something."

"What that your gay? I mean, I always suspected Adrian was, but you! That's quite a surprise!" I joked.

"Hilarious, Hunter, but if I recall correctly, Adrian use to date your baby mother back in high school." Luke dug inside his front pocket. "Hunter, I haven't told nobody else this, not even Sadie. I wanted to tell you first because I know you would understand." Luke pulled a ring box out of his front pocket, holding it his right palm, opening up the top with his left hand. I thought we all were making paper, but I see now that Luke was making a lot more than Floyd and me. That ring had to cost him a grip. He smiled and confidently said. "Yo, bruh, I'm gonna ask Paige to marry me." "Nigga are you out your fucking mind! We making money. You're in your early twenties, and you want to get married. Are you fucking stupid?" Paige pussy done turned this nigga brain into mush… Well, at least that's what I wanted to say to

Luke, but instead of telling him that, I just shook his hand, gave him a hug, and said, "Congratulations, my nigga! I knew it was gonna be you first, so when you thinking about proposing to Paige?" Luke ashes the blunt and then spits over the balcony. "Well, her and Kelly get back from Napa Valley Friday afternoon, so I'm gonna purpose Saturday night on the beach under the fireworks." "ON ADRIAN'S BIRTHDAY?" I asked. "Yeah, Hunter, on Adrian's birthday! Besides, it's not just Adrian's birthday; it's America's birthday too." "That's the dumbest shit that you have said all night, but I'm happy for you nigga. I just think maybe you should wait till after we leave next week, or at least tell Adrian before you do it." Luke French inhaled, smiled, and rubbed the diamond in his left earlobe. "Look, bruh, I told you first for a reason. I know Blue better than anyone, and if I tell him now, I know there is a possibility that he might get drunk and tell Paige before I can and ruin the moment. You know Blue don't fuck with Paige." "So you're gonna possibly ruin his birthday by telling him then." "Look, Hunter, I know what I'm doing. I'm gonna get Blue so fucked up he's not even gonna care. Plus, once he sees these birthday gifts, I got him, and what I got planned for both of y'all tomorrow night, that shit definitely is gonna soften the blow." As Luke was talking, I could hear Adrian and Vinnie come through the front door laughing and talking loud as shit. Vinnie started yelling out, "Luger! Homie, where you at? Aye, Luger!" I looked at Luke, confused, and asked, "Who the fuck is Luger?" "Oh bruh, that's just some shit Vinnie be calling me," Luke responded.

Vinnie slides open the balcony door, he has a bottle of Patron in his hand. Vinnie cracks open the bottle and drinks out of it before he passes it to Luke and says to him, "Aye, Luke, your fam Adrian funny as shit homie! That nigga was clowning while we were waiting for our food at the taco spot." "Oh, word for real. Adrian is funny when he wants to be. Where he at right now?" Luke asked. "Oh, he's in the bathroom," Vinnie responded. Luke paused for a second, titled his head, and looked Vinnie in his eyes, "Yo Vin, did you give Adrian some yayo?" Vinnie smiled and rubbed his nose. "Cuz, I don't know what you're talking about!" Luke snickered and shook his head, "I knew I should have sent Hunter with your ass!" Vinnie laughed as Luke slid open the balcony door yelling back to Adrian as he closed the door behind him. "Blue, I know what you're doing back there, you fucking druggy. Save me a little bitch!" Vinnie and I both laughed; he handed me the Patron bottle and started rolling up another blunt, "So how long have known Luger Hunter? I mean, Luke!" "Shit, I've known him for like ten or eleven years." I answered, He thought a second and asked, "Where y'all from again?" "Waldorf, Maryland! So how did you meet Luke Vinnie?" I asked. "Oh, he never told you?" Vinnie was surprised. "Nah, I didn't know you existed until tonight." I admitted. "So there must be a reason for that, then don't you think Hunter?" It was quiet for a moment, with only the sound of ocean waves crashing. I held the bottle in my hand, sipping out of it, and heard a Bic lighter flick. The weed smelled like the same shit we were smoking earlier. Vinnie passed me the blunt, and then I passed him the bottle and then asked him, "So why do you call Luke Luger?" Vinnie sips out of the bottle and looks over at me. "One night, Luke took one of my burners, this nine-millimeter, and started yamming at these niggas." I couldn't believe what Vinnie just said. Luke has always been down to fight any nigga, but gunplay that's not like him. "Luke really did that?" Vinnie nodded, "Yeah, Cuz that night was crazy. I guess you don't know Luke as well as you thought you did, huh, white boy?" "Well, Luke doesn't know me as well as he thinks either because he would be utilizing my connections out here." I could tell what I said intrigued Vinnie. "What kind of connections you got out here, Hunter?"" My little cousin goes to college out in San Diego, he's in this frat, and those boys move serious product down there. I talked to him two weeks ago, and their source went M.I.A. My cousin knows I can be a source, he just doesn't know if I can be one out here, so maybe you can help me with that." I said casually. Vinnie paused before asking, "What about Luke?" "Luke is my mans, and I'm gone make sure he eats something, but this would be more like my thing," I said looking for a reaction. Vinnie took a sip out of the bottle, and a drag from the blunt, then passed it to me, "You surprised me, Hunter. I didn't see you as the bossing up type. You seemed more like a sidekick to me!" Did this milk-dud head nigga just call me a sidekick? I just laughed it off as I smoked, "Nah, Vinnie, I think you got me confused with Adrian." "You crazy cuz I ain't got you confused. You violating by even saying some shit like you just said to me. You lucky I'm in a good mood." "Or what?" I asked. Vinnie begins to hold his side as he broke down from laughter. He went into a coughing fit from laughing so hard, "White boy, you crazy, you almost made me throw up from laughing. I kinda see why Luger keeps you around, but I might be able to help you. Let's get ready to ride out to this titty bar. You better get some taco's before Luger and Adrian smash on the whole box."

That night and the following days leading up to the 4th of July where something out a fucking movie, we all went to Vinnie's homie's strip club that night, and I ended up getting head in the Champagne room from this badass Caribbean bitch. That bitch is in my top five dick suckers. Luke definitely threw some of them hoes money cause Adrian had a threesome with two black bitches after we left the club. I didn't fall asleep until that Thursday morning. Adrian woke me up around two that afternoon and told me to hurry up and get dressed we were going to Vegas, and our plane was leaving at 6:30 pm. When we got to Vegas, Luke had already rented two luxury sports cars, he rented a Powder Blue Lamborghini for Adrian, and Luke and I rode a Yellow drop-top Porsche. That shit was surreal. I can't believe how fun that night turned out. After we picked up the cars, we hit the Vegas strip, stunting hard as shit slim like I felt like a fucking rap star that shit was Jah like unbelievable. There were celebrities in the same V.I.P. section that we were sitting in. Right hand-up may God strike down if I'm lying, but I fucked a C level R & B singer who shall remain nameless. The only thing that I didn't like about that night is I didn't hit it off with Luke's connection. He was out in Vegas as well, but he only chilled for like an hour, and when I tried to chop it up with him, he was acting like he didn't really understand English. To make it even worse, he ended leaving the club with Adrian in the Lambo. Adrian didn't get back until a few hours before we had to leave for the airport. We had to catch a 12:30 am. flight out of Las Vegas into the Los Angles L.A.X. airport. We all tried to get some sleep as we sat in Luke's car, waiting on Paige and Kelly's flight to arrive at 3:45 pm at the same airport. Initially, Luke's plan was to take the girls to eat and then just chill back at his spot, but Adrian, who was still lit from the night before, convinced Luke and the rest of us to go to Universal Studios. I will give it to Adrian, bruh knows how to have a good time. He came across some mushrooms from some random surfer dude

127

while walking on the beach before we rolled out to go to Universal Studios. We all ended up eating some before we got to the theme park. I ended up eating like two grams, and I felt like I was Brad Pit in "Cool World" (for y'all who don't know google that shit). I felt like a kid at Christmas in that theme park. I don't know why, but I had an extreme craving to eat seafood after leaving Universal Studios and not just any seafood; I wanted raw oysters. That definitely was a bad idea because I ended up getting sick. I mean, I was fucked up! It wasn't just the oysters. It had to be a combination of things, including the cocktail of drugs that I have used in the past three days. When I woke up to take a shit for the twentieth time, it was four something on Saturday morning. It was officially the fourth of July now as I climbed back into the bed in the guest bedroom I stayed in. I took a sip out of a two-liter bottle of ginger ale that sat next to the plastic trash can I was using just in case I threw up. I could hear Luke and Adrian through the bedroom window that was to the left of the balcony. I had the window cracked a little bit to get some of that Pacific Ocean breeze. I was sleepy enough to pass back out, but as I tried, a part of the conversation on the balcony pierced my soul as I heard Adrian tell Luke in a disappointed manner, "Bruh, you know I always have minded my business with what you got going on. For the most part, I only know what you tell me. But as your Brother, I can't act like how you're moving is cool with me. It doesn't seem like just business that you give Floyd a lower price than Hunter, especially if Hunter is moving more." "First off, lower your fucking voice, Blue!" Luke and Adrian started to talk at a little bit lower volume, but I could still hear them. "Secondly, Floyd sells twice as much as Hunter."

"Additionally, you said that you mind your business about what I got going on, and then proceeded to question what I got going on, and finally! I'm treating Hunter like he treated me." Luke said.

"And how is that Luke?" Adrian asked.

"Well, Hunter thinks I forgot about that shit that happened when I was up at Morgan State, or he doesn't think I know that he went around my back to one of the plugs that I have in New York. Shit, even last night out in Vegas, he let it slip that he was mad that you got to hang with Allen, and he didn't."

"Allen did tell me something about Hunter this morning." Adrian admitted.

Luke frowned, "What he say?"

"I can't remember really because I was high as shit, but he made it seem like Hunter was trying to undercut you," Adrian struggled to remember.

"See, Adrian, that's the shit I be talking about! I be seeing Floyd and Hunter when they don't think I'm watching. The bottom line is Blue. The shit is just business!" I could hear Adrian coughing from the blunt they were smoking. Adrian recovered from coughing and told Luke, "Well, Loot the shit sound like bad business to me, and that goes for Floyd and Hunter too!"

I wanted to get up out of bed and crush Luke. I've known this bitch ass nigga since he was wearing black Airforce ones. He still really holding on to that shit that happened while he was up at Morgan. If that nigga was in my shoes, he would have done the same thing that I did. The full knowledge of knowing how Luke felt made me even more nauseous. I tried to gather thoughts, Luke is supposed to be one of my best friends, but I can't trust this nigga. It's all good, though! Now I just know how I gotta move with him and Floyd.

BORN ON THE 4TH OF JULY

This is probably the most sleep that I have got since we've been here. I woke up and had a Bloody Mary with my 4:00 pm breakfast. Luke left a note by the food in a Styrofoam container that awaited me, the note read. "Blue, we figured you needed some sleep. We're on the beach behind the apartment. Happy birthday, Brother. I left a few of your gifts in the guest bedroom you're sleeping in. Love you, Blue!" I took my food to the room with me placing it on the dresser along with the Bloody Mary. I went to the closet and immediately started opening the gifts that awaited me. Luke brought me some alligator shoes, a cold-ass designer outfit that's definitely my style. I cried when I opened the second gift. It was a custom painting of an old picture of Me, Manny, and Juice from when I was younger. I had to be three or four years old. The last gift I opened was a fourteen karat gold Movado watch and a cannabis vape pen.

After I finished my breakfast and Bloody Mary, I showered up and then met Luke, Hunter, Kelly, and Paige down at the beach. When I got there, Paige, Hunter, and Kelly were in the ocean playing around. Luke was under a beach tint, lying back on some beach towels drinking a beer. I got myself a beer and sat down in one of the chairs. "What's good, Blue! Happy Birthday!" I toasted beers with Luke and gave him a hug, "Aye, Bruh, that painting was beautiful, thank you!" "Bruh, I still got more gifts for you," Luke smiled. "Damn OK! I'm making money at my job, but when your birthday comes around, I'm not gonna be able to match you on gifts!" Adrian responded laughing. Both of us laughed and talked shit to each other. Paige walked over. She was wearing a sunflower yellow two-piece bikini, water dripped from her caramel skin, and curly brown hair that hung down past her shoulders. Paige opened up the cooler, removing the bottle Carbonadi Vodka and a bottle of Orange juice. She used a plastic cup to scoop up ice and then mixed her drink. Even when Paige is trying to be nice to me, the shit comes off as condescending and fake as fuck! She cheers her plastic cup with my beer bottle and said, "Happy Birthday Castro!"

Now I don't care when people call me Castro, but she never does, and the way she said it rubbed me the wrong way. Hunter and Kelly came over eventually. We're all drinking, listening to music, and having a good time until Paige and Luke started arguing. They went back and forth a while, and then Luke said smugly, "You know what! I was gonna save this for Adrian and me until later, but fuck it, we're drinking it now. Adrian! You want some of this Codeine I was saving for later?" I looked at Paige with the most pompous expression that I could muster up and said, "Hell yeah, you know I do, Bruh!" Paige ended up storming off. Kelly followed behind, grabbing the bottle of Carbonadi Vodka before she left with Paige. Luke, me, and Hunter all stayed behind chilling, smoking, and drinking beers. Luke opened the bottle of Codeine and mixed it with some water and ice. I was waiting until later. I just said I was drinking it now to piss Paige off. Hunter ended up going inside like thirty-minutes after Paige and Kelly left. Luke and I stayed behind and played a football game with a group of people on the beach. I don't know how Luke was balling even though he was already wasted, and it was only like seven o'clock. I went inside while Luke was making friends with some of the people we met. I had to use the bathroom really bad my guts were bubbling. When I got In the apartment, music played over the speakers, and Kelly was passed out on the couch. I hurried to the bathroom before it was too late. When I got out of the bathroom pleased and refreshed, the music playing had gone off, and I heard something coming from Luke's bedroom. I put my right ear to the door, and I could very faintly hear moaning. I got out of the apartment as fast as I could without making too much noise. On my way out of the apartment, I glanced at the couch and noticed Kelly was faking like she was sleep. I had a million thoughts running through my head as I walked back to the beach. My first thought was I should have just burst into the room and confronted them. I thought, what the fuck is wrong with Paige and Hunter? If that was Luke instead of me, he probably would have killed Hunter. What the fuck am I going to do? When I got back to the beach, Luke was under his beach tint talking to a few of the people we played football with, "A bruh Anastasia said that she and her roommates are having a party at their Beach House tonight if you wanna go." "Yeah, Adrian, you should come. It's gonna be entertaining," Anastasia gave me the I want you to fuck my brains out expression. I definitely was intrigued, but I had more pressing issues on my mind. I was able to get Anastasia and her friend to leave as I attempted to get an intoxicated Luke to focus. I wipe the side of my mouth and then told him that I wanted to talk about Paige, and he got pissed, "Blue, this shit is getting fucking played out! You've been jealous of Paige and me since Whitney dumped you before we graduated college. Look, bruh, I'm not trying to be mean, but you need to realize that Paige is going to be around whether you like it or not, so you can get on board, or you could step the fuck off. She's gonna be my wife one day, and you need to accept that shit!" I didn't know how to respond. I wanted to blurt out Hunter just fucked Paige, but instead, I just stayed trying my best to hide my emotions. I ended up taking the rest of the bottle of Codeine and put it in my cup with soda and ice. Luke ended up changing the subject by telling me about the five grand worth of fireworks he brought me for tonight. I couldn't decide whether to confront Paige or Hunter. We ended up going to that party at the Beach House that Anastasia invited us to. My chest was burning the entire ride there. I wanted to say something. I can tell by how Hunter looked in my eyes that he knew that I knew something I could sense his trepidation. The party was a little bigger than I thought it would be. I was looking for the right opportunity to confront Hunter, but Anastasia was on me as soon as I walked through the door. She grabbed my wrist, getting me to follow her to take some shots. I ended up taking a few Jell-O shots off of her torso as she lies on the dining room table. After I did some lines of cocaine and fucked Anastasia I left her in the bathroom and made way to outside. I figured that's where Hunter and Luke were, people were on the patio drinking and talking, but most of the people were on the beach around the bonfire. As I walked down the spiral staircase towards the beach, I could hear Luke and Hunter's voice. I stopped so I could listen in to their conversation…

"I told you Adrian was gonna be straight Hunter, he's on right now, feeling good! He's not gonna care after I purpose to Paige. He's having too much fun to care." Luke bragged to Hunter. I hear you nigga, I'm having too much fun to care.

Luke continued, "Like I told you when you got here, Hunter. I know Adrian better than anyone, and I know how to work him when I need to. Why do you think Anastasia so friendly with him?"

Hunter starts laughing. "Yeah, bruh cause I was about to say because that's a pretty ass, blond bitch!" I walked down the spiral stairs, and Luke spoke to me as soon as I appeared. "You ready to light these fireworks, Blue?" I had a tightness in my chest, standing there looking at Luke. All I could say was, "Hell yeah, I'm ready!" I watched as Luke and Hunter and four other guys set up and light the fireworks. I feel guilty sitting back and watching as Luke purposed to Paige in front of the entire party, knowing what I know. I watched Paige light up like the fireworks she was standing under when she saw the ring, and I watched Hunter smile and cheer with Kelly along and the rest of the crowd. I watched all of these things on my twenty-third birthday with the Pacific Ocean's backdrop in my

CHAPTER XII: THE ADVENTURES OF ADRIAN & ALLEN
"If I die tonight, Imma die high!"

-Two8G

We were in our suite at the Wynn Las Vegas Hotel and Casino and this was probably going to be the most that we were going to be in our hotel room. It was me, Luke, Hunter, and Luke's old College roommate Devon. I remember Devon from driving up to Morgan to hang with Luke. When I first met him he weighed like three hundred and fifty pounds. In December of Luke's Junior year of college Devon and him drove in an a RV with Devon's brother and his friends (who were ignorant to the fact that they were caring Forty pounds of cannibas) across the country. Devon took some of that money he made, and invested in some tech stocks and starting up his own company. He seemed ten times more confident than he did when I first met him. Devon was still big but not morbidly obese like he once was, he wasn't wearing sweats, comic book tee-shirts, and K-Swiss any more. Now Devon was trying to dress like a plus size GQ model, he actually was the one to make the toast as we all stood in our hotel Luxury suite with our champagne flutes raised to the sky. "To Luke! Dude you changed all our lives for the better when you decided to take that gamble, because of you I got my own business and I'm getting pussy on the regular without paying for it." I shouted out, "Amen to that!" We all laughed a little before Devon finished his toast. "And to Vegas! Let's go have the fucking time of our lives!"

The plan after we finished pregaming was to go down to casino, meet up with Luke's boy Allen, gamble a little bit and then hit up the club, Luke already had a VIP table reserved for us. I ended up drinking and playing on the slot machines with Devon for like forty minutes. I got lucky and wound up winning two stacks playing Russian roulette for the first time ever. I hit off my third bet and walked away from the table right after that. Devon and I reconnected with the Luke and Hunter and by that time Allen had arrived and they were at the blackjack table. After another twenty minutes of watching them play blackjack we made our way to the club. I give to my brother he really went all the way out for my birthday this year. I don't think I have ever had someone put so much thought into me having a good time. I know he probably paid for those two pretty ass stripers to have sex with me yesterday, but I don't care, sex and drugs have been some of my happiest nights, and so far tonight has been no different. Luke stood on the couch dancing with a bottle in his hand, Devon had disappeared somewhere into the crowd, and Hunter drunkenly talked to Allen who seemed to be annoyed by him. I was sitting back soaking up the whole scene it felt completely amazing.

Allen eventually got up from sitting next to Hunter and walked over to me talking to me in my ear, "Hey Adrian come with me." I wasn't sure what this was about. I didn't wanna leave the club yet. I asked Luke what's going on and he told me. "I don't know, but I would go!" I remember Luke describing how he first met Allen, he said that they didn't vibe initially, but for some reason Allen and me hit it off immediately. I can tell Luke has spoken positively about me to Allen, he kind of seemed disappointed when he tried to speak to me in Spanish and I didn't understand that shit. As we drove the Vegas strip Allen told me the story of how him and Luke almost didn't do business.

Luke flew out to Cali with Devon and was supposed to meet up with Allen at three-o-clock on a Thursday afternoon. Luke told Allen something had come up and he was gonna be late for their meet up. This was Allen's first time officially doing business with Luke and he didn't trust it enough to wait around it as it could be some kind of setup. Luke was about to be out of luck, he took his life savings and got two planes tickets all for nothing. Allen said he got back home pissed that he just wasted his time with Luke. Luke talked all that good game, but when it came down to it he ended up being late to their first deal, and that's someone he didn't wanna do business with. When Allen's wife got back they were both pissed at each other. Allen said his phone was going in and out of service. His wife said that her phone died from calling him so many times. Allen's wife told him her phone died while driving on a road on the outskirts of Fresno California, she was fifteen miles away from the house seven months pregnant with no phone, she told her husband if it wasn't for those guys outside she doesn't know what she would have done. He asked her, "What guys outside?"

Allen's wife told him about the guys that helped her, and she told them she could get them a little weed for helping her out, she said she was thankful and they seemed like they really could use it. Allen was upset at his wife for bring two strange dudes to their home, but his wife was eventually able to convince him to give the guys something. Allen went to take half an ounce of weed outside to the guys that helped his wife and much to his surprise it was Luke and his fat friend. Allen had to respect Luke's character. He had so much money on the line but he was willing to risk it to help a pregnant woman in need. Allen laughed as he said, "I wouldn't have done that shit! But you got to respect it, and luckily for him that pregnant woman just so happen to be my wife caring my baby!"

I felt like a fucking celebrity going down the strip in that powder blue Lamborghini chicks where definitely checking us. It took us a little over an hour for us to get to our destination that was on the outskirts of Vegas. Allen said he had to talk to someone about some business for like an hour and then he was gonna take me to a surprise. I was thinking to myself man this was bullshit. I could still be at the club in the V.I.P. with Luke, Hunter, and Devon but instead I have to wait around in some fucking office building for an hour while Allen does business. Whatever surprise he has better be fucking awesome. This is definitely not an office building. It's a fucking whore house! We walked through the door the bulky guard stepped to the side and nodded at Allen. There was marble everywhere, a woman stood behind a marble counter at a cash register in pink lingerie, she smiled at both of us, "Hey Al nice to see you again. Pierre is back in his office. Who's this cutie pie that's with you. Allen laughed and said, "Oh this is my amigo Adrian. It's his birthday today!" The woman walked from behind the counter and gave me a hug, I smiled at Allen as he smiled back at me with his thumbs up nodding his head. "Well Adrian, while Al talks to Pierre why don't you come with me and I'll make you a special birthday drink." Her name was Haley, she took me to the bar area that was lit up by hot pink and turquoise lights. There where man in the bar area whom ages range from their earlier twenties to my dad's age. All the woman looked amazing, and like they were all under thirty. Haley sat me at the bar and then begin to tell the bartender how it was my birthday and to make me a special drink, "Becky's going to take care of you Adrian I have to get back to the register." Haley left a big lipstick mark on my cheek. "Happy birthday cutie, "Becky handed me a drink and when I asked her what's in it, she winked and smiled. "It's called Molly's birthday special!" Well okay! I was already feeling pretty good from the pregaming that we did back at the hotel. Add whatever is in this drink to the mix, and you have a man who is about to be feeling amazing. I was about half way through "Molly's Birthday Special" when she approached me. She had a really pretty face, dark hair, dark eyes, and a huge rack with a pretty decent ass. She sat next to me a the bar, her name was Eva. She got a drink and started to talk to me. I told her how I was having the time of my life. "Your energy is amazing Adrian I can tell it's a special day today. Two is a very good number." She flirted. "Well my birthday actually isn't till the forth but we've been celebrating since I flew into LA last night," I said. "Well that's alright. You're with Eva close to the eve of your birthday. I was told that I would meet a special Cancer tonight and here you are. I've been off for the last hour how about me and you go back to my place? It's only six miles away!" She suggested. "I would love to but I can't I'm here with my boy Allen and he should be out in the next thirty minutes." Eva started to lick my ear while rubbing on my penis. I definitely started to chub up. "If your friend is in the back he's going to be longer than he told you. I'll make you cum twice before he even knows you're gone," she whispered in my ear. At this point I was hard as a rock but I just couldn't leave Allen without telling him. That's when Eva said, "You can ride back with me and just leave your keys with the bartender, she's knows who your friend is right?" I just shook my head mesmerized by Eva as I handed her the keys, she place them behind the bar. I walked out the back of the brothel hoped in Eva's black Corvette and rode with her to her house, but unbeknownst to me back at the bar Haley had returned searching for me, "Hey Becky where's the birthday boy at?"

"Which one?" Becky asked.

"The cute one that you gave the Molly birthday special to, the one that was sitting right here earlier," Haley responded laughing.

"Oh he must have left with Eva." Becky picks the Lamborghini car key up from behind the bar. "This is the car key to the Lamborghini he said his brother rented for him." She said as she dangled the keys.

"Becky what the fuck!" Haley yelled.

Confused Becky responded, "What do you mean what the fuck!"

"You know Pierre hates when we take customers home, and he specifically said to never let a customer leave with Eva again!" Haley panicked.

I had no clue where I was and I had absolutely no service on my cell phone, we drove at least sixteen minutes away from the brothel to a old house in the middle of the desert in what seemed like nowhere. I was kind of nervous, but I was more horny and increasingly high by the minute. Eva was massaging my balls on the car ride, she parked her car in front of the spooky desert house and told me. "Hecate" showed me that I would meet a Cancer, under his star at its full power. My star at its full power," Eva gently grabbed my chin and titled my head towards the full moon. "The moon is the ruling planet of the Cancer. C'mon so I can feel on your energy inside of me," she said. Eva licked my face and got out of the car looking back at me as I sat in the passenger seat feeling kind of weird. I was definitely having second thoughts. This chick was super-hot, but I should have at least drove here. I figured fuck it since I'm already here I might as well complete the mission. I got out of the car and moved towards Eva as she waited. We walked inside of the single story house I told her that she had a nice ATV to which she responded, "The keys are in the ignition. You can take it for a ride if you want!" "Very tempting, but remember I have to get back," I responded. When we got inside she closed and locked the door behind me, she pressed me up against the wall and started kissing on me and feeling my cock. She then walked me back to a room. It was pitch black. Eva guided me the whole way, because I couldn't see shit in that dark ass house. When we entered the room Eva pushed me on the bed and then started to light up candles one by one in the room. I was just in a tank top and my draws by the time she finished with the candles. She pulled off her top, and her bra and those big ass titties came plopping out. She took her skirt and panties off, she put on a robe and said, "I'll be right back?" She needs to hurry back I've been gone for almost thirty minutes I think. Eva returned in the room six minutes later caring some incense, a glass of water with a leaf in it, and an album under her arm. Eva gave me the water and told me, "This is to help enhance your element." Okay I could use a water because I feel this Molly kicked in but we have to speed up this process. I have to get back! Eva put on the album on the record player in the corner took off her robe and said, "I'll be right back." Okay! Now I'm like what the fuck? This girl better hurry up, my dick has literally been rock hard for the past eleven minutes. I got up from the bed dick poking through the hole in my boxers and started to look around the room. I went over to the record player to see what album she put on. It sounded like some groovy shit from the seventies. The cover had eight white guys sitting and standing around a table. The album was called the *Banquet* and the band was called Lucifer's Friend.. Now the sound of the band definitely doesn't match the name, but the band's name plus the pictures on the wall had me feeling really uneasy. I attributed it to the drink I had at the brothel, but something didn't feel right. I'm not a theologist by any means but I know Pagan symbols when I see them. At least I feel like I do! She had all kinds of crazy looking dolls and statues around her room, she had a painting on her wall that looked like it was straight out of the film "Wicker Man!" Eva came back in the room dancing erotically as the music played, she had stars drawn on to her titties. Eva pushed me on the bed and started licking me in places that I had never been licked. She started to give me what was probably the best head that I ever had. This woman was with no question a professional! She put a condom on me, got on top of me and started riding me. She got off of top of me, and told me to sniff something that was in this tiny bottle. I had no clue what I was inhaling but it gave me an insane head rush. Eva pushed me down and started to lick my butthole. That shit felt so fucking amazing, She lifted her head and said fuck me from the back. I kissed her and then bent her over the side of the bed. I know I technically just tasted my own asshole, but I was so caught up in the moment that I didn't care. As I was fucking her from the back I didn't notice that she had already did it, but at some point she started squeezing some oozey substance into a shot glass. I don't know why I didn't stop, maybe because it felt so good, but I asked her what the fuck she was doing as I was stroking and she said, "Baby don't stop just let me know before you cum!"

Now I have done enough drugs in my life to know what I'm feeling even when they're mixed. I know what it feels like to be on Molly, Cocaine, Weed, and Liquor at the same time because I've been there before. I went to up to Towson University to visit Caden one weekend and I got lit with him and his frat brothers. So I knew that there was a different element that I thought might be present, but I wasn't sure until I asked Eva. "Hey what was in that water you gave me?" "Water! Oh yeah baby keep hitting it just like that! A mint leaf! And a few hits of liquid LSD!" She said. I pulled out of her when she said that. I was pissed as shit that she would give me some ACID without telling me, but I was also close to climaxing. Eva pulled off my condom and started sucking my cock after I pulled out. I came before I know what was going on. Eva kept sucking after I came, it hurt so good I was crying stop like a little bitch. Eva poured wine into the shot glass that contained the mystery substance, took the shot and then looked at me. "We're gonna have another round where I will make you cum in three minutes guaranteed, and then I will take you back to your automobile. Eva pricked her left palm with pocket knife that sat one her nightstand, and placed it at the center of my forehead and started to chant in some langue that I have no idea what the fuck it was. Maybe it was Irish, maybe Scottish, maybe fucking Gypsy! Whatever she just said translated to I should have been the fuck out of here a long time ago! Or better yet I shouldn't even be here. Eva left the room and went to bathroom I think. That's when I decided to get the fuck out of there! I wasn't sure where the fuck I was, but I know we made at least three turns and headed south, at least I believed that was what we did. I was about to make two turns and walk North. I wasn't sure what this girl put in my water but it Definitely slowly started to feel like it was what she said it was. The music playing from the record player was becoming too amazing. She more than likely gave me some L.S.D . I have to try to remember this album. This shit sounds awesome!

I was somehow was able to unlock the front door and started to run as soon as I smelled the desert air. As I was in the motion of beginning to run something in my head said ATV. I stopped in my tracks and looked over at the white and green ATV. I probably have only road a ATV a few times in my life, but you couldn't tell by how I hoped on it and started riding. I was completely full of Adrenaline when I pulled away from that house. I forgot my shirt inside, I just had my tank-top on, lucky for me I didn't forget my phone, or my wallet. I thought I forgot the keys to the Lambo until I remembered I left them back at the bar. I could barely see what was in front of me because it was so dark outside, as I drove the ATV through God knows where the fuck. The full moon that disappeared illuminated like it was the morning sun. I had absolutely no idea how long I had been riding, or how far I had went. When suddenly as I drove the ATV I stumbled upon something sent from heavens. It caught my eye like a flame catches a moth. In the middle of the Las Vegas desert there I was. I couldn't tell if I was hallucinating are if what I was seeing was real! From a far I saw what looked like a mountain of neon boulders. I stopped in my tracks to view something magnificent. I felt like I was right up on it even though I had to be miles away. I had some music stored on the hard drive of my phone and I was listening to Pink Floyd as I looked at those neon rocks on this plain. But in reality I had traveled to another one realm past the "Dark side of the Moon." A realm where time was non-existent. I don't know where the fuck I was but something told me to just ride. My phone was on fifteen-percent at this point, but I just kept riding. I came to a point where there was only cars traveling at sixty plus miles an hour and me on my ATV. I was almost certain I was going to die on this road, but Fuck it if I can't say it hasn't been an epic time! At certain point I wasn't sure if what I was hearing was real, but a car that I felt like was honking at me pulled up like a thousand yards away and stopped on the side of the road. At first I kept driving on Eva's ATV, but then I stopped in my tracks. I felt like that's what I'm supposed to do! Dirt flew around me in the night sky as I walked towards the light blue car." Without question I could hear someone screaming Adrian over here!" The voice that was speaking to me felt so honest that I just followed it! At some point a dope woman ran up to me and said Adrian come on! I decided to roll with the sky blue horses and hop inside of the gold chariot, that's when I discovered that I was valued in this earthly realm. Haley was sent by an angel that spoke Luke's name! The pink lady told me I had to hurry up and hop in the car. Apparently forces have been looking for me for the past sixty plus minutes, and I needed to get my shit together. The space ship door opened up, the pink lady sat on my lap as we flew away. The space pilot Allen laughed at me asking. "What the fuck happen? You look high as shit!" Well Captain Allen I left to have sex with a beautiful temptress, who turned out to be a witchy women that tried to do some kind of Celtic magic spell on me. I think that Bitch was going to kill me, she marked her blood on my forehead!" The pink lady named Haley told me that I wasn't in any danger and that the witchy women just believed in some really weird shit. I asked Haley did the witchy women cast a spell on me, and she said. "Well she thinks she did. She once told me before that she only cast good spells, and to those whom she performs her rituals on shall blessed with multiple lives." Allen and I both started dying laughing after what the pink lady said. Allen dropped the pink lady off back at the house of pussy. After we left from there Allen said he was finally gonna take me to my surprise. I told him how high I was as we hoovered over the freeway. He laughed saying, "I know you're high as shit bro the girls told me they gave you some Molly and liquid THC."

"There was liquid THC in that drink too?" I asked.

Allen nodded saying, " Yeah Adrian I told the girls to get you right brodie!"

I shrugged and said, "Well Allen that witch that I had sex with told me that she put some L.S.D in some water she gave me, so I'm feeling pretty fucking unbelievable right now! Can you do me a favor and play some "Kid Cudi?"

 Allen laughed and smiled at me as his eyes glowed like the stars, he spoke to me before turning on the music, "Adrian you're about to have the time of your life amigo!" We flew on what felt like a completely dark freeway all I would see was little flashes of light passing through. We had to be on a mountain because the stars became closer, at some point we rode into a valley with a carnival. Lights from every color in of the rainbow shine through the night sky, EDM music radiated all around as an incredible energy grew the closer we drove. "Adrian we're gonna use valet service, this is the underground carnival. It's this big fucking EDM party that they threw four times a year, and there are actually carnival rides, games, cotton candy all that stuff! DUDE THEY HAVE COTTON CANDY?" Allen couldn't stop laughing at me, as he walked normal and I skipped inside. Allen gave me a walkie talkie so we could communicate when we got separated, because there was absolutely no service out here. Plus my cell phone has been dead for like the past hour. There were so many people there. I pretty much lost Allen as soon as we got into the place. The glow in the dark bumper cars caught my attention, I went straight to them. I made friends bunch a friends, as I went from rides to booths, and exhibits. The way they had the lights designed throughout the carnival looked fucking insane. I rode a carousel were the lights coordinated with the music. The DJ stage was set up in front of a Ferris Wheel the lit up different colors. I would periodically run into Allen and the four girls that were waiting on us when we first got to the carnival. I can't remember their names I just think I remember where they were from. People told me the Carnival was over at eight-am. Time was none existent to me at that point. I was just flowing where ever the energy took me. I ended up on the Ferris Wheel with one of the four girls Allen knew, she was from Salt Lake City, we waited in the line when it was at longest point she said she wanted to make sure I can see the sun rise when it was our turn to ride. The girl from Salt Lake City was right, our timing was perfect I was right at my peak got to see the sunrise as we ascended to the highest point of the Ferris Wheel I was smoking some amazing weed getting head from a fun awesomely amazing chick, all while I watching the best sunrise ever. I have had great times so far in my twenty-two years on this plant, but this is possibly the greatest, and the craziest part is that it's all been with people that I just met for the first time in my life. I let Allen drive the Lamborghini from the festival back to my hotel where his car was parked. I needed to hurry because my flight leaves at noon I think. Luke was calling Allen's phone soon as he got reception as we drove closer towards the city. They must have been having a good time too because Luke didn't call to check on me until damn near nine-am. Luke called Allen after he called my phone. I needed to hurry up because we still had to check out and drop the rentals back off. Allen and I were having really dope conversations the whole way back from the festival, we both laughed so hard until he said some shit that made me uncomfortable. "Adrian you were a wild man tonight. I wish you could have seen how happy you were making people. I been thinking about this all night. Have you ever thought about making some extra money?"

"Extra money doing what?" I asked sitting up straight.

Allen puffed on the joint and then passed it to me, "Just using your social skills Adrian. I could set you up nice, Hunter already let me

143

know that he would be down, but I like you better, and I would rather it be you." "

"What about Luke?" I asked.

"Luke is my homie I already told you that Adrian, but I'm looking expand, and you could help with that, "Allen explained.

I was still really high at that point, but what Allen said to me made me angry enough to where I temporarily snapped back into sobriety, "Yo dude I don't know what kind of misguided vibe you got from me, but let me look you in your eyes when I tell you this. Luke is my brother and I'm loyal to him no matter what. I would take a bullet for that man. I can't fight, but if you ever ask me something like that again we can throw hands!" Allen laughed as he pulled into the hotel valet. "What's so funny Allen? I'm not playing!"

"I know you're not Amigo! Luke's lucky to have you as his friend. The other one Hunter not so much." He said.

I grabbed my head, "Hold up this was some kind of test?"

"Yeah!" Allen laughed.

"Did Luke put you up to this?" I asked.

Still laughing he said, "Hell no Cutty. I'm just high and thought it would be fun to fuck with you."

I sighed with relief, "Fuck you asshole that's not funny I'm still tripping." We continued to laugh as we walked to the entrance of the hotel and through the front lobby, Allen put his arm around me and joyously said. "Adrian what a great adventure we just had, well mainly you just had! Happy Early Birthday Amigo!"

CHAPTER XIII: CHRONICLES OF THE JUICE MAN VOL.3

"Todo Por Familia"

-Christian Mendoza

JOHNNY BLACK

I've been going to this diner for almost a decade, and I hadn't crossed paths with Jimmy in the hundreds of times I've eaten here. But one evening, the legend I had been searching for my whole life walked up to me at the lowest moment in my life. His name wasn't even Jimmy Brooks. It was Johnny Black! And my theory was right. He was lying low as a business owner. Johnny had always kept his ear to the streets. Johnny was friends with Bill Perez from the seventies. Bill was the uncle of the "Perez Brothers who Manny came up under, so Johnny kept an eye on Manny during his run. Johnny told me I was doing the right thing by going back to school. I told him I was just waiting to get back in the game. Instead of telling me that I shouldn't, he told me how I could have longevity and grow old in the game. I would end up spending so much time over Johnny's house. I know that my chess skills are remarkable because of him. I know the reason I went to school for linguistics is because of him. I know the reason that I'm going to be a billionaire before I'm fifty is because of him. I know I'm alive because of me! I tell Blue all the time that either you control the future or you're going to be acting surprised when tomorrow comes. I would be less of a man if I didn't honor JB for helping guide me! The lost will look at JB as someone who just passed on another perpetrator of destruction to the community. Let me tell you something about JB. He was one of the biggest cats in the game at his time. He gave it all up, not even in his prime, but the ascension to his prime. JB has been disciplined enough to anonymity for thirty years. People that Johnny was taking care of cursed him for disappearing. Johnny's favorite cousin killed Johnny's only sister, trying to get to some money that Johnny had stashed away. You know what Johnny did? He killed his cousin's wife. Well that's what I thought he did after he told me about what happened to his little sister. Johnny's first cousin ended up getting life in prison, his cousin thought he was getting money on his books from his peoples, but it was Johnny! Johnny said to me one day, "When you're God like you were created to be, you can't spare a second on human thoughts or actions." It took me until I lost everything that I loved most to begin to understand what that truly meant. Johnny is in his fifties now, and I see him when time is permitted! Johnny wasn't a father figure, because any man in your life that's in your father's age bracket could be a father figure. Johnny was more than that. Johnny was a street, Shulman! He helped guide my spirit to what I was always destined for. This world is full of predators. In the underworld, even more so! Johnny taught me that every good and bad deed matters, but the bad weighted heavier on the scale. That means a man must have a tremendous amount of good deeds to overcompensate for the bad. And when you're born with the conquering spirit, you have to have it ten times more. I'm still alive, and so is Johnny Black! The greatest accomplishments are undocumented. Johnny told me that he had been watching me for years. If I stuck by his side, I would be what he could have been, but even greater! I met Johnny Black on July 24th, 1997, twenty-one days after Manny was murdered. Johnny took me to a spot that he lived at in PG county Maryland right outside of D.C., we played a bunch of games of Chess, and I lost everyone, but every minute I spent playing Chess gained me a wealth of knowledge. I was looking at the game wrong, Manny had me on the path to eventually becoming a hundred-kilo man, but Johnny schooled me on how I could become a man who dealt with tons. Johnny told me the only way I could truly achieve that level was to develop a relationship with someone in the government who would be around regardless of who was in The White House. I had to question Johnny when told me that. "What you saying? I gotta be a snitch?"

Johnny shook his head, took a sip out of his fifty-year-old wine, and said, "I told you young blood if we're gonna have these talks. Your ass is gonna leave that street shit at the door. Now don't be no fool like the rest of these knuckleheads or you gonna end up like them. I'm not telling you to be no stoolie. I would have never spoken to you if I thought you ounce of a coward in you. No, you bet not ever be no rat, but if you smart like I think you are, you can see that if you wanna have longevity in this game, you're going to have permission from the world's biggest kingpins. The United States Government! I bet you think most of the dope comes in through the borders, don't you? I figured you would shake your head, yes! The majority of the narcotics come in through this country's ports, not no god damn boarders. You see, young blood, the trick is not to find someone who works on the inside, but someone you control instead. Checkmate." That was the fifth game in a row that Johnny beat me. Even though I detested losing at anything, I enjoyed every moment and got better with every game.

During the last game we played, Johnny told me how I had to handle the Aruban Alejandro situation. Based on what I told Johnny about my time with Manny and what he knew from keeping his ear to the streets, he told me limited options. The first was to take him off the map before he takes me out. Stone Face Ernesto trained Diego, Isaac, and me up before he died. I wasn't ready to take him on. Not to mention who Aruban Alejandro was and who he might be connected with. Johnny and I both heard the word of mouth that Manny was killed by a woman's husband, who he was smashing. Supposedly the dude is a detective for the City Homicide unit, and the police are erecting that "Blue Wall" around him to protect him. Johnny straight up told me that no matter how minute the action was, Aruban Alejandro played a part in Millie Mac's death. I lost a couple more games and then caught the bus and train back home.

After Manny died, I moved back with Delilah. I had my GED by then. My aunt welcomed me back home with open arms. Delilah and Johnny both wanted me to continue my education all though they were for different reasons. Ms. Zhao had forgiven me for quitting the restaurant by then. The sight of me walking with a limp and my arm a in sling definitely brought Ms. Zhao around to reconcile faster. Ms. Zhao convinced her son to give me my job back that I had quit, he fired my replacement. Mr. Zhao definitely didn't wanna fire the Chinese American kid he hired for the Black American kid he didn't care for. I kept living with Delilah and working at the China Hut for twenty-one months after Manny died, and I met Johnny. I went to Johnny's house and played Chess with him two times a week since he accepted me as his pupil. We talked about everything and every aspect of my life during my visits. Johnny kept me from taking out a few nigga's. Johnny always kept me on my square, he actually had the same feeling about Killa Ken that Manny had, but that still couldn't sway my feelings about Ken. Johnny also warned me about Rose.

JB told me that he knew Rose's Grandfather as a youngster coming up and that the Jenkins family was cursed like the Kennedy's. Rose's mother was killed by a cop. In retaliation, her father shot up a police station. Mason Jenkins became a legend, serving life in prison for his crimes. Rose's Grandmother started raising her at the age of ten. Rose was different from any female I had ever met, but Johnny would always stress that a relationship with her would only end in tragedy! After a close encounter with the law, Delilah convinced me to move to Virginia with Barrette's mother to get away from my environment and continue school through community college and maybe a university.

Once again, the move with the best intentions to get me away from the life turned out to be something that only enhanced my skills. Isaac and Kenny have always been my brother's and the universe blessed me with another to complete my pyramid. I met Braxton Turner A.K.A. Boogie on the third day, staying with Barrette's mother. I became familiar with Tina and Tammy, my older cousins, and they introduced me to Boogie. Tina and Tammy linked Boogie and me just off the strength that he had an uncle that lived in Maryland. Tina and Tammy didn't know it at the time, but that little introduction helped put on the path Johnny foresaw. I humbly built my relationships out in "Hampton Roads" Boogie and I became tight in the first six months of living out there. Boogie's game at the time was guns; he had out of state connections but not like me. With the type of artillery that Boogie can get, I certainly can link him up with plenty of out of state customers. Boogie helped me expand my network of connections. Boogie's mother was from Memphis, Tennessee, and even though he grew up with his father in Norfolk, Virginia, he spent his summers in Memphis, where he acquired his gang affiliation and local connections that would become invaluable to me, things were coming together at that point in my life, before I knew it the new millennium was at hand. New years eve of 1999 was a good night.

I was celebrating more than just the New Year. Ken got out of prison a few days prior. Isaac was back on this side of the map. After graduating from Military school, he enlisted in the Army, Isaac is now on his third assignment, currently stationed on a base in Northern Virginia, and he just got a promotion. Boogie just had his first child four days ago. My godson Prince Jamar Turner and I recently connected with one of the country's biggest traffickers. At that point, everything was moving ahead. Aruban Alejandro still had me under his thumb, but that wasn't going to last forever. I connected with Alejandro before I left D.C. he was lying low, but I located him in Delaware. I offered to take care of the reason that he was lying low. Aruban Al told me if I could somehow do that, I could live my life; however I wanted without looking over my shoulders. When you're as quiet and as close as I was to Manny's organization, you learn a lot. I was their errand boy; I would do shit for all four of them. Manny, Alejandro, Juan, Ernesto, and in the process, I discovered things that the four of them might not want me to know. Like I found at the Juan had a boyfriend. Manny knew about the shit, but he didn't care. Jalapeno Juan made them the most money, so Manny decided to keep it between them. He knew it could cause problems with Alejandro and Ernesto. I knew where I could possibly find Juan, and fortunate for me, I lucked up and was able to locate him. Jalapeno Juan was at his boyfriend's spot, and after a week of recognizance, I made my move entering through the fire escape, catching them off guard. The feds on Juan's detail was trash, and they didn't discover that Juan was dead until the following morning, and by that night, I was standing in front of Alejandro with my proposition. Once Aruban Al accepted. I presented him with the evidence that Juan was gone by giving him Juan's ring that never left his finger. Alejandro gave me his blessing to live my life, but once I resurfaced making money with Boogie, he put me back under his thumb.

This new connection that I made is drawing me closer to being able to rid myself of Aruban Al once and for all. I was looking forward to The New Millennium. I have a woman I love in Rose, my crew had come full circle, and I'm a little over two years from finishing my four-year degree in Linguistics, and I'm close to being fluent in three languages other than English. As the ball dropped to bring in the new year, I was surrounded by nothing but family and friends. I knew what Johnny and I had been discussing for years was beginning to unfold right before my eyes.

THE SUMMER OF '04

By the summer of '04, I was in complete control of my own destiny. One of the worst days in this country's history was one of the best days of my life. 2001 September 11th was the beginning of the never-ending war and the birth of the New World. It was also the beginning of the end for Aruban Al. Alejandro made a deal with a Mexican cartel, but because of 9/11, Al wasn't able to make good on that deal. On the other hand, I had just received an influx of product for dirt cheap and was one of the only shows in town after the towers fell. The mark up on those bricks put me over the top, and Alejandro's newfound enemies presented me with an opportunity to finally take Aruban Al off of the map. It took me a few years, but in 2003 I was able to take out Alejandro Gomez A.K.A. "Aruban Al" with a sniper's bullet shot from four hundred and twenty yards away. Isaac was dishonorably discharged from the Army after doing two tours in Afghanistan. Isaac came to work for me once he got back home. Isaac pulled the trigger of a high caliber sniper rifle that ended Aruban Al.

I cleared Alejandro out of my path, and I made a few friends south of the border in the process. By 04' I was the owner of a legit business specializing in providing interpreters and translators for businesses and foreign nationals. Boogie had a legit business that I helped him establish in Maryland. Best of all, I was the father of a beautiful two-year-old girl named Rosetta. I'm not in the right space to be what Rose wants me to be, but I'm a great father. I got Rose and Rosetta set up in a house in Ashburn, Virginia. When I wasn't out of town or on the move, I was at the house with them. The last week of June in the Summer 04' Adrian's birthday was a week away. I promised that I would take him and Luke out of town to do something to celebrate his twelfth birthday. Time flies so fast. It feels like just yesterday, I watched these little dudes swim in the kiddie pool. Now they're a couple of years away from High School. Blue has some of his father's features, but for the most part, he looks like his wicked bitch of a mother. I don't know how much Blue remembers about Manny, but he does some of the exact same shit that Millie Mac used to do. When Blue laughs really hard, he grabs the back of his neck with his left hand like his big brother. Blue is so smart and such a sweet kid,

Manny would cry with joy if he could see him. Blue is growing up so fast it's scary, and speaking of growing up too fast. This little nigga Luke is going to be a problem for Willie and Anna in the future. I had to convince them to let me bring him on the trip. Loot got suspended the last two weeks for selling test answers to kids in a class that he didn't even take. This kid has been all about his money since he was four years old. That's why I started calling him Loot. This past spring Luke lost his virginity to this thirty-one-year-old bitch named Keisha that works for Gold Watch. Sadie was pissed once she found out. She overheard Loot describing what happened to Blue. Sadie said she knows he was telling the truth by the details he was giving to Adrian. Sadie is a sweet-heart, but if you violate her, she turns into "She-Hulk!" Sadie went in on Keisha, she broke her jaw and knocked out five of her teeth. She was mad at me like I set the shit up. Like I would do some shit like that! I try to keep Adrian and Luke away from the same shit that happened to me, but the fact is they're both growing up, and Loot was gonna be fucking soon anyway. I'm just happy that the little nigga ain't no homo. I haven't talked with Luke about what happened, so I promised Sadie I would on this trip.

We got to Orlando, Florida, on a Thursday morning, we went to Disney World and Universal Studios. By Friday night, we were heading down to Miami to spend Saturday and Sunday on the beach. As we rode down the freeway, I decided to have "The Conversation" with Luke. Blue was in the back seat passed out, and Loot was riding shotgun. I told Luke that what happened was wrong. That bitch is twenty years older than him. If that had happened with a man and a girl his age, the man would turn up missing. I talked to Luke for about twenty minutes. After everything, I said this little nigga asked me, "Aye, do you think that bitch will still give me some pussy?" Following the car drive from Orlando to Miami, we arrived at the spot. Blue and Loot went crazy when they saw the beach house I got us for the weekend. That Saturday morning, I brought them breakfast and then let them explore the beach while I handled some quick business. I had to settle a dispute between two of my connections down here. It's always over money or a bitch. Two of their soldiers got in a beef over a female, and somebody ended up dead. Now I gotta prevent these niggas from potentially fucking up money. Once I sat the both of them down, the expressions they had, once I told them how much money they could make said it all. Both of their faces were blank, but I could read everything. Money makes most things make sense. There was a mutual agreement, and all parties moved forward. After the meeting with them, I met up with this cat named "Cuttlefish" I met through JB three years back. Cuttlefish could make a body disappear like no other. Cuttlefish is from the Caribbean, but JB told me that he had CIA training. Up to this point, I've looked out for Cuttlefish in many ways, we've built up a good relationship. Cuttlefish wants me to meet him at this driving range so he can introduce me to someone. There's only a hand full of individuals who can get me to meet new people, and Cuttlefish is one of them.

I arrived at the driving range and walked down to the space where Cuttlefish and the man he wanted to introduce me to were set up. Cuttlefish was placing the ball on the tee as I approached. He looked up at me, joyful, then introduced me to Christian Mendoza. I was twenty-three years old, Christian couldn't have been that much older than me, but I could tell that he was on a different level. Apparently, some of the moves that I made caught Christian's attention in a good way, and he wanted a mutual friend to introduce the two of us. Christian thought I could help him with something and help myself at the same time. I spoke with Christian for over an hour. Cuttlefish vouched for Christian, and Johnny Black has always vouched for Cuttlefish, so I decided to leave the driving range that day with a new business partner. Within nine months of beginning my partnership with Christian, I made Sixteen million dollars and had two additional shell accounts. Before I met Christian, the only places I traveled outside of the country were Jamaica, Mexico, and China. In no time, I added thirteen additional countries to my passport. Christian introduced me to his father along with his older sister Hanna in the Winter of 06'. By that point, Christian and I had built up a solid relationship. It was time for me to be introduced to a few of the other family members.

MELTED CROSS (2012)

I was thirty-one-years-old and more focused than ever! So much had changed at that point! Isaac was dead, as well as my Aunt Delilah and Ms. Zhao. I hadn't seen Rose in five years. My business relationships with Boogie and Gold Watch had changed entirely. The days of us being a crew were well over. Everyone was doing their own thing individually. The main rule upon our mutual decision to move on our separate ways was to "never step on your brother's toes." Boogie was doing his thing with his crew that he built up, and Gold Watch was slowly becoming one of the biggest cocaine dealers in the country. And me, on the other hand, has not seen or touched a kilo since 2006. I was on the logistics side of the game, I was bridging connections between dealers, and most importantly, I was supplying cutting agents globally through a link that I established with a group out of Beijing, China. Even though we were all individually doing our own thing, we would help each other out sometimes. I had the most powerful connections and have sometimes utilized them to assist both Gold Watch and Boogie.

There were a few times that I helped them out without their knowledge, especially Gold Watch! I hadn't seen any of the family for quite some time. It's been over two years since I saw Blue or Loot. I attended their High School graduations in 2010. That was the last time that I've seen the family except for Benny. Benny was the one man I could really talk to outside of JB, and I needed someone I could confide in with the information that I found out in the fall of 2011. I was gonna be a father once again. I developed a fling with Hanna, and she ended up getting pregnant.

Hanna was a lesbian, and this was hard on her heavily catholic father, so much so that he put a million-dollar reward up for the man who could turn his daughter out and provide him with a grandchild. His oldest son died before he had kids, and Christian and his wife have been trying to have a child for years with no success. Mr. Mendoza was approaching eighty and wanted a grandchild, and as fate would have it, I would be the one to provide him with that grandchild. Senor

Mendoza was prejudice, but those prejudices subsided once he found out he would have a grandson, he gladly awarded me my million dollars, which was cool, but I was worth over a hundred million by then. I had my money so spread out that even if I were ever to get caught, the government wouldn't even be able to confiscate a quarter of my money. Adrian and Luke didn't know it, but they had a couple of million in trust-funds to be received if they reached thirty. When I found out that Hanna was pregnant, I discussed it with Benji. I confided in him how I was concerned that Hanna and I having a baby together could lead to problems between us, which would be bad for business. Christian always thought that I could be the man to get Hanna. He would talk about how she looked at me sometimes—what she used to say about me. Hanna and I had a one night stand back in 06' years before I got her pregnant.

I never will love another woman like I loved Rose, but my admiration for Hanna is only second to Johnny Black! Carlito Isaac Knight was born on April 1st, 2012, in Hickory, North Carolina. Christian became my brother, second to only Benny. Christian was the second person to meet Carlito outside of his grandfather Francisco. A few months before Carlito was born, I agreed with Hanna and Mr. Mendoza that Carlito would be my son on paper, but he would stay in Venezuela with the Mendoza family. It's been a couple of weeks since Carlito's first birthday, and I was able to see him in person for the first time in four months. I saw a change in the Mendoza family once Carlito was born. I witnessed the most change transpire in Christian. He looked at his nephew Carlito like he was his son. Christian felt like Carlito was a miracle baby because six months after his birth, Christian got the news that he and his wife will finally become parents after trying for over a decade. By the time I visited Venezuela to see my son and Hanna, Christian's wife, was already seven months into her pregnancy. My two-day visit was productive and pleasant. I was there to see Carlito, but it was business first. He was only turning one anyway. It's not like he's gonna remember any of this shit. I landed in D.C. when I got back to the States. I had to take care of the legitimate side of my business life, "Babel Communications" was expanding to another city, bringing the number of locations to three. I was still the CEO, but I rarely dealt with day to day operations at that point. I paid people to deal with shit for me. The only time that I was involved was when there existed some kind of problem that the people I paid couldn't take of themselves, and one the managers in our Chicago office fucked up in a major way. This fucking nincompoop working for our Chicago branch. Moonlighted as an interpreter for a crew out of the Midwest under investigation by the feds. After years of hard work, I was able to place someone deep inside Federal Law Enforcement. I would have heard if my company or myself were under investigation, but the last thing I needed was the feds snooping around Babel Communications! Babel is one-hundred and ten percent legit, but I was not! Christian and I have something in the works currently, and I can't afford to have the feds anywhere near any aspect of my life. It will only make our potential partners back out of our deal that we have been working on for over two years. I went to Babel's D.C. office unannounced, I can't remember the last time that I was here, but I see now that I'm going to have to engage in some theatrics to get this office back on point. No wonder we've been losing money here the past two quarters. I ended up firing two of our reps before making my way to the company's Vice President's Office. She was out at lunch with a client. I decided to wait around in her office until she got back. I actually got a kick out of firing the kid who was fresh out of college. I was speaking like Samuel Jackson before and after I fired him. When our Vice President Monica got to the office, I could tell that her secretary gave her the heads up that I was there. Monica tried her best to act like everything was under control, but I knew it wasn't, or else I wouldn't have been there. Monica ended up revealing to me that it was worse than what I was initially told. This little shit causing all of my current headaches wasn't just moonlighting for some crew who was just being investigated for narcotics. They were also investigated for links to terrorism. This was way worse than I thought, but I couldn't afford a second to stress. I had to look for solutions both immediately and long term.

I was able to arrange a meeting with Christian a week after I got the news about Chicago. Christian would be in Houston, Texas, for a night before he went south of the border to meet with one the Cartels that his family had diplomatic ties with. When I got down to Houston to inform Christian of the new developments, I didn't receive the reaction that I was expecting. Christian acted as if what I told him wasn't that important. Like something that could affect a deal worth hundreds of millions of dollars was insignificant. Christian was more worried about celebrating that he was about to become a father, and the new alliance, his family, forged in Mexico. I rarely drink or smoke, but I did that night because Christian was so happy about his upcoming child, and honestly, I needed a few hours to take my mind off of my stresses. "We stopped at a Whataburger to grab something to eat a little after midnight. Christian loved women from Texas, and we had a whole flock of females waiting back at the spot that he was renting. We were riding in a 2013 W Motors Lykan Hyper-Sport Christian was well connected in Houston, so my comfortability was at its normal paranoid level as we moved through the city. The girl working the drive-through window was ready to quit her job for Christian as we picked up our orders, and he flirted with her. Christian gave the broad two thousand just because he was feeling good, and she had a kind personality. I was feeling more optimistic as we pulled out of that Whataburger! At the end of the day, Christian was right; I was overreacting. My inside man has reassured me that I'm good, so have my lawyers but comfort is a feeling I rarely allow myself to have. We left the Whataburger going to a carwash a few blocks away. Christian and I sat outside of the carwash, eating our food and laughing. Things were looking up; there was no reason for me to be so worried about Chicago. A young attendant pulled Christian's Hyper-Sport around as it sparkled from its fresh wash and shine. Christian tipped the kid a hundred dollars as he was about to pull off. I wanted to use the bathroom before we hit the road. The last thing that I heard was Christian say, "Todo Por Familia!" The bomb planted on Christian's car had a timer delay, so it didn't explode until I got back out of the bathroom and was only moments away from entering the Lykan and being blown-away along with Christian. I suffered a server brain injury and received third degree burns to three percent of my body.

CHAPTER XIV: WORK LIFE

"Towards the light of wrong, and right take your feelings, and roll the dice, only regret is a regret of not living your own life."

-Marcus Auraylius

Thursday is usually my busiest day of the week. I work four hours in the morning from 8:00 am to noon. I have a class for my major on campus at 12:30 pm till 3:00 pm, and then I have to work my second shift at the restaurant from 5:00 pm till closing. I only have an hour and some change after my class before I have to go back work, I usually use that time to nap, but I promised Krystal that I would meet in her dorm at Blount for an afternoon delight. I smashed Krystal a month ago in September and shorty been acting like a dick fiend ever since. Krystal is a freshman, and I should have known what would happen before I piped her down. Well, ever since then, this bitch has been worse some as shit. I want to cut her off, but she got some good ass pussy, so I went to her spot before I went back to work instead of taking my usual hour plus nap. I parked my car and then hauled ass to my class at Holmes Hall! I swear I've only been on time to class like four or five times, and today I'm late again. I'm lucky the professor is cool and somehow managed to have the highest grade. Dr. Danchimah's class was cool, as usual. I left Holmes, making my way across the bridge to Christal's dorm in "Blount." When I got there, her roommate answered the door. She was bad as shit! I know she wants to give me the pussy too. In due time. In due time! Krystal was ready when I got to the room; she was butterball naked. She was dosing off by the time I left her spot. It was 4:08 pm, so if I was lucky with traffic, I might be able to sneak in ten minutes where I could close my eyes before I had to clock into work.

I was smoking the last of the ounce I got from Hunter the previous week. It wasn't even worth what I paid for it, but I needed something before I stepped into that kitchen. I was bumping Big Krit - *Hydroplaning* before I walked into work. I had to put a game face on as usual when I opened that back door. I wholeheartedly believe that everyone should have to work a year to six months as a server! I've learned more from being a server in a year that I have from school. You see human nature when you're serving Mothafucka's food! I've been working like a slave since I started community college in

Southern Maryland. I was able to work my ass off, and after two years, I transferred to Morgan State. I wanted to transfer to the University of Maryland to attend school with Adrian for the first time since Junior high, but my parents wouldn't take on the tuition I would have had to have at Maryland compared to Morgan. I moved to Baltimore in August of 2012. I started working at this restaurant a month before I moved here. It's not the job that bothers me but more so the environment. The shift manager is an uncle Tom who hates on me. He's salty that the head manager and the owner fuck with me so much. Plus, he hates the fact that I can fuck any one of these girls in the restaurant from the hostess to the servers, but the main thing I hate about working here is how people treat me sometimes. Mothafuckas be so rude, shitty customers are truly universal, no race holds a monopoly on that bracket. I saw my name was already on the board when I got inside. I clocked-in to work and said, what's up to the uncle Tom manager. His name is actually Thomas, so you know I use that shit for my own personal amusement. I clocked-in and did my usual routine. I made myself a drink, root beer a lot of ice. I'm probably only cool with five people at this job, a cook, a dishwasher, a bartender, and two servers at this the restaurant. The rest of these Mothafuckas in here are predominately corny. Kyle is one of the servers that I'm cool with, and he's talking to me nonstop like always. Kyle's a white boy from Calvert County he's going to Loyola University Maryland. I think he's in his third year like me. Kyle was telling me a story about how he smashed one of the hostesses after work last night. Little does he know, but I fucked her first. I had to wait about eight minutes before I was at the top of the board. I had a party of seven. This family was celebrating their father's 80th birthday. I got their appetizers out before I got hit with my second table. A couple and they already know what they wanted when I got there, which is always good. My shift was cool. All my tables were tipping well. I didn't have any problems until my second before the last table. It was three dudes around my age. As soon as they got seated, they were loud and obnoxious, and these Mothafuckas kept calling me servant instead of by my name. I took them their drinks and took their orders. I had to put up with more insults. I was about to reach my breaking point. I ended up going outside so I could get some fresh air and calm down. I don't smoke cigarettes, but if I did, I would have smoked three. These Mothafuckas are talking to me like I'm a pussy or something. I ain't Floyd Mayweather, but I know for a fact that I would hurt one these boys if we went one on one, especially the way I'm feeling right now! I was able to calm myself down before it went back in there I put on my Obama politician face and greeted my last table, it was an older Black couple, and they were nice, so that chilled me out even more. I made my way back to the kitchen to get those three rude guys food, but someone had already dropped their orders at the table, so I just went over to make sure everything was alright, and of course, it wasn't. One of them told me that he asked for a well-done steak when I know for a fact that asked for medium-rare, garlic mash potatoes, with asparagus. I wrote the shit down in my pad, so I know for sure that he's full a shit. One of the guys wanted his forth refill of Iced Tea, and I knew the other guy would complain about something. I could see that shit in his face, and they still were calling me servant. I took his food back so his half-eaten steak could cook longer and get the refill for the thirsty nigga. When I took his drink back to the table, I overheard one of them say. "Fuck this, Henry; we should just leave Yo!" I played it off like I didn't hear them, but I thought, I wanted to slump one of them in the back of my head, but I'm not superman; I'm not beating up three niggas at once. Even if I did, I'm almost certain one of them niggas would try to shoot me. The older couple ended up leaving a little early, so they took their food to go. I gave them two deserts on the house, and they left a twenty-five dollar tip on a bill that totaled sixty-two dollars. When I went back to the three bama's tables, one asked to see the manager. I wasn't expecting that, but okay. Tom was at the bar flirting with this blond-haired server Kathy. Little does Thomas know I already smashed Kathy too. He would be sick if he knew that. So Tom goes over to those three bama's table, and for one, these mothafuckas tried to front like I was being rude to them, and then said I gave him a medium-rare steak when he ordered well-done, and the dude who asked for Tom that I knew was about to complain about something said that he didn't want one of his pieces of chicken because one of them was pink in the middle. Now mind you, this nigga ate both of the sides and the other three pieces of chicken, and the one he didn't has pink in the middle because that particular piece of chicken is cooked with Prosciutto, which is an Italian dry-cured ham, but the dude said he didn't know and he wanted his money back because he felt like I should have told him that. One of the guys told Tom. "And we shouldn't have to pay because of my steak!" Tom ended up doing a whole song and dance but still comped their meals, only charging them for their drinks, which were about ten dollars because those bama's only ordered sodas and no alcohol. When I got back to their table, I wasn't expecting a tip, but I wasn't expecting what happened next.

I placed the bill on the table and the Bama they referred to, as Henry said. "Hold up, servant, don't go nowhere. I'm about to pay right now!" This Bama pulled out a big ass roll of cash and started counting it in my face telling me, "Damn servant, I can't find no small bills. Here just take this fifty. That's as small as I got!" I bit my lip and told him, "Alright, sir, I'll be right back with your change!" They all started laughing, as Henry said. "Yo said he gone be back with my change. Nigga you fucking right, you're gonna be back with my change. Hurry up!" They all laughed as I walked away, and they cracked jokes. At that point, I was trying to get these mothafuckas out of here before I did something stupid! I brought back his change and told them to have a good night and to drive safely. Henry picked up the forty dollars that I gave him in tens, fives, and ones. Looked at me in the eyes and put that shit in his pocket. The dude who kept getting refills rudely stared at me. Crumbled a dollar bill in his hand like it was trash, placed it down in front of me as they exited the booth. At that point in my life, I've never felt more like a bitch and angry than when that Bama slammed that dollar bill in front of me, and you know what I did? Do you know what I did? I put that dollar and my pocket and smiled back at him and said thank you like it was a hundred dollar bill. Working those next forty-five minutes was stressful as fuck! I felt like I had a panic attack. I've had customers treat me worst, but this felt different. Maybe it was because I was at one of the many crossroads that Benny told me I would reach in my life, but I was so angry that I could have started to tear up. I listened to Kyle talk as usual, but I felt like I was in a different realm! I felt like I was a bitch for letting them bama's talk to me as they did. I felt like I was letting myself down by being a cooperate coon! And most of all. I've been feeling like I've been feeling since my first year of Community College. Like I was going in a direction where I wasn't Luke Lamar Beck!

HAPPY BIRTHDAY FAT BOY (OCTOBER 2012)

It was officially about three weeks until my twentieth birthday, but today is one of my roommates Devon's twenty-first born day. I promised Devon that I would take him out to "Dave and Busters" for his B-Day up at Towson! Straight up, Devon is one of the coolest niggas I've ever met in my life, but he's awkward as fuck! Devon was the only nigga that I've ever met from Dundalk, Maryland. Not to say there aren't any Black folks in Dundalk, but Devon was the only that I knew. Devon was about six foot five inches and weighed at least 330lbs, and that's being generous. Devon was a legit gamer, and I'm not talking about PlayStation or Xbox! This nigga was a PC gamer. Besides school, the only thing he did was play games on his PC and watch *The Big Bang Theory.* We had one other roommate, but he never was at the apartment. He stayed at his girlfriend's house in Baltimore County most of the time. I promised Devon I would hang out with him for his twenty-first birthday because he wanted to do something. I tried to take him to a party that was going down off-campus, but Devon wasn't the going to parties type of guy. I got Devon some pussy earlier this week. He said he had sex before, but I think he lost his virginity with that chick. I didn't tell him, but I paid her to have sex with him. When we got to "Dave and Busters," Devon fat ass was like a kid in a candy store. He adjusted his glasses on his face and asked, "Luke Beck, are you ready for the time of your life?" I couldn't help but laugh as I replied, "Yeah, I'm ready, Devon! I'm about to bust your ass in basketball!" Even though I wanted to be at that party, I was having a good time with Devon. This is probably the first Friday that I didn't have to work at a job in almost two years. I sat down with Devon to eat some pizza and sip some of his Long Island Ice Tea! Devon and I were debating about who would win in a fight between Superman and the Incredible Hulk. When that anxiety I felt from yesterday kicked back into my system. I don't believe in coincidences, the fact that I saw Henry from yesterday up at "Dave and Busters" I knew the universe was trying to tell me something. That mothafucka was with his family. At first, I'm not gonna lie, I pulled a sucker move and tried to play like I didn't notice him, but this Bama decided to walk up to me and Devon's table and spark up a conversation. "Yo, what's up, servant! That's when I looked him in the eyes and stood up from my seat, telling him, "Aye, slim, I'm not working! We can step outside if you man enough?" Henry lifted his shirt to show me the gun on his waistband, "Nigga please, this ain't what you want, I promise you!" I was about two seconds away from breaking that niggas jaw when Devon grabbed my wrist and said. "Hey, Luke, it's my birthday chill out, dude!" At that exact second, I had what drug addicts classify as a moment of clarity. I knew for a fact that where I was at that point in life was not where I wasn't supposed to be. Luke Lamar Beck wasn't meant to serve any humans food. I was born to be a boss, and that is what I was about to become. Henry walked back to his table, not too long after he showed me his pistol flash dancing. I sat back down with Devon and had the conversation that would change my life. I passively told Devon last month about the encounter I had with Allen at Terence's boy's bachelor party, but at this point, I was no longer passive in my approach, and I was going to use Devon to help me. Devon told me that his stepbrother was going to drive from California to Maryland in an RV for winter break. Devon didn't fuck with his brother, but his brother asked him if he wanted to fly to Cali and take the cross-country road-trip with him and his friends. I straight up asked Devon. "How about we take that trip with your stepbrother and friends and load that RV up with pounds of weed?" I asked that question in a joking manner, but Devon responded seriously. "Fuck, we can do that, dude. I fucking hate my stepbrother, so if we happened to get pulled over, we could just blame it on him! Plus, I could use the money." At that point, I started to talk to Devon dead ass serious. We talked about how we could make it happen. I had enough to buy a little over thirty-five pounds, which amounted to my life saving, but I was ready to take that risk. The following day I called Allen's phone to no answer, but he ended up hitting me back a day later, and six weeks after that, I took a flight and the road trip that would change my life. I didn't realize it then, but Henry helped guide me to the path that I was destined to walk. I found my future on a random day in my work life!

ADRIAN FEELS BLUE (December 2015)

I didn't go to sleep until three in the morning, but I was somehow able to wake up at five to get ready for work. I looked at my phone and saw

I had a text message from Caden that he sent at four in the morning that read. "I still can't believe we didn't hang out for over a fucking year, dude! I don't blame you for ignoring me after what happened between us. I didn't bring that shit up earlier at the bar because I didn't want to fuck up the vibe, but I've been thinking on this shit since that night. I feel like I'm the one to blame for what happened. I feel like we were both in a vulnerable position. After that fight you had with Luke and then divulging your child-hood abuse story. And then me having my mother die a month prior, breaking up with Vicki the day before Luke's party. Maybe it's just because I'm drunk, but I almost feel like what happened was mostly my fault. Sorry for this long-ass text. I just wanted to say that you're my best friend in the world, and we should never let anything get in the way of that. Anything! Alright, Castro, I love you, bro. Make sure your ass wakes up for work."

Adrian sits on the side of his bed, reflecting on Caden's text…

"MORNING OF DISILLUSION" (OCTOBER 5TH 2014)

Caden and Adrian are sitting at the kitchen table in Adrian's dining room. A glass of water rests in front of Adrian, along with Alka-Seltzer tablets and two Tylenol pills. Caden has an uneaten piece of toast in front of him and a full coffee cup that is becoming colder by the minute. Both men have their eyes focused on something in the kitchen beside one another. Caden finally breaks the awkward silence that filled the room. "Look, Adrian, I should probably head out, but I can't leave without saying that regardless of what happened last night, Caden finally drinks some of his coffee, "It shouldn't change our relationship with one another. You're my best friend. I want it to stay that way."

Adrian replies to Caden in a low tone, "It's a little too late for that!"

"I'm sorry, bro, I couldn't hear you, what did you say?" Caden asks.

Adrian now looks up at Caden, locking eyes with him, "I said it's a little too late for that, Caden! "But it doesn't have to be though it was something that happened, and shit happens!" Caden said.

Adrian covers his face with his hands, "Yeah, Caden, and when certain shit happens, there's no coming back from it."

Caden's tone becomes more defensive towards Adrian, "Dude, you're acting like we committed murder or something!

"Caden, I don't think what occurred has hit you yet, so let say it more bluntly. You and I... You know what? Never mind! I don't wanna talk about it! I just want to ask you this and tell you the truth, in your dozens upon dozens, to hundreds of sexual conquest that you have had. When have you ever slept with a woman you were friends with, and things were the same afterward?"

 The awkward silence fills the room again. Adrian gets up from his chair, placing the Alka-Seltzer tablets in his water and grabbing his Tylenol off the table, as he tells a still silent Caden, "I'm about to go to bed. I still really haven't sleep yet. Make sure you lock up before you let yourself out!" Adrian walks out of the kitchen, leaving Caden at the table with his hand out as he attempted to give Adrian their trademark handshake that they had done since they were sophomores in high school.

CASTRO'S WORK LIFE (DECEMBER 16th 2015)

I was still drunk when I got to the office about ten minutes to seven am. I've been working for C&S technologies corps since I graduated from Maryland with a Bachelors' in Computer Sciences. Juice knows everybody, and he was able to get me a job pretty much right after graduation. He got Luke a job working with a non-profit organization, but he quit after a few months. I'm really not in the mood to deal with anyone at this job today. I already knew what I had to do the Head

Security Compliance Officer is out of the country, and he wants me to make sure that malware software audits get completed for two of the companies that we are contracting for before he gets back to the office on Monday. It was Wednesday, and I was going to have all the audits done before lunch. The way I'm feeling right now, I knew I was going to take an early day. I went and threw up in the bathroom shortly after having my third cup of coffee. One of my co-works came into the bathroom as I was throwing my guts up and commented, "Adrian! You sound like you like had a good time last night, bro! Why didn't you invite me?" I was at the point that I was throwing up stomach bile and barely had the strength to respond, but I told my co-worker, "Austin shut the fuck up and leave me alone, please!" Austin kept talking to me as he finished using the urinal, he rolled a water bottle and a pill bottle under the stall, and then he popped his head over the stall. "Damn Adrian, you look shit, you're sweating bullets! Look, go home after lunch, and I'll cover for you. The boss isn't here anyway she won't be back until after New Year's! Austin went and got napkins out of the dispenser and handed some to me from underneath the stall. "And by the way, take it easy with those pills those aren't Tylenol there Percocet ten's. You can keep the bottle, call us even for that money I owe you, plus for finishing my compliance reports last month. Hey Castro, how far are you from being done with those audits? Never mind, I'll let you finish throwing up. Call me next time you party, dude!"

A little past noon, I got to my house, put my phone on vibrate, and passed the fuck out. I've been in a deep depression since about April, so it's been about eight months now. I'm like a walking zombie. I think the last time that I happy was when I went to visit Luke for my birthday. A few weeks after I got back from my trip to the West Coast. My depression was ten times worse than it was before I left. Depression is something that I have dealt with since I was younger. It's only got worse with age. At this current juncture in my life, I wake up and go to sleep with a tightness in my chest. Even when I'm in a room full of people who want me to be there, I still feel that I have to wear the mask of an unauthentic smile to hide my true emotions.

Last weekend I found myself sitting on my bed in the dark, holding the gun that Terence brought me as a house warming gift to my head.

167

Tears rolled down my face as I contemplated pulling the trigger, but I wasn't numb enough yet. It was dark outside when I awakened from someone knocking and ringing the doorbell. I looked at my phone with one eye open, and I saw I had twenty-two missed calls. Fuck! I forgot that I promised Sofia that I would go out to dinner with her tonight. I've been dating Sofia for about three months. My mother is the one who introduced me to her. My mom goes to mass with Sofia's parents, and she is the one who set us up. Maybe that's why I don't treat Sofia like I did my Ex because she reminds me too much of my mother. The only reason I think I'm dealing with Sofia is that I'm vain, and she's stunningly beautiful. Not the mention the fact that I have had some of the best sex in my life with Sofia, church girls can be the biggest freaks!

Sofia smelled and looked amazing when I opened the front door, and she was pissed at me, "Babe WTF I told you like a hundred times about tonight. When I talked to you last night, you said we were going, but you were probably too wasted to remember. I knew you were going out with your friend Caden was a bad idea!" I did not wanna go to dinner with this girl, but she's been making such a big deal out of it that I just apologized, conceded, and got ready as fast I could. I would have been ready faster, but she kept making me switch outfits. I ended up wearing the outfit that Luke brought me for my birthday for the first time. Come to find out Luke only picked out the gators. Paige coordinated the rest of the outfit.

The restaurant was in Crystal City, Virginia. We took Sofia's car because she thought mines was a bucket and didn't like riding around in it. When we got to the restaurant parking lot, Sofia was excited as she told me. "Babe, I have a big surprise for you!" Sofia looked at me with her green eyes, smiling as she fixed my hair and kissed me, telling me. "You've been acting like such a downer lately that I wanted to do something to cheer you up. Come on, let's go inside. We're already late!" Sofia held my hand as we walked through the Japanese restaurant. She was getting looks from guys, the host was a little too friendly to Sofia for my taste as he walked to the table, but I didn't care enough to be jealous. Our table was around a corner, so I didn't see Sofia's surprise until we made our turn. Sofia shouted out, "Surprise, Babe!" Santino walked up to me and hugged me, joyously proclaiming, "It's so good to see you, little cousin, it's been so long. Jesus man! You're still short but not as small as your dad, and you have some facial hair now. Where has all the time gone? Hey Adrian, I would like for you to meet my wife this is Emilia! Emilia, this is my cousin I told you about. Adrian, the party animal who's too cool to answers his big cousin's phone calls!"

I was completely numb as I smiled and introduced myself to Emilia. My heart rate was up and racing like the Indy 500! I haven't seen this piece of shit since I was seventeen years old. I thought I was strong enough to confront him then, but I didn't. I figured I'd be strong enough to confront him now, but instead, I just sat there and let him control the situation like he always has. Santino has always been a charming guy. Everybody loves tall, handsome, smart, funny Santino! My mom's side of the family has always treated Santino like he's better than everyone else, and that is how he has always acted. Santino made Sofia and his wife laugh as he passively disrespected me. Santino made slick comments about my father and Manny, but he made sure that he said may Manny rest in peace before he made his condescending comments about him. Santino made slick comments about Juice and Luke. He talked about how I'm closer to that black kid's Luke family than my own, but the devil has charm, so his wife and Sofia just ate it up under the guise that he was joking, being his fun-loving self. I just sat there getting drunk off my ass. I shared sushi with this piece of shit as he smiled in everyone's face. The only time that I asserted myself at that dinner was when the bill came, and he smugly said, "Jesus, Adrian, calm down, you can pay the bill. Somebodies had a little too much Sake!" The whole ride home from the Japanese restaurant felt like an out-of-body experience. I can't even remember how I was replying to Sofia. My answers must have been enough for her because she was in the best mood I might have ever seen her in.

We were about a mile away from my house when she said. "Adrian, I'm so glad your mother made me reach out to Emilia to set up that dinner. Your cousin Santino is so amazing. I don't know why you weren't answering his calls. Your mom said he's been trying to contact you since he and Emilia moved to the area last year. I see what she meant. Like, your friends are kind of cool, but you're a higher class than them. You have to start surrounding yourself with people who are like you. People who don't have a victim mentality!" Sofia gently rubbed my cheek and kissed me as she continued, "Either way, Babe, I'm so excited for you. You're only about a year or two away from a mega promotion."

"Pull the car over!" I yelled.

"I'm sorry, what did you say, Babe?" She asked, confused.

I said louder, "I said, pull the fucking car over!"

Sofia's mood went from giddy to concern as she probed, "Babe, what's wrong?"

"Sofia, I wanna break up with you!" I said plainly.

"Oh my god! What the fuck did you just say to me? Are you serious, Adrian? I know you're not fucking breaking up with me!" She yelled.

I spent the next eighty-eight minutes, breaking up with Sofia. If this was two years ago, I don't know how I would have done it, but I manipulated Sofia into believing that it was because of her. If she were a woman like Sadie, I probably would have told her my layered, complex life, but instead, I lied to Sofia like I was trying to run for President one day! Sofia was playing Candy Land, but I was playing Chess! I used all the manipulation tools that I had at my disposal to make Sofia understand that I was breaking up with her because she wasn't good for me. Which was the truth? I just like Sofia because she is pretty and comes from money. I don't think I ever had a girl cry over me as Sofia cried over me. I left Sofia in her car, crying on the road's side as I walked back to my house. When I got home, I started popping those perc's that Austin gave me like they were candy. I was trying to make myself numb enough to do what I had to do. I felt my depression was a stage five cancer at this point, and it was time for euthanasia. I shouldn't have to live feeling like this. No one should. I was a burden to myself in everybody in my life. The world would be just fine without Adrian Luis Castro. I was numb enough to do what I had to do. I went to my nightstand and started to pull the gun out of it when I heard a knock on my front door. At first, I wasn't going to answer, but I knew it could only be one of two people by the knock on the door. I knew it wasn't Luke because he's still in California, so if it's who I think it is, I don't know what he's doing here, but I would like to see his face one last time. I took a minute to put on my mask as I answered the door. Terence was standing there smiling at me, looking like he's been training with Bruce Lee and Muhammad Ali. Terence was in the best shape that I had ever seen him in, including when he returned from The Marines. Terence gave me dap, which was equivalent to him, hugging me by his standards. I don't know what the fuck Terence was doing stateside, but I was thrilled to see him.

I didn't have to wear a mask with Terence. "Damn Blue, what the fuck is wrong with your phone, boy? I called you five times."

"My bad Bruh. I had my shit silent," I told him.

"It's all good, Blue. So are you going to let me in, or are you going to keep me waiting outside?" He asked laughing. Terence came inside the house. I open up a bottle of Hennessy that I had in the freezer and started chopping it up with him the things that were going on in my life. I told him about my trip to California to visit Luke. I told TT how I caught Paige cheating on Luke, but I wouldn't tell him who. I told him how I just broke up with Sofia and was miserable at my good paying job. I told him how I was at a crossroads in my life, but I didn't tell him how depressed I was.

I felt like Terence would view it as a weakness and wouldn't understand. All those perc's I took were kicking in by the minute, and it became increasingly difficult to maintain a conversation. I was able to get a reluctant Terence to leave eventually to finish what I intended to do. I didn't feel it would be right to do it with the gun that Terence brought me, so instead, I downed the rest bottle of Hennessy and took the rest of the pill bottle that I got from Austin and then topped it off with some sleeping pills from my bathroom cabinet. I figured all that and a blade to wrist would do the trick. I no longer wanted to live this life I was living. I know it was time for me to exit stage left. I was done with this pain. I was done looking at the enemy in the mirror. This life was work, and too much for me to manage. It was time for me to resign!

"Some say the good die young in the worse way, and the bad live with nightmares and enemies."

-TWO8G

LITTLE MS. MIA (FEBRUARY 19ᵀᴴ 2016) 3:29PM

It's an unseasonably warm day in Maryland to be Mid-February. Four inches of snow fell two days prior, and now the temperatures are in the Mid-fifties. A group of kids has taken advantage of the warm weather playing a basketball game in the middle-class Bowie, Maryland neighborhood. A white BMW pulls up in front of a mailbox to a white house with green window shutters. Floyd is listening to Go-Go music Backyard Band- *Thug Passion* plays as Floyd gets out of the driver side of the 2010 BMW. He opens the backdoor carefully, removing his almost two-year-old daughter Mia out of her car seat. Mia remains knocked out sleep from the car ride as her arms draped around Floyds' shoulders. Floyd carries Mia in his left arm as he pops the trunk of his BMW, removing an Adidas duffle bag and throwing it over his right shoulder. Floyd rings the doorbell as his mother comes and answers, excited to see her granddaughter and eldest son. Floyd tries to keep his mother from awakening Mia, but to no avail, a groggy Mia sees her Grand Mommy and instantly smiles. Floyd's mother plays with Mia as he goes downstairs into the basement with the Adidas duffle bag to break down the thirty pounds of Marijuana inside. Hunter gets five pounds out of thirty. After making a sale in Upper Marlboro, Maryland, about twenty minutes away from his mother's house, Floyd plans to stop by Hunter's baby mother's house. His client in that area wants two pounds of weed and has a gun that Floyd has wanted to purchase.

Floyd has had a hectic day dealing with his child's mother, although they have a great co-parenting relationship. Mia's mother resents that he has slept with so many women she personally knows, whether friend or foe. Floyd has also been trying to find out who robbed Hunter a few weeks prior. Floyd has also been questioning his business relationship with Luke. He feels like Luke has been too distracted in California and is making careless decisions affecting their bottom line. Floyd was also one of the primary voices to warn Luke about Paige. Floyd knew how Paige was, but Luke was too sprung to see what was

173

clear as day. Floyd is getting older and is questioning those around him. He also feels like Hunter is doing something behind both he and Luke's backs, and is questioning if Hunter was even really robbed in the first place. Floyd finishes sealing and separating the packages of Marijuana as he smokes a Backwood stuffed with an exclusive strain of weed only grown by Luke's California connection. He goes upstairs to see Mia in her playpen smiling, and watching a Disney film entitled "The Princess and the Frog." Floyd goes into the kitchen, where his mother is preparing dinner. Floyd can talk to his mother like she's one of the homies. She knows about every aspect of his life. It's no one that he trusts more. Floyd's father died in 2014 of Lung Cancer. Only a year after his parents moved from their Waldorf Maryland Townhouse into a bigger, more spacious Bowie Maryland home. Floyd's mother pulled out a bottle of Bacardi and made drinks as she cooked and spoke to her son.

Floyd's mother told him that he had to be more respectful of Mia's mother. The fact that he was sleeping with some of her enemies was a slap in the face and pointed out that Floyd would be angry if the roles were reversed. Floyd sips his Bacardi and pink lemonade; his moms made him as he tells her. "Yeah, I shouldn't being fucking bitches she ain't cool with, but the difference between her and me is the niggas who I ain't cool with is trying to kill me!" Floyd eventually conceded to his mother's point of view. She also spoke on him and Luke. She knows how successful they have been, but stressed to her son that he and Luke's friendship is more important and valuable than money. She even went as far as quoting a Notorious BIG line. "Money and blood don't mix like two dicks with no bitch. Find yourself in serious shit!" Floyd barely could contain his laughter, especially when Mia started repeating the word shit. Floyd's mom also talked about her distrust for Hunter and how Luke was lucky that the high yellow bitch he was about to marry left him. Floyd told his mom about the thirty thousand Paige stole from Luke, which she replied. "You know I raised you to never put your hands on a woman, but if a female ever does that to you. Punch that bitch in her gut," Floyd laughs at his mother and tells her, "Shit Imma smack a bitch if she steals three hundred dollars from me! But thirty G's! Imma shoot that bitch in her titty! Floyd talks to his mother for eleven more minutes before he grabs the duffle bag, hugs and kisses her, and gets Mia out of the playpen. Floyd's hoping that the car ride will put Mia back to sleep.

It's dark out when he exits his mother's house due to short winter days. Mia keeps repeating, love you, Daddy. Floyd already started the car with push start before they left out his mother's house. He pops the trunk of the car, he throws the duffle bag inside but doesn't close it all the way. Floyd opens the backdoor and safely places his gorgeous daughter Mia in her car seat. Floyd tells his daughter he loves her, he gives her a big wet kiss and closes the car door. Floyd goes to the trunk to retrieve some weed edibles that he left in his duffle bag's side pocket. Floyd's phone rings again like it has been all day. Once again, it's Hunter asking for his ETA! Floyd is annoyed and tells Hunter he'll be their soon and to stop fucking bugging him. Floyd hangs up the phone and closes the trunk. Before the next minute could tick, Floyd's mother's middle-class neighborhood turned into Fallujah. A gray minivan driving from the opposite direction pulls up to Floyd's White BMW. A short man carrying an automatic rifle hops out the van and shoots indiscriminately in Floyd's direction. The man who did the shooting had purple tips on his dreadlocks. This was one of his only identifying features besides his height and race as he was wearing a mask along with the driver. The man shot all thirty rounds in the clip, running to grab the Adidas duffle bag out of the white BMW's trunk before hopping back in the gray minivan. Thirty-three seconds, and just like that, Luke's goddaughter and partner in crime were gone forever.

"I WANNA COME HOME!" (JUNE 2016)

Luke sits in the living room of his quiet, lonely apartment. Eamon – *I Don't Want You Back* plays over his top of the line Bluetooth speakers. Luke has a bottle of Champagne in front of him, an ashtray with several cigarette butts and marijuana roaches. Luke is doing lines of cocaine on a picture frame. Inside the frame is Luke and Paige's picture when they took a trip to Cancun, Mexico. Luke's inner thoughts are racing as he sits all alone in his living room. Expensive furniture but no Paige to share it with the trauma of his big homie being killed in front of him constantly hunts his mind. Luke almost feels like he could have done something to save D-Ro from getting killed. D-Ro's funeral is only a few days away, and Luke is in a deep depression. He has moments where he feels empathy and regrets not being more supportive of Adrian now that he knows how depression really feels. But Luke tells himself their situations are different. Luke lost his goddaughter, his big homie D-Ro was murdered in front of him, and Vinnie was killed driving his car when he was the intended target. Allen dying in his car crash, and of course, Floyd's murder. Luke feels like if he never was on his reckless tare. Fucking any attractive female, the sensitive, weak boyfriend wouldn't have tried to kill him, and Vinnie would still be here enjoying life. Luke's empathy towards Adrian slowly devolves into resentment. Luke sees Adrian as weak!

Luke thinks to himself that he has every reason to be suicidal. He has lost four homies and his goddaughter in four months. On the other hand, Adrian is just a weak ass bitch who has it all, but instead, he wants to be a soft ass, emotional coward! Luke chops up more lines of cocaine out of the six grams leftover. Luke does a big line, finishes the remainder of Jamison's bottle, lights up another cigarette, makes his way into his dirty kitchen, grabbing an IPA beer out of the semi-empty refrigerator. Luke uses his Zippo Redskins lighter that Paige brought him to open his beer. Luke plops back down on his couch and changes the music playing in hopes that it would make him feel a little better. Luke puts on Willie Hutch, and then he hears a knock at the door. Luke isn't expecting any visitors; he becomes extremely paranoid and fearful by the knock on the door in his coked-up state. Luke grabs his pistol that Vinnie gifted him with a few months before his death. Luke cocks the gun back as he cautiously approaches the door asking, "Who is it?" The voice on the other side of the door says calmly. "It's me, Loot. Open the door!" Luke scrambles to get himself together. He quickly puts all the evidence of cocaine and cocaine paraphilia away; he rushes to the guest bathroom running water over his face to clean up and conceal the fact that he has been using coke. Luke takes a deep breath, puts on his poker face, and opens the front door. Jalon stands at the doorway threshold in a three-piece navy blue Dormeuil Vanquish II Suit, a white shirt, and a salmon-colored tie. His dress shoes are polished and are without a flaw. His Daytona Rolex watch goes without a tick, and his diamond pinky ring is the cherry on top. Jalon smiles and asks Luke, "Are you going to let me in?"

"Yeah, my bad bruh. I fell asleep. Come on in, please excuse the mess! I haven't had a chance to clean up today."

"I can tell Loot!" Luke opens the curtains to the balcony to brighten the dark, gloomy apartment. He looks at the sun for the first time in two days. Jalon is impressed by the apartment even in its condition, he was told by Adrian that Luke was in a nice place, but he didn't know the extent to how nice. Luke paid for every piece of furniture, but he allowed Paige to decorate the entire apartment. Paige has many flaws, but her taste is impeccable, and she elegantly decorated the apartment. The view of the Pacific Ocean really sets it off. Luke pays an extra five hundred dollars a month in rent just to have that view. Jalon sees Luke's gun on the leather couch and he notices ruminates of cocaine on the glass table with an Onyx stand underneath the table is an Alpaca rug. Jalon sees where all Luke's money has went and the extent to how Luke allowed Paige to make him recklessly spend. Jalon drapes his suit jacket on the back of the cream leather sofa. He sits down and tells Luke, sitting in a chair that matches the sofa, to sit next to him. Luke sits next to Jalon and attempts to hide his depressed state of mind. He fronts as if he's in a good mood asking Jalon, "What you doing over here? I can never get you on the phone! And now, here you are just showing up all the way across the country out of nowhere!" Jalon pats Luke on the knee, smiling at him, "Come on, Loot, you know the Earth is my turf. Sadie said you called her last week, and you didn't sound good! She's worried about you!"

"Nah, man, it wasn't nothing. I'm just still feeling a little heartbroken over Paige," Luke says as he shakes his head.

Looking him in the eye he says, "Yeah, Loot, I know man, but Sadie said you called and told her one your friends got killed in front of you."

"Yeah, man, I was just messed up over it, but I'm cool now!" Luke says as he tries to sound upbeat.

Jalon gets up from the couch, making his way to the balcony looking at the beautiful sunset over the Pacific Ocean, "I talked to Blue! He said he calls you all the time, and you don't pick up!" Luke speaks with an agitated tone. "Adrian, is just being a drama queen, I've been busy as fuck! I got a lot going on right now!"

"What happened to your car? I didn't see it outside? Blue said you had a dope cherry red Jaguar," Jalon asked.

Luke doesn't answer, and Jalon has to repeat himself. "Loot, I said what happen to your car?" Music over the Bluetooth speaker mildly plays, as Jalon still hears no response to his question. Jalon turns around and sees that Luke is standing shaking and is in the process of breaking down! Luke starts sobbing uncontrollably. Jalon has known Luke since he was four years old and has never once hugged him. He walks over to Luke and hugs him, as Luke whimpers and tells Jalon, "I wanna come home! I wanna come home! I wanna come home, Jalon! I'm sorry! I'm sorry!"

After reassuring Luke for a while, Jalon settles him down, as the two men sit on the balcony looking at the Pacific Ocean view, smoking a blunt together for the first time! Jalon sits and attentively listens to Luke as he tells every intricate detail of the past twelve months. Luke details how his relationship with Paige failed. He tells Jalon how he beat up the Swedish man at Paige's modeling event. He tells Jalon how the man was going to press charges, but Luke used Vinnie to intimidate the man who was easy to locate due to his social media activity. Luke also tells Jalon how he became like family with his connection Allen who died in a tragic car crash. Jalon interjected three times while he and Luke smoked and talked for hours. Jalon tells Luke that he was once almost married to a woman who he loved very much. He told Luke how his personal vanity cost him what he loved most in the world. When Luke asked what it cost most that he loved? Jalon began to explain what it was but then redirected the conversation back to Luke. Jalon told Luke that he had been disappointed by him over the years in multiple ways. But his neglect towards Adrian upset him more than anything he had ever done.

Luke knew he could not justify not seeing Adrian in the hospital after his suicide attempt and made no excuses for his treatment of Adrian. Luke told Jalon that he loved Adrian as if he were his twin brother, but expressed how he felt Adrian's mental illness could be detrimental to him one day. Jalon's interjects, "I can understand that! Adrian went through a lot as a kid. Manny was killed right in front of him, and his mother has never been shit! Even with all that, Loot! Adrian's has one of the most loving hearts in the world. "He loves you, Loot! You should be there for him!" The two men continue to talk as Luke tells Jalon about all the money he made and lost. After Luke wrapped up the story of his past year in California, Jalon broke down how he would help Luke move back home. Jalon was going to help him sell everything of value that was in the apartment. He told Luke that everything they talked about would stay between them and that he would say to the family that he was in good health and would be moving back to Maryland soon.

Jalon would hug Luke one more time before heading out. Jalon tells Luke before he left that he knows he has been using coke and hoped it was temporary. Luke assured him it was just him working through shit and wasn't a habit. Stating weed and pussy was his only vices. Jalon shakes his head. "And look where those vices have got you Loot!" The two men shake hands, and then Luke begins to walk Jalon to the door. Jalon gave Luke a book that Sadie wanted him to have before he exited entitled "The Isis paper" By: Dr. Frances Cress Welsing Sadie felt it was time for her little brother to read the book and gain some knowledge that she thought would be helpful to him! Luke would leave California, moving back to Maryland shortly after Jalon's visit.

"The Sad Boy" - Malibu California (December 2015)

Its day four of Adrian's stay in a five-star mental health rehab facility in Malibu, California. Adrian was initially admitted to a Baltimore Maryland mental health rehab facility where he was held for seventy-two hours. After his release, his father and Jalon convinced him to do twenty-one days of additional treatment in a mental health rehab facility in Malibu, California. Adrian refused because he felt that he was okay and didn't wanna miss Christmas and New Year's. Although his father had trouble selling it to Adrian, Jalon invoked Manny's memory and essentially guilted him into going. Adrian Sr. would use the hospital's proximity to Luke as the final selling point.

On December 16th, 2015, Adrian was admitted to a Prince Georges County hospital after trying to overdose on prescription pills. Mr. Castro also tried to slit his left wrist. Mr. Castro's extremely high level of intoxication prevented him from cutting deep enough to hit his Radial Artery. Mr. Castro was discovered unresponsive in his Indian Head, Maryland, home by a friend who left Mr. Castro's house twenty minutes before his suicide attempt; he only returned to retrieve his cellular phone! Mr. Turner is why Mr. Castro was rushed to Fort Washington hospital, where he received medical and psychiatric care. Mr. Castro was transferred to the Baltimore Maryland Mental Health Rehab Facility, where he received additional treatment.

DR. GREENE

On the fifth day of Adrian's stay in the Malibu Mental Health Rehab Facility, he has his daily one on one session with his appointed therapist. Dr. Greene is a fifty-year-old black woman originally from Oakland, California. Dr. Greene received her Doctorate in Physiology from Stafford University; Dr. Greene is a widow and a mother of four; two of her children were casualties of the war on drugs. Her eldest child committed suicide by driving off a bridge. Dr. Greene's daughter was five months pregnant at the time of her suicide. Dr. Greene is an extremely compassionate, non-judgmental woman. Dr. Greene is the doctor that is most compatible with Adrian in the entire facility. Adrian and Dr. Greene start off with their typical scale of one to ten on how he is feeling. Adrian tells Dr. Greene that he feels like a six a number that he thought was believable even though, in actuality, he felt like a negative three. The two went over the reason that Adrian was there. They briefly talked about his mother, but only for a moment because of Adrian's disdain for her. Then they begin to talk about Adrian's suicide attempt, something that he is still evasive about. Dr.

Greene tells Adrian why the hospital in Baltimore kept him for six days as opposed to 72 hours. In Baltimore, Maryland, at the mental health rehab hospital, Adrian stated how he would be released, get really drunk, take the revolver gifted to him as a house warming gift, and play a Russian roulette game. All of which Adrian does not remember stating in his drug-induced state of mind. Towards the end of the session, they get to the subject of Adrian's childhood molestation. Adrian's cousin Santino sexually molested him from the ages of six to eight. The molestation only stopped because his cousin went away to college. He would see his cousin at the age of eleven when his mother married a third time and hasn't seen him since. Well, that's what Adrian has told Dr. Greene. Adrian eventually becomes agitated with his molestation questions, and Dr. Greene reroutes the subject to something more positive, and Luke's topic is brought up. Adrian expressed how he was looking forward to Luke's visit. Day after day, Adrian waits for Luke to visit, but he never does. Luke would come up with some weak excuses that Paige told him to say; before Adrian knew it, his release date was at hand, and Luke never visited him.

JUNE 6TH 2006

"I've been in and out of town for almost nine months straight! Shit has been really hectic, and Rose doesn't understand that the timing of this girl's trip is about to fuck with everything. I would not let any of her decisions directly affect my business, but I have to give her ten percent of my mind is a problem for me. Not to mention that one day I have to rest! The one day, I have to finally fucking get some rest, relax and enjoy what I love most! Rose has me fucking playing chef for her, MiMi, and Brandy. I gotta stop by the store just to get some shit that I specifically told her to buy. I told Rose, you lucky I'm even giving you this! Don't make this inconvenient for me and do some careless shit like forget something that I'm gonna need to cook for you! And what does she do? How Imma make macaroni cheese with no cheese? It's cool! I got ten hours before I gotta fly out to meet Christian. I really wish Blue could stay all day and watch Rosetta, but I got him for more six hours! Rose and her chicken heads won't get back from the spa for a few more hours. By that time, I'll have most of the sides done, and I'll have some appetizers ready because I know MiMi weed head ass is gonna want have the munchies! Aight bet I'm making good timing! I got five hours left. These Apple Barbeque Salmon are fucking perfect! Rose, better give me some head before my flight because I will throw these wings on the grill. Then run and meet up with Boogie real quick. This is some random shit, so it better to be important! Rose is inside of the house, getting faded with her Chicken Heads! Rosetta is in the pool playing with her Uncle Adrian! I'm making good timing! Now let me go see what the fuck Boogie wants! Now see, this is the problem when you let dumb ass nigga's in your family mess with your business. Boogie wants me to clean up some shit one of his dumb ass cousins fucked up! I ain't got time for this shit! Either dumb ass gonna eat the murder he gone catch, or he gone get dealt with. Boogie can't afford to have homicide and Narcos on him because dumb nigga's making the block hot. Terence is Boogie's only good cousin, and that little nigga still crazy, but at least he's smart! Well, at least I thought he was, but this little nigga is the one who caught the body! Two days before he was about to graduate from High School. Terence is lucky I look at him like family, so I gonna have expend a lot of capital and connections to clean this shit up. I connected Boogie with my fixer, Cuddle Fish, and assured him that Terence would be fine if he kept his story straight. He needs to act as if nothing happened, walk across that stage, and get his diploma in two days. I met Boogie about fifteen minutes away from Rose's house. The meeting took longer than I expected it would, but I was still making good time. I got back to the house, took the wings off the grill that Blue was watching for me, and left them on low in the oven. When I went back outside, something didn't feel right. MiMi and Brandy were sitting poolside, and Adrian was in the shallow end playing with Rosetta. Now I know Adrian very well, and he didn't seem right. It was like he was trying to give me a warning with his eyes. I knew it wasn't a life or death situation, so I threw the corn and the grill and headed upstairs to change and pack my bags. When I got upstairs to the master bedroom, I discovered what Blue was trying to warn me about. I knew shit was bad by how calmly Rose said! "Jalon, I always forgive you, and I never ask for shit! But out of all the bitches in the world, the one I ask you not to fuck! You fuck!"

I was one hundred percent sure it was about Hanna, but I wasn't sure how she found out. Until I realized it was the new phone that I just brought that morning. Rosetta dropped one of the phones I kept as a clean line in the pool last night. I just got the phone this morning. I didn't even take out the box. She probably was just trying to activate it, or she was just fucking noisy. Either way, I didn't have time for this shit right now! I knew it was about to go down. I was ready to use any trick in the book to get it over with quick. I just knew it was about to be a long, intense argument. And I didn't have time for it! "Jalon, you talk all that "La familia es unica" shit or whatever you be saying, but when it all boils down to it, you don't give a shit about anybody, but yourself! Before you bring up Rosetta, let me stop you right there. You niggas kill me with that 'well, I'm a good father.' Nigga you're supposed to be a good father.

What you're not is a boyfriend. You're not a good brother. The fact that you hide Rosetta from everyone in your family but Benny, Sadie, and Adrian says a lot. You've had Adrian lying to his best friend for four years now! What kind of shit is that to teach your "little brother, Jalon?" She yelled as she paced the floor. Rose really trying hit me with some body-shots right now! I'm protecting the family, and this bitch is trying to act like I'm doing something conniving. Before I could counter-punch, Rose me with hit me with the proverbial knockout blow. "You know this bitch is just kicking a dead horse at this point. I haven't loved you in months, Jalon. If you love 'Us' your family so much, then call Isaac over!" Rose kept repeating, "CALL ISSAC OVER HERE!" She begins to cry as she stood in front of me and punch me in my chest. Rose gathered herself after a while, didn't say another word. She just left out of the room!

You dirty bitch! She knows exactly what she's doing. She doesn't know that I know she's been sleeping around too. And then she going to try and bring Isaac into the mix! Now I got more than half of mental energy directed towards her! Fuck! I ain't got time for this shit! I finished showering and getting dressed quicker than usual. After all that and packing my bags, I probably got about three hours left. I started to make my way downstairs, and that's when Gold Watch hits me on one of my phones. Ken and I never talk on the phone. Ever! But we have a system set up. Certain ring tones we program into our burner phones represent a coded langue that only he and I understand. The first call represents the time, the second the location, the third call the reason. It takes a while, just waiting on him to hit me from different lines. After about 5 minutes, I get the code. In one hour, Ken wants to meet at a Chinese restaurant to talk about some Dominician dudes from New York. It was James Brown, Wu-Tang, and whoever sung *Sweet Home Alabama*. If that doesn't make sense to you, then good! I rush backed to the grill because I forgot all about the corn. Rose was poolside, holding Rosetta as she slept on her chest. She laughed and joked with MiMi and Brandy as if everything was okay. She really was trying to play mind games, but I ain't falling for it. I gotta worry about whatever curveball Gold Watch is about to throw at me. And whoever's outside beeping their horn needs to shut the fuck up! It's Adrian Sr. I forgot all about Blue; he's here to pick him up. As I begin looking for Blue, he popped up, spraying me with his water gun. He was justifiably doing something that I gave him permission to do. It was retribution for when I threw him in the pool when he had his street clothes on earlier today, so I told him he can shoot me if he were to catch me off guard, outside of the house. Of course, he did, and Blue couldn't have picked the worst time to do it. After fake laughing with Blue for a few seconds, and telling him that I would see him later. He just kept telling me something about a drain inside the pool that needed to be fixed for some reason. The combination of him repeating himself, his father honking his horn, and Rose playing her mind games. I went out of my character! I allowed my frustration with Rose to make me impatient with Adrian. After Blue told me to fix whatever he was talking about again. I just snapped! I'LL FIX IT! GO TO THE FUCKING CAR! SO YOUR FATHER COULD STOP BEEPING THAT GOD DAMN HORN! I knew it was terrible when Brandy shut up, and there was just an awkward silence. I could tell I really hurt Blue's feeling. I could feel how much he wanted to cry, but I'm proud of Blue. He held that shit in like a man! He didn't cry in front of those women. I arrived at the Chinese restaurant an hour on the dot. This shit gotta be quick because I forgot my passport at Roses house, and I gotta double back and get it. Ken was already sitting down eating. He had a meal already ordered for me. I knew it was about to be bad news! I sat down with Kenny, and he said they know it was me, which was something I didn't give a fuck about. I'm mad he even made me take an hour out of my day for something I already knew about. I got two hours to get to the airport, and I'm ten minutes away from Rose's house.

"ROSE"

Jalon arrives at Rose's Ashburn, Virginia, resident to see her car is gone. Her flight didn't leave until the following day. Rose knew Jalon didn't like anyone in her family watching his daughter except Rose's Grandmother, so the fact that she has left MiMi or Brandy to look after Rosette has Jalon highly irritated. Jalon goes through the front door looking for a confrontation; his angry becomes worry when he hears crying from the living room. Jalon grabs a gun hidden by the front door and begins to try to figure out what's going on. MiMi is in the living room curled up on the couch; she stutters as she talks, incapable of finishing her sentences. Jalon tried his best, not to panic; he knew someone had kidnapped his Daughter and Rose. Jalon tells MiMi that she has one minute to get herself together. The coldness in Jalon's voice made MiMi understand that her life depended on it. Not to mention Jalon put a nine-millimeter pistol in her mouth.

MiMi gets herself together in twelve seconds as she tells Jalon that Rosetta was playing in the pool and got caught in the drain that Adrian was telling him about. The contractor who built the swimming pool did a poor job. The draining system was improperly installed. Swimming pools of that size are supposed to have at least two drains per pump so that one drain can handle one hundred percent of the water flow. There also should have been a raised or doom shaped drain cover, but there was not. The pool only has one drain located in the shallow end instead of the deep end. Rosetta could swim but got caught in the suction of the pool-drain and was unable to free herself.

Rose pulled Rosette out of the pool as fast as she could. She was barely breathing. Rose and Brandy throw her in Rose's Lexus and drove to the hospital instead of waiting on the ambulance. That was thirty minutes ago, and neither Brandy nor Rose was answering calls; both woman's phones were going straight to voice mail. Jalon had to decide if he was gonna rush to the hospital. It was only fifteen minutes away, but it would cause him to miss his flight. Jalon didn't know what to do. He knew at this point he only could pray and be there to support a distraught Rose. This meeting he had to attend in Costa Rica was everything he had been working towards, and could literally mean life or death. Jalon stood in the living room, unsure what to do as MiMi began to cry again. Jalon stared at the "Basquiat" painting that hung on the living room wall before deciding to go upstairs to grab his passport and head to the airport. Rosetta was ruled brain dead and kept alive through ventilators. Once Jalon arrived back from his trip overseas, he and Rose decided to turn off the machines that kept their daughter alive. Rosetta Josephine Jenkin's official date and time of death were June 13th, 2006, at 2100 hours. Rose and Jalon would part ways after that day. Although Jalon has kept tabs on Rose, he has not spoken to her since Rosetta's funeral.

CHAPTER XVI: WELCOME HOME LUKE PT.3

"Living for the moment bet you make the limit your moment."

-Two8G

Luke is authentically laughing for only the second time all night as Liam recalls the party from his perspective. Adrian returns from the bathroom nudging Liam to the inside of the diner booth. After fleeing Jackie Flower's house, Liam convinced Adrian to drive to another party. By the time they arrived at their destination, an hour away. The party was already over. It ended hours earlier, and Liam didn't divulge the tidbit of information that he was specifically explicitly told not to come in the first place. He almost got into a fight with the homeowner when he knocked on the front door. Adrian, Liam, and Luke decided to stop by a 24 hour diner to get food to balance out the drugs and alcohol before heading back to Southern Maryland. It was after 3:00 am at that point! A middle-aged red-headed woman came over with three glasses of water for the table. She takes the guy's orders. Liam compliments the waitress on the quality of her breast for a woman her age. The waitress, whose name is Jody, didn't find Liam's compliment amusing as she took his order of Steak and Eggs with a glass of milk. Luke and Adrian both ordered the Meat Lovers Omelet. Adrian got a ginger ale while Luke got a cranberry juice. The waitress Jody took the guys menus and then checked on her other customers seated by the front door. Luke cosigns Liam's complement of Jody's titties as she walked away. Luke tells Liam to treat people better who serve his food or someday someone might do something nasty to it. Liam responds to Luke in a forthright manner, "Luke, I ate a random girl's ass out at Jackie's party like four hours ago! I don't think the old woman with the young titties can do much to my food."

"That was funny as shit Liam, but in all seriousness, you ain't smoking after me no more! You roll your own shit!" Luke says laughing. Liam insults Luke and then asks Adrian if he finally fucked Jackie Flowers? Adrian lies and tells Liam that he hasn't and eventually directs the conversation to how drunk Liam was earlier that night. Liam proudly brags about his drunken state from earlier, and then he tells Luke stories about Adrian that occurred while he was living in California. Adrian's house became party central. Liam tells Luke about the time that Adrian threw up on a girl they were tag-teaming, or how Adrian got a disorderly conduct charge on his front lawn. The police were frequently at Adrian's house because of his rowdy parties. That particular night Adrian was extremely drunk, and he was aggressive towards the police in his behavior and tased as a result. Charges were pressed initially but dropped because Adrian wrote an apology letter to the officers for his behavior and completed sixteen-hours of community service. Luke listened to Liam's stories of Adrian that he had never heard before. Luke was surprised by some of the things that Liam said Adrian had done, but then again, they hardly have been around each for almost two years, except for Adrian's visit to California last summer. Both men attempted to deny that they had grown apart, but it was something neither Adrian nor Luke could ignore. After seventeen minutes of Liam's stories. Jody comes over with their meals and drink refills. Luke goes to use the bathroom before chows down on his food. When he leaves out of the bathroom, he ends up running into one of Floyd's cousins.

Craig was just about to leave out of the diner carrying a To-Go order. Luke follows Craig outside because Craig didn't hear him calling his name initially. Craig finally turns around as Luke approaches him. Craig and Luke haven't seen each other since Floyd's funeral. They talk outside for over ten minutes. In the middle of their conversation Craig just abruptly stopped talking and left. Luke returns inside the diner, confused by Craig's sudden departure; he eventually chalks it up Craig just being his strange self. Craig's drug of choice is PCP, so that could have been a reason as well. Luke arrives back at the table. Liam just finished his steak and eggs. He was ordering a dessert from Jody, the waitress. Luke sat back down at the diner booth looking at Jody's breast as he started to eat his lukewarm omelet. Adrian was still slowly eating his omelet; he made a wager with Liam on whom would throw up out of the two of them. Luke and Adrian began to listen to Liam, tell another one of his stories. In the middle of Liam's story, two men sat down in the booth directly behind them, talking excessively loud. Both men have on the same brand shirt and have dreadlocks. After a few minutes of trying to tell his story over the excessively loud man, Liam gets upset and asks them to keep it down a little; both of the men burst out in laughter at Liam's request. The man sitting directly behind Adrian begins to imitate Liam. "Like bro, could you dudes keep it down a little bit? Jesus Christ!" Luke begins to laugh at the man's imitation of Liam; eventually, Adrian and Liam begin to laugh along. Luke notices something familiar about the man that was facing him. He notices a scar on the right side of the man's cheek, and the end of his dreadlocks are dyed purple. Luke stares a little too long, causing the man to ask Luke, "Is something wrong with your eyes nigga?" he asked aggressively.

"Huh?" Luke said snapping out of it.

"I said, is there something wrong with your eyes nigga?" The guy repeated louder.

Luke shakes his head, "Oh Nah, my man, I'm just high and spacing out."

The man points at look as he says, "I don't give a fuck what you on nigga. You better focus your eyeballs somewhere else!"

Luke and the man have a brief stare down as Luke focuses attention on Jody as she arrives at the table, she drops off Liam's Pecan Pie and Maple Ice cream before taking the table across from them orders. Luke brushes the man's aggression off and goes back to eating his meal. Liam and Luke sit at their table, waiting for Jody to bring over two additional Pecan pie and Ice cream slices. Adrian is outside of the diner seated in his 2016 blue Ford Fusion. Adrian smokes a cigarette with the driver's side window down with his eyes closed as he waits for Luke and Liam. Jody has already been paid and tipped nicely. Luke and Liam wait for their desert To-Go-Orders. Liam found a tiny baggie of cocaine in his wallet when he went to pay his portion of the bill. Upon discovering the baggie of coke, Liam tried to get Luke to do some with him, "Yeah, Liam, I'll think about it. But back to what we were discussing. How's Blue, I mean, how's Adrian been?"

"Dude, this is my first time hanging with Castro in like eight months, and when I saw him back then, he just seemed like he was exhausted and had a lot on his mind. Then like the next month, I hear he's in rehab." Liam admits.

Luke frowns, "Who told you Adrian was in rehab?"

Liam shrugs as he answers, "Caden! We were supposed to play poker that weekend, and he canceled because he said that he was flying out California to see Castro, and when I asked what Castro was doing in California, Caden said that he was in rehab. I would have gone with him, but I couldn't take off work. Was the rehab as nice as Caden said it was? Luke!"

"What did you say, Liam?" Luke responds distracted again.

"I said, was the rehab as nice as Caden said it was?" Liam repeats.

"Yeah, it was nice!" Jody brought over Luke and Liam's slices of pie but had to go back to the kitchen because she forgot their Ice cream. Neither man cared that the ice cream was going to melt. Something that Jody emphatically pointed out to the intoxicated duo. Jody was on hour ten of her twelve-hour shift, but both men insisted on waiting. Liam tells Luke some of his sexual exploits' graphic details with the random woman at Jackie Flowers' party. Luke lightly bangs on the table as he laughs at Liam's facial expression while Liam describes eating the random woman's butt. Luke suddenly stops laughing as his ears ring! Liam sits blankly, staring back at Luke. The top right side of his head is covered in blood and brain fragments. A masked man walked into the back entrance of the diner, where no one was seated. He walked up to the two men behind Luke and Liam, firing two shots from a high caliber handgun. The first shot hit the man facing Luke directly in the head. The second shot also hit the man in the head. His friend seated across from him and began to flee for his life as the second shot rang out. He caught a bullet in the leg as he escaped. Liam was lucky that the bullet went into the man's leg instead of his back. Luke was able to grab Liam as he sat in a state of shock.

They bolted to the front entry behind the rest of the customers and staff escaping the disturbance. Adrian was already waiting at the front door with the car running facing the parking lots exit. Liam hops in the front seat, and Luke leaps in the back. Adrian drove off, asking Liam if he and Luke were okay. Liam answered in an adrenaline-filled manner. Liam was eventually able to quiet an excited Adrian down by yelling at him. "Castro shut the fuck up! Adrian becomes mute after Liam's outburst. A few minutes of complete silence permeates the car. Adrian pulls over to the side of the road, scrambling to open his car door. Adrian immediately began to vomit once the door was open. While Adrian was looking over at Liam, he noticed human brain fragments on his neck. Adrian became nauseous by the sight of Liam's collar and couldn't hold his food. Liam tells Adrian as he throws up. "I won the bet bitch!" Liam looked back at the expression of a numb Luke's face who hasn't spoken a word, "Hey Luke, now you wanna do a line?" Luke numbly stares at Liam as he slowly nods his head up and down.

CHAPTER XVII: DEEP CREEK LAKE PT.2

"Opportunities are presented to us on a daily basis. Either we take them, or we don't. Most of these decisions have no major impact on the rest of our lives, but sometimes they can be the difference between life or death or death in life!"

-Misfit Z

T he escorts Curtis ordered have left after three hours of servicing the drunken high group of men. Luke and Curtis talk outside of the Cabin Luke drinks a beer while Curtis smokes an American Spirit cigarette in his left hand and holds a Corona in his right hand. "Yo, Curt, quick question…" Luke says.

"What's that, Luke, my man?" Curtis responds.

"Why would you bet that much money on me? What made you think that I could fight?"

"Well, for one, when the guys and I get together, we tend to gamble." Curtis laughs, ashes his cigarette looking at Luke in an extremely confident manner, "And two, because I'm extremely observant, for instance, you didn't start drinking much until after the fight. You had two drinks, maybe while Connor, on the other hand, was drinking since 10:00 am yesterday and hasn't slept since Wednesday evening. Plus, you haven't done any coke or scripts. You've just smoke and babysat your drinks. I can't forget to mention that your brother-in-law, who was supposed to go to the Olympics, used to train you in boxing when you were younger." Luke stares at Curtis in an upset, confused manner, as Curtis snickers telling Luke, "Settle down, Beck! You see, there's this thing called Facebook, and on Facebook, once you accept someone's friend request, you can see all of their pictures, not only the photos that they post of themselves, but you can also see what someone else post with them in it. And your brother-in-law tagged you in a picture when you were boxing in a tournament back in the day." Luke's anger subsides as he recognizes Curtis's talent for observation. "I wanna ask you a question, Mr. Beck!"

"What's that, Curt?"

"Why didn't you bet on yourself? Did you think you were going to lose?"

"Nah, not at all. I never for a second thought I was going to lose. I never underestimated another opponent, but I understand psychology and knew that if I put up money, at least half of the guys betting against me might have reservations about betting against me. That's why I decided to play it like I was a nigga with a big mouth who put himself in more of a position than he could handle!" Luke exaplined. Curtis blew his cigarette smoke out of the side of his mouth as he looked at Luke with a big smile on his face. The two men stand outside, having amusing conversations. Conner's flunky makes his way outside. Conner has his left arm around wrapped around his flunky's shoulder as he helps him into the passenger side of his Red Lamborghini Countach. Conner could barely talk because of the shortness of breath. Conner's flunky walks over to tell Curtis he's running Connor to the hospital because Connor is in terrible shape. Curtis sternly reminds the flunky of the agreement that Connor made with Luke; he assures Curtis that they are sticking to the agreement. He shakes Curtis's hand and acts as if Luke isn't even there. Four of the other guys have already left the Cabin, and besides Luke, Curtis, Joshy, and his cousin are the only ones left at the Cabin. Luke would eventually run Joshy and his cousin to a hotel roughly forty minutes away. The guys got pulled over en route to the hotel, but the police would let them go after running everyone's identification. Joshy lit up some weed he had rolled up as soon as the cop pulled off, "Glad he didn't search us! We're dirty like Conner's poopy leg!" Luke and Joshy's cousin laugh as they smoke and drive off. They finally reach the hotel, and Joshy's cousin has to help a drunken Joshy out of the car. Joshy hands Luke a stack of money out of his gambling earnings to his cousin's objection' "Hey, Luke. You're the fucking man, bro! Make it rain on some stripper hoes! Who was that we were listening to just now?" "His name is "Travis Scott" Joshy." Luke laughs.

"I like that shit, dude!" Joshy gives Luke another drunken handshake and hug, "Peace out. You're my nigga, Luke!" Joshy's cousin helps him inside of the hotel. Luke drives off, laughing at how much he came up from a trip he didn't even want to make. Luke has never made more money in one night in his entire life, and all he had to do was drive the speed limit and beat up a racist cracker that he would have fought for free.

It takes Luke an hour and a half to get back to the Cabin because he got lost on the way back and also had to stop for gas. 2:00 am is right around the corner as Luke enters the Cabin as the fireplace illuminates the living room. Music plays from the basement as neon lights partially glow between the basement door threshold and stairs leading to the living room. Luke enters the Cabin he thinks Curtis is upstairs with another woman. Luke sits in the living room as he surveys the damage to the nice luxury Cabin. Luke lights up a doobie out of the ashtray as he looks at a painting above the fireplace, smoking and slowly falling asleep. Luke gets cotton-mouthed and goes into the kitchen to get something to quench his thirst. Luke is high and sleepy, and he doesn't notice Curtis passed out on the kitchen floor until he trips over him. Luke laughs, sitting up leaning on his elbows with his feet resting on Curtis's back. Luke gently taps Curtis with his left foot, but Curtis doesn't budge an inch. It takes Luke ten minutes to carry Curtis into the master bedroom. He is completely dead weight; Luke hurts his shoulder, carrying Curtis into the master bedroom and placing him in the bed. Luke sits down on the bed's side, attempting to catch his breath. Curtis lays out, arms spread passed out, snoring. The master bedroom is well designed. The king-size mattress sits on a custom wooden bad frame with carved with tribal symbols. Luke looks over at the nightstand with coke and prescription pills, Percocet, Xanax, and Viagra on its surface. Luke shakes his head, laughing about the whole scenario and night in general. Luke plans to sleep until 9:00 am or 10:00 am, wake up and then head to Adrian's house. Luke has his nice lump sum of money stuffed inside his left pocket.

Luke gets up from the bed laughing at Curtis as he gets up from the bed's side to use the restroom. Luke opens the bathroom door, and his heart instantly drops. There is a young girl on the bathroom floor with her eyes open and blood coming from her nose. Luke immediately tried to perform CPR. Luke had training from a course he took for a previous job. He does everything he could to revive the girl but to no prevail. Luke almost knocks the bathroom door down as he darts to the bed, attempting to wake up Curtis, who is in a coma-like state. Luke screamed in Curtis's face as he slapped him and shook him. Luke dumps a bucket of water that melted from ice on Curtis's face. Curtis came to as Luke shook him after dumping water on his face. He initially pushed Luke off of him and threw a punch that made him fall off the bed onto the floor. Curtis got to his feet, yelling at Luke, who had a look on his face that made Curtis instantly realize that something was wrong. Curtis stood over the girl's body in shock, and he asked Luke what they were going to do?

"WHAT DO YOU MEAN WE???"

Curtis made four different suggestions on what should happen, and every one of them was a bad idea. Luke understands at this point; his life has changed forever. There was nothing he could do to get out of this situation. Regardless of his ignorance and innocence, he was a part of it all the way the moment he opened that bathroom door. The best thing he could do is get the police involved. Well, Luke is a man who barely graduated from college and came from a Black American middle-class family. On the other hand, Curtis is blue blood whose family has been wealthy since the early 1900s. "Yeah, officers. My black ass sold drugs to this wealthy white man, and when I came back to his Cabin from dropping his wasted friends off, I found this dead underage girl in the bathroom!" The girl couldn't have been older than sixteen. Curtis, on the other hand, was twenty-eight. A million scenarios played out, in Luke's head and the only one he could come up with as he sat with his hand on his head, smoking his first cigarette ever. Luke modestly asks Curtis, "If you are who you say you are, maybe you should call your father?"

Luke figured the best-case scenario would be Curtis's father appreciating him for holding his son down and keeping his wits about himself. Maybe they wouldn't throw him under the bus if he played it smart. Curtis quickly shot the idea of his father getting involved down. "He said he wouldn't help me with something like this again!" "AGAIN? How many little white bitches have you killed?" Luke screamed. Curtis is agitated in his response as he sips his beer. "Luke, I didn't fucking kill her! And it wasn't a girl last time; it was different."

"Look, Curtis, I don't give a fuck what it was, he, she or they. We need to figure something out!" The sound of music playing from the basement is only sound in the living room. "Maybe we can get some kind of sulfuric acid." Curtis thought aloud.

Luke looked at Curtis even more upset, "Curtis, this ain't no fucking 'Breaking Bad'! Besides, where would we get the sulfuric acid from at three in the morning?"

"Luke, I don't know! I don't hear you coming up with any ideas!" Curtis said pacing back and forth.

"I did! I said, your father," Luke reminded him.

"And Luke, I'm saying no, that's out of the question!" Both Luke and Curtis are smoking cigarettes as they try to find an answer to their solution. Curtis asks, "What about who you know?"

"What do you mean who I know?" Luke asks as he narrows his eyes.

Curtis puts his hands up in defense, "This isn't the time to be PC Beck. I know you're not a thug, but you know them. And don't mean a thug! Their fucking useless in this case! There's gotta be somebody who you trust within your life. Someone that can call to help us with something like this! You need to fucking think, Luke! You and I both know how this scenario looks if the police get involved."

Luke looks Curtis directly in his eyes, "And what the fuck does that mean, Curt?"

"It means that both of us need to think!" Luke begins to consider Curtis's first suggestion of wrapping her in a garbage bag with rocks and throwing her in the river. Luke found out that after he left to drop Joshy and his cousin off at the hotel, Curtis called a young woman up that he met at the lake earlier in the day. Curtis started taking Xanax to come down off the coke, he calms he doesn't recall anything after letting the underage girl inside the Cabin. Luke was in an awful position and had no idea who he could call for help. Maybe he could get? No, he couldn't reach out to him. But at this point, what choice did he have.

Luke goes outside to his car, and he digs in the glove compartment of his Impala, searching for a burner flip phone. Luke turns on the phone, still charged even though it has only been turned on once, and that was weeks ago. Luke scrolls down to one of the few names that were programmed into his phone. Luke calls the person who doesn't answer at first. They call him back six minutes later on an unknown number. Luke knows how to talk in code on the phone. But he doesn't beat around the bush too much in this situation. "Luke, you need to calm the fuck down! Imma take care of you, but you gotta do exactly what I say! "Gold Watch tells Luke that he would call someone for him and have more details once upon completion of the favor! Luke would be indebted to Gold Watch. Luke calls the mysterious number given to him by Gold Watch. He talks to the stranger who tells him he will be at the Cabin in two and a half hours. Luke calls Gold Watch immediately after hanging up. He waits on the callback, as soon as he picks up the phone, Gold Watch says. "Luke, you're very welcome! Never forget this favor! The call disconnects as Luke gazes into the starry "Deep Creek Maryland" sky.

"CUTTLEFISH"

A light brown station wagon pulls in front of the Cabin two hours after Luke made his phone calls. Luke and Curtis were seated in the living room when the station wagon pulled up to the Cabin, but Curtis ran upstairs to the master bedroom bathroom and locked the second door where the shower is located behind him. Luke explained everything, and he convinced Curtis that it was the best option, but Curtis still wanted to remain anonymous. Luke walks outside, greeting Cuttlefish, whose leaning against his station wagon soaking in the Deep Creek Lake scenery. Cuttlefish is a fifty-five-year-old Caribbean male with a heavy accent; his clothes freshly pressed, a peppered gray and black mini afro rest under his fedora. Cuttlefish rubs his tongue across his beige teeth as he smiles. Luke is trying his best to hide his fear. Cuttlefish smiles and tells Luke, "Let's go inside, bredrin!" Cuttlefish marvels at the inside of the Cabin as he inconspicuously investigates every detail of the Cabin. He compliments Luke on the weed that is out on the table. Luke is uneasy about Cuttlefish's casual demeanor. Cuttlefish hasn't even asked any questions as Luke explains the predicament that he and Curtis are in. Cuttlefish acts as if they were at a cookout instead of getting rid of an underage white girl's body. "It smells blessed in here, bredrin!" Luke directs Cuttlefish to the master bedroom as Cuttlefish comments on the Cabin's smell and music as if that were relevant. Luke points, "The bathrooms back here, man!" "Well, lead the way, bredrin!" Cuttlefish enters the bathroom with Luke examining the dead girl and the bathroom. He talks to Curtis, who is in the shower area, with the door locked. Cuttlefish tries to convince him to come out so they can talk eye to eye, "Curtis, come out, we're all friends here." "What the fuck Luke? I told you not to tell him my name!" Curtis yelled through the door.

"He didn't tell your name, bredrin. It was on the pizza boxes in the kitchen! Now come out of there so I can see those blue eyes and that sandy brown hair," Cuttlefish joked. Almost a minute of silence goes by as Curtis slowly opens the door, he sees Cuttlefish smiling at him. Luke sits on the tub by the dead girl's body, "How did you know what I looked like?" Curtis slowly extends his hand to Cuttlefish, who already has his hand extended, "I didn't know bredrin, I guessed." Cuttlefish tells Curtis that he needed to tell him every detail that he remembers about what happened. What the girl knew about him and what he knew about the girl. Curtis tells Cuttlefish how he met the girl at the lake earlier the previous morning. He told the girl a fake name and gave her his burner cell phone number that he uses certain women and people like Luke. The girl was with a few other girls at the lake. Although they saw her briefly speaking to him, he was confident that they couldn't positively identify him because of their intoxicated state. "Those Bitches were already wasted before noon, Bro!" Curtis becomes frustrated as he explains the details to Cuttlefish, as Cuttlefish paces around the bathroom, acting as if he were ignoring Curtis.

Curtis starts becoming red in the face as he looks at Luke, "What the fuck Luke we're in this together. Your life is on the line! You said you could take care of it, and instead, you get some fucking Jamaican cab driver. WHAT THE FUCK BECK!" Cuttlefish allows Curtis to finish his rant, as Luke sits with mixed emotions in silence. Curtis wipes sweat from his nose as Cuttlefish laughs and pats him on the shoulder, speaking with his heavy accent and laid back tone, "It's okay, Curtis, my brother!" Curtis shrugs Cuttlefish's hand off his shoulder, "I'm not your fucking brother!"

"Yes, you are Curtis, man!" Cuttlefish manages to temporarily calm Curtis down as he gives a quick explanation of what they're about to do. Cuttlefish leaves Luke and Curtis in the bathroom as they sit on opposite sides, looking at each other. Curtis is now soberer minded, less emotional, and is in his normal controlled state, as he speaks to Luke in a calm, confident manner. "Luke, I hope you know what you're doing. I can't believe someone like you has me in this position!" Curtis lights up a cigarette as he looks Luke in his eyes, "Luke, this better work because if it doesn't!" Luke walks over to Curtis and grabs the cigarette out of his hand in a seamless manner; he faces Curtis as he puffs the cigarette, "It's going to work! Cause I don't lose the big games, Curtis! And this is one I can't lose.

"Curtis shakes his head in disgust at Luke and replies in a grandiose manner. "You're God Damn right. You can't lose! You're God Damn right!"

Cuttlefish returns to the bathroom with a heavy-duty toolbox; he makes Luke and Curtis wash and sanitizes their hands before giving them a pair of latex gloves. Luke and Curtis carefully listen to Cuttlefish as he explains what he needs them to do. Cuttlefish provide both men with cleaning supplies. He instructs Luke to clean the bedroom while Curtis cleans the bathroom. Cuttlefish takes care of the young girl's body; he strips her completely naked and removes all of her jewelry before placing her in a black body bag. Cuttlefish asks Curtis if he wants to say any last words before he zips up the body bag. Curtis rolls his eye, unamused by Cuttlefish, as he cleans around the tub. Within thirty-six minutes of starting, the whole cleanup is complete. Cuttlefish inspects both the bathroom and the bedroom with his UV light before giving his stamp of approval. Cuttlefish has already stored the body in a secret compartment in the back of his station wagon.

Cuttlefish tells Curtis and Luke to burn every article of their clothes and shower once he leaves. Curtis walks Cuttlefish downstairs along with Luke. The two men shake hands as Cuttlefish goes over the story Curtis and Luke would tell if they ever were questioned one additional time before he exits the Cabin. Cuttlefish shakes hands with Curtis and Luke before he leaves. Curtis and Luke briefly watch Cuttlefish walk to his car. Curtis is at ease after the whole fiasco and walks to the kitchen to make himself and Luke a drink. Luke realizes he forgot to tell Cuttlefish something and rushes out to his car before he drives off. Luke catches Cuttlefish in the nick of time. He walks up to the driver's side window that is already down. "What's up, bredrin? I got a long drive make it quick." Luke digs in his pocket and hands, Cuttlefish a smartphone with a hot pink protective case. "I found this while I was cleaning up the room. I almost forgot to give it to you. It's definitely her phone." Cuttlefish looks at Luke and smiles at him. "If Curtis is what you say he is. You might want to hold on to that phone just in case. Cuttlefish hands the phone back to Luke, telling him, "Tell Juice I said hello!"

Luke stands and watches Cuttlefish drive away. He returns inside the Cabin. Curtis is at the fireplace with a drink, slowly removing his clothing articles, throwing them into the fireplace. Luke walks over and grabs the drink that Curtis made for him off of the living room table. The men talk as Curtis puts his clothes in the pit using the fire poker. Curtis emphatically expresses to Luke how he has a friend for life now, how he would never forget what Luke has done for him! But he made sure that Luke understood that if he crossed him, he would see what real power was like. Luke left the Cabin at 10 am that morning as planned. When Luke arrived at Adrian's house, Adrian was still in the living room. You could tell he was feeling better. Adrian was eating some soup that Mr. Banks made him and watching "Coming to America" Luke stands by the front door watching the movie repeating the lines. Luke doesn't even notice Adrian talking to him. "Luke!" Adrian shouts as he tries to get his attention. "I asked how was it up at Deep Creek Lake?" He tells Adrian that it was just alright, downplaying the whole sequence of events. Luke stays with Adrian for a few hours, and then he returns to his parent's house.

Luke lays on the couch in the living room, watching a movie with his parents. In the middle of the film, Luke goes outside to call Paige. Luke tells Paige, who just recently moved to California. That he can't live without her, Luke tells Paige he's going to move to California and make something happen for the both of them. The couple talks on the phone for hours as they plan out Luke's move to California. Luke goes inside after he hangs up with Paige and tells his parent's about his decision. They both disapproved of Luke's plan move to California and were adamant in expressing how stupid the decision is that he is talking about making, but Luke would ignore his parent's pleas and move to California less than 40 days later.

CHAPTER XVIII: APRIL IS FOR FOOLS

"I gotta hold fast speaking to the enemy, because the realization is it's the inner me"

-Two8G

Hanna was overjoyed to see the father of her three-year-old son Carlito. Her Ethiopian girlfriend accompanies her along with two other South American women. The Luxury Suite in Santorini, Greece, was more so for the adults and business than celebrating Carlito's third birthday. Regardless of the location, Carlito was happy to see his father for the first time in almost a year. Carlito was born in Hickory, North Carolina hospital, so he is an American citizen like his father. While Hanna's girlfriend, along with the other woman, showered young Carlito with gifts and affection, Hanna and Jalon sat out back soaking in the amazing view. "Christian would be proud if he could see how well you have done for us." Hanna kisses Jalon and rubs his clean-shaven face. "Are you still having those migraines at night?"

"Nah, I haven't a migraine in months," Jalon responded.

"You're lucky to be alive, love. I may have lost my baby brother, but at least little Mijo still has his Papi, but enough catching up, let's get down to business. My father is thrilled with the way things have been going. What you were able to do with that cryptocurrency was spectacular!" Hanna kisses Jalon once again, "My father and I think it's time for you to maybe closer to us instead of staying stateside." The Frank Muller watch on Jalon's left wrist glistens as he rubs Hanna soft hand, asking her, "Is it you or Senor Mendoza that wants me closer?"

"Well, that would be me, of course. I feel we should give it another try. Little Mijo loves his Papi so much, and he should see you more than he does!"

"Hanna, this arrangement was always your idea. You and I both know I want Carlito with me, but your father is who your father is, so I fall back and play my part. Now you're telling me all of a sudden. It's time to be closer?" Jalon pours more wine and both glasses as he peers into Hanna's eyes. "I think it's more to what you're telling me." Hanna twirls her hair with her seductive devilish smile, "Of course, there's more, sweetie, but its little Mijo's birthday, and I would hate to spoil the mood." Jalon has pulled his hand away from Hanna; he pushes his glass to the side. "Then what is it, Hanna! You know I don't like riddles. I promised you I would never lie to you, and you promised me that if me or mines were in jeopardy, you would give me a heads up."

"Aww, sweetie, you're still a little naïve!" Hanna kisses her index finger, places it on Jalon's lips. "If I didn't love you and our son so much, where would you be? Love, I'll give you a heads up. A friend of yours is doing business with a friend of ours rival. Now, this hasn't become an issue yet, but if it does... Papi will clean your house because we don't think you're capable of cleaning it yourself, and it would devastate me if you somehow refused our offer to clean it for you. So now it's not so much of a riddle is it?" Jalon understands exactly what Hanna's is getting at, but he is still in disbelief that Gold Watch was able to accomplish something of this magnitude by himself. Who else could it be? One of Jalon's main traits that have kept him alive and free in the upper levels of the underworld is his ability always to be thirteen steps ahead of everyone he deals with, but somehow this slipped pasted him. He realizes that it all started around the time of Rosetta's death!

Jalon was more so disappointed in himself that he underestimated Kenny's ambition and patience. He overestimated his ability to manipulate and never thought Gold Watch could connect to anyone past upper-middle management. So now how in the hell was he able to gain a close working relationship with one of the Mexican cartels. Well, it could only be one of two cartels. The other cartels the Mendoza family has good diplomatic ties with. And why is Hanna warning him instead of just letting things play out? There had to be other dots that he wasn't connecting. Jalon hates when he is unable to understand things that he should, and he realizes that Hanna might understand that as well, and she might be allowing him to put the puzzle together. It's his only living child's birthday, and this time is for him! He knows for a fact that his son is safe and is fifty percent confident that he, or the people he considers close family is in no danger, but he didn't know how deeply Gold Watch connected to this cartel, or how much damage he has done with his other business relationships, and thinking deeper about cleaning his house. Maybe Boogie was in on it on a lower level as well. Carlito didn't have it in his blood to be a fool, but he was born on the day of fools, and his father felt like one for the first time in a long time.

ISLA MARGARITA (APRIL 3rd 2018)

Little Carlito is placed to the ground by his grandfather as he sprints into his father's open arms. Carlito is now six years of age but already speaks with a high school student's vocabulary. Carlito and his father play well into the evening, as Hanna and her father chat the hours away. Eventually, Hanna gathers a fussy Carlito inside of the Mansion while Francisco and Jalon have a one on one conversation. "Jalon, I'm an old man who has been blessed with three beautiful grandchildren in his Autumn years. Carlito, our little Einstein. And Christians last blessings to my family, his twin boys, Able and Justice. At this point in my life, all I want is peace. Before Christian died, he told me how much you sacrificed. You were willing to sacrifice, Isaac, as Abraham was. I'm a straightforward man Jalon," Senor, Mendoza takes a puff of his Cuban cigar as he continues. "Hanna is like her little brother was, their ambition knows no bounds. Although we have everything, we need built. Hanna still wants to build more, which has only brought more complications into my life, and I would like to thank you for handling some of those complications personally. I know you intended to make it appear that Hanna took care of these complications independently, but I know the truth as it is, and I want to show my gratitude. Jalon, you are a loyal man and have my utmost respect for that characteristic, but your loyalty will destroy you and everything you've built. Now you know about your associate's "Gold Watches" relationship with an organization who is enemies with friends of ours for quiet some time. Hanna informed you about this three years ago, and what once was a minor concern has grown to be a significant problem. I understand friendship, so I empathize with your inaction, especially after the unfortunate situation with Isaac. But you have to ask yourself this, Jalon. Will I allow my love for Judas, put me on the cross?" Jalon hasn't broken eye contact with Mr. Mendoza as he smokes his cigar sipping Jamaican rum and orange juice.

After cashing his Cuban cigar, Jalon finally responds, "Senor Mendoza."

Senor Mendoza puts up his hand, "Please, Jalon, you're the Father of my eldest grandson. Call me Francisco."

"Well, Francisco. I'm not Jesus, and Kenny's not Judas. We just happen to have conflicting interests, but I assure you that I have had this taken care of for the past year. My kingdom is under control, and all those who I consider family, including Braxton." Francisco leans forward, patting Jalon on his shoulder before he leans back, puffs his cigar and tells Jalon, "La Familia Es Unica." As a sign of good faith. I feel that it's only necessary that you oversee a small favor for me, as a sign of action. There's a man who is essential to your friend Kenny, whose name is Dean Dotson. Orlando will give you the details." Mr. Mendoza shakes Jalon's hand before he gets up from the table, outside of the South American villa

.

"THE SIT DOWN (APRIL 6ᵀᴴ 2018) 2:22 AM

Boogie walks up to his townhome, pulling his gun out of his waistband as he slowly opens the unlocked door, he hears Curtis Mayfield playing as he cautiously investigates the front hallway along with the kitchen. Boogie enters his living room gun still drawn. He lowers it as he sees Jalon, looking at pictures on the entertainment stand. Boogie calmly asks Jalon, "When did you get back?" Jalon puts the picture of Boogie's little brother Tyrone back on the entertainment stand, as he replies to Boogie's question with a question, "What I tell you about putting pictures up where you are resting?" Boogie sits down on his brown coffee sofa; he lights up a blunt that sat in an ashtray beside him. Jalon sits down on the love seat to the left of the couch, "What's it matter anyway those are all pictures of dead people."

"Those dead people still got family, don't they? And I flew into JFK this morning." Jalon responded.

Boogie looks at Jalon, "How was your trip? Wherever you were."

Jalon shook his head, "Come on, Boogie. You're smarter than that. You know where I was."

"In all honesty, I don't know, but I can guess, somewhere tropical, I suppose," Boogie shrugged.

"Tropical you say?" Boogie ashes the blunt as he French inhales, "What you getting at Juice? Jalon stares at Boogie, looking at him in a manner asking if he had his safe house swept for bugs or wires from law enforcement. Even though Boogie has his safe place swept weekly, both men leave their phones on the coffee table and take an electronic walk free down the sidewalk of the Silver Spring Maryland townhome complex.

Jalon makes it known to Boogie that he is looking for wire without speaking a word. Boogie is offended that the Godfather to all but one of his kids would even think that he was on some funny shit, and tells Jalon as they walk down the street. In his unfiltered manner, a quarter-mile away from his townhouse, "Aight Juice on GD! You know what it is from Memphis to the Midwest! And you ain't never came at me like this. And yeah, we all built our own castles. Yours may stand a little higher, but best believe my energy ain't going nowhere! Should my castle fall. Now speak, you're mind nigga!" Jalon stops with Boogie as they talk on the Silver Spring Maryland sidewalk, realizing, "Oh, shit, you don't know!" Jalon begins to tell Boogie about some of his business ventures while not explicitly painting out a small percentage of the picture. Boogie is the person he trusts the most in his lonely position. Heavy is the head that wears the crown. Jalon divulges enough to give Boogie a better understanding of the current level he has been operating on for the past two years. At this point in their lives, Jalon is now thirty-seven years of age while Boogie is thirty-five. The two men are on two different levels. They still maintain the old crew's original principles from the early two-thousands have lived by, but they haven't done business face to face together in years. Although Boogie has many legitimate avenues, he still is very much involved in the underworld with the majority of income come, from guns to narcotics, and prostitution.

On the other hand, Jalon has legitimized himself by insulating himself from the criminal underworld through several conduits and only deals with a few major American traffickers from San Francisco to Boston,

Philadelphia, Chicago, Memphis, Tennessee, and Miami, Florida. Besides those few people, he only deals with representatives like his child's mother, Hanna, or heads of the organizations. Jalon has spent the last twenty years building connections both in the cooperate and the criminal world. Juice is connected with Chinese and Russian people in business who are fully backed by their governments. In particular, Juice's Chinese connect has a company which producers product for a major American company, but in actuality traffics Fentanyl and other narcotics through American ports from Virginia Beach, Chicago, to San Francisco. Jalon has reached a level and status that Black Americans have rarely been able to obtain! And then we have the overly ambitious Gold Watch. Even though Jalon has kept Gold Watch alive through many of his connections, Gold Watch has always resented the fact that Jalon has always kept his most important relationships to himself. Both Boogie and Gold Watch have accomplished many things on their own accord, but one the main rules since the crew has ventured out on their own post nine-eleven is to never step on your brother's toes. Jalon has turned down millions of dollars off this principle alone, but it's been apparent for years to Jalon, and now Boogie that Gold Watch hasn't held these rules to high regard, or as gospel as the both of them have. The time reads 3:15 am on Jalon's watch as the man continues to walk and discuss Kenny's deception.

LUKE'S HOUSE OF CARDS: Vol. 1

Luke sat on the hood of his plum Impala, waiting in the Fridays Restaurant parking lot. A business meeting located him that Curtis was attending is close by. The past twenty-two-months since Luke moved back to Maryland has been a world apart from the one he was living in California. Luke is currently living with his parents and works for a cell phone company and makes ten dollars an hour plus commission. When Luke first moved back, he was living with Adrian, but after three months of being roommates, both men decided it was best for their friendship not to live together. Luke would discover the answers to mysteries surrounding the night of his return as he reaccumulated back into living in Maryland. Luke found out through Adrian that the fire at Jackie Flowers farm-house started because of the "Halogen

Torchieres" lamp that was located in the master bedroom. For months following the party, Adrian believed that he was somehow the cause of the fire. Luke also discovered the story behind what happened at the diner where that guy was killed. Floyds, cousin Craig, was the masked gunman. Craig saw the man he thought was behind Floyd's murder while he and Luke talked outside of the diner. The man drove a similar car to Floyd's killer and had the same hairstyle. Craig felt that it was enough for him to return to the diner after smoking PCP and avenge his cousin's death. It turns out Craig killed a kid who was about to attend "Virginia Tech" in the fall on a full academic scholarship. The man who killed Floyd was arrested five months later for another homicide he committed. He was murdered two months into serving his double-life sentence. Luke hasn't seen Paige since she left, but she called him on his birthday last year to wish him well. Luke smokes his third cigarette, awaiting Curtis's arrival in the "Friday's" parking lot.

Luke gets a call from an unknown number telling him to meet someone at a pool-hall. Luke hangs up the phone as a cold chill circulates through his body. He knew this day might come, but didn't know when. Luke texts Curtis that he has to leave. Curtis replies. "No worries, bro. I wasn't going to be able to make it anyhow. I'll see you at the party tomorrow, right?" "You already know Curt." "Alright, be great, my man. I'll talk to you tomorrow night. I have some important people I want you to meet."

Luke arrives at a pool-hall, located in Suitland, Maryland. He makes a phone call and then walks to the back alley like instructed. Luke smokes another cigarette as he somberly waits in the alley. Luke applies the façade of a confident demeanor as the back door slowly opens. A light-skin man with dreadlocks approaches Luke. The first thing Luke notices about the man is his diamond necklace. Luke's time in California and his relationship with Paige sharpened his eye to the cost of meaningless items such as fashion and jewelry. That necklace around ole boy's neck had to cost at least seventy-six-thousand. He picks a piece of lint off of his "Hugo Boss" shirt before he extends his right hand to a standoffish Luke.

"How are you doing, Loot? My name is Live!" Luke couldn't disguise his reaction to what the man just declared his name to be, squinting in an offended manner. "I know what you're thinking. That's my real name though nigga! I also know you were expecting to see Gold Watch, but he couldn't make it. Now I don't know all the thoughts flowing across your mind right now, but I think I can guess at least a couple. Your thinking does this random nigga that Gold Watch sent possibly know what is going on between us. Am I right? Don't worry! You don't have to answer that. And then you're thinking. Why should I even talk to this nigga? I'll tell you why because our time to build could be years down the line. Right now, all you have to do is hear what I was told."

Live begins to explain the information that he was told to pass on. Luke is presented with new information that only adds to the convoluted thoughts running through his mind. At the forefront of Luke's mind is the person that he has looked at as his older brother for almost his entire life set him up for failure. Luke remains indifferent in the way he responds to what Gold Watches associate is telling him. Live talks to Luke for over twenty minutes before inviting him inside of the pool-hall for a few games of nine-ball.

April 6th, 2018

Luke stands outside of an auto repair shop, waiting for his ride to arrive. Luke didn't sleep very well after returning to their parent's house following his departure from the pool-hall. He's trying to become ok with the decision that he's planning to make. A tan Honda Prius quietly pulls up Luke as he tosses his cigarette. Luke opens the back door of the Prius, gently lying his black garment bag on the backseat. Luke extends his right hand as he sits in the passenger seat. "Damn nigga! Hoping in my car smelling like cigarettes."

"Nice to see you too, Terence. And nigga this a rental this ain't your car," Luke advised.

"Luke, I don't give a fuck if it's stolen. While I'm driving, it's my car. Roll down your fucking window, please," Terrance complained.

"Aight nigga, damn!" Terence turns the volume on the car radio down as Luke rolls down his window half-way. "But it is good to see you, Luke. It's been so long I don't even remember the last time we kicked it."

"T, how you don't remember? Don't you remember that scuffle Blue and me had?" Luke asked.

Terrance laughed, "Oh yeah, now I do. Adrian, pluck the shit out of you, with that flip-flop."

Luke replied irritated, "Yeah, real funny nigga. Blue is lucky that you tripped me into that table, or I was about to fuck him up."

"Bitch I ain't trip you! Your angry drunken ass tripped yourself up. And what the fuck are you and Adrian still doing fighting?" Terrance continued laughing.

"T, that was almost four years ago. I'm not talking about back then. I'm talking about what you told me over the phone."

"Yeah, and I told you what happened. Luke, regardless of what happened. You and Adrian are twenty-two years old, fighting like y'all in middle school," Terrance chastised.

Luke sat up straight, "Nigga I ain't twenty-two! I'm about to turn twenty-six in November."

"That's even worse. Both you and Adrian are damn near thirty. Acting like y'all kids! At least one thing I can say about Blue is although he's a fuck up. Adrian has been doing what the fuck he is supposed to be doing. Adrian has been maintaining his home, has a new car, and got a promotion at his job. On the other hand, you had all kinds of money, and you have absolutely nothing to show for it, but clothes and stories. You let Paige and whatever happened to you in Cali fuck your mind up. What the fuck are you planning to do with your life? What the fuck was the point in getting a degree in whatever you went to Morgan for, to end up working as, cellphone salesman?"

Luke pointed at Terrance, "See! That's y'all problem."

"Who is y'all?" Terrance questioned.

"My mom, Willie. You. Adrian, Benny, Juice! Pretty much everybody, but Sadie thinks. I'm on some depressed ass nigga shit like Adrian, walking around without a plan." Luke said sounding disappointed.

Terrance glanced at Luke, "Are you sure about that?"

"Yeah, T.T. I'm sure I have a plan," Luke nodded.

"Loot, I'm not talking about that!" he said.

"Then what do you mean?" Luke asked loudly.

Terrance softened his tone, "I mean that Sadie ain't thinking like Benny and me?"

Luke looked confused, "Why do you say that?"

"Because, while you were out with whatever chick you said you were with last night. I was over Benny and Sadie's house, and you know what your sister told me?" Terrance explained.

"What did she tell you?" Luke questioned.

"She said T.T. at this point, I feel Luke is going to get a job in his field eventually. He's going to be doing good, and end up with Paige, two-point-zero!" Luke starts laughing as he picks a water bottle up off of the passenger side floor mat." Yeah, Loot, you laughing like it's funny, but you should probably hear the rest first, and who fuck said you could have that water?" Luke sarcastically responds to Terence, "Oh, I'm so sorry, Mr. Turner! May I please have this bottle of H2O? My throat is parched."

"Aight Mr. Beck, since you want to be a smart ass. Your big sister straight up looked me my eyes and told me. I don't even know my little brother anymore. When I hug him, I feel like I'm hugging a stranger." Terence voice begins to pick up in intensity. "And this how I know Sadie was fucked off thought of what you have become because her eyes were starting watering as she was talking to me. And you and I both know that that's not even Sadie's style! Sadie is the girliest tomboy that I ever come across, including all of the women I was in the service with. The fact that Sadie had to wipe tears from her eyes talking about your dumb ass is why I'm talking with the tone that I' am talking with right now! So you can take offense to the shit all you want, but since you asked me for a ride. You're going to take this shit how I want to serve it to you. I'm not going to sugar coat shit like most of the fake ass people you have consistently put yourself around. Who don't give a fuck about you! Luke! If you don't stop being so selfish and self-centered in your world view. You're going to do something attempting to get ahead, which will be detrimental to the one's you call family in some capacity."

"Is that how you feel, T.T.?" Luke asked.

"Nigga, those were Sadie's words, not mines, but after our conversations over the phone the past two days, and talking to Sadie last night. Yeah, that's how I feel!" The Honda Prius is almost silent as they approach the I-95 south interstate, with only the sound of music faintly playing in the background. This is the first time that Luke has physically seen Terence for almost four years, and this is how their first interaction is transpiring. Luke is bothered by what Sadie told Terence. But he feels that Terence has only given him more conformation to the actions he has decided to take. Luke breaks the silence as Terence drives on the freeway lost in the thoughts of his own life and current circumstances. "Aye T, can you slide by Boogie's store for me real quick?" Luke asked. "I was on my way there anyway, but why are you trying to go?" Terrance inquired.

Luke sounded irritated, "I want to see your big cousin. What's up with twenty-one questions?"

"Because I don't know who I'm talking to anymore!" Terrance said in a matter of fact way.

ADRIAN GETS SUPPLIES (APRIL 6TH, 2018)

How can I explain the past forty-eight hours? Well, I guess I'll start with me confronting Santino at my mother's house. My piece of shit grandfather died earlier this week, making his way to hell where he belongs. My mother was having dinner at her Sterling, Virginia house, and Santino's family, my aunt, and uncle drove down from New Jersey. I showed up to the dinner drunk and high as shit. I'm not a fighter at all. I have never been, but I beat the shit out of Santino in front of everyone, including his pregnant wife and my mother, who told me she wished I never was born. She told me if I wasn't for the church, she would have had an abortion. Which bounce right off of me. My mom has said shit like that to me since I was ten years old. After all these years of dealing with my childhood trauma, I always thought finally confronting Santino would make me feel better about myself, but it didn't. I didn't feel anything! I feel like I did three years ago when I tried to kill myself. All fighting Santino did for me is showed me that I could fight if I'm furious and don't give a fuck. The feeling only worsened, and I decided to go out Friday night to numb the demons floating around in my head. I went out to U-street with my Co-worker, Austin, after a twelve-hour shift. Austin and I drunkenly stumbled inside of a Pizzeria that specialized in jumbo slices after three-am. Out of all the people in this great area, I just so happened to run into Paige's BFF Kelly. Now I haven't seen Kelly since we were both in California visiting Luke and Paige two years ago, but the universe wanted me to run into her and remind me that I was a shitty brother and friend. Austin and I were behind a group of three women and a couple holding hands. I had the group of women and couple laughing as we all stood in line. One of the women began to tear up from laughing so hard. Her friend took a snap chat of me as I did my drunken goofy stand-up routine. I waved goodbye to the couple as they left out of the Pizzeria. The girl who took the snap chat of me walked over to Austin and me as we sat down, she put her number in my phone before she left out with her friends. I got in line to order another slice to take with me. Austin was beginning to dose off as he sat at the table. I sparked up a conversation with two drunken guys who looked like they could be extras in The Soprano's. As the line moved forward, I looked back towards the door, and I saw Kelly and a man getting in line. I allowed five people to go ahead of me just to be in line next to Kelly. She really didn't seem like she wanted to see me; we have always had hatred with a sprinkle of like relationship. It even got sexual on a few occasions. Apparently, Kelly recently got engaged, her fiancé Billy a thirty-eight-year-old Caucasian man, held her hand as I introduced myself. Billy was authentically laughing at my jokes, which I could tell was getting on Kelly's nerves. Well, I somehow managed to get into an argument with Kelly in the middle of the Pizzeria; she was saying all kinds of foul shit about me trying to commit suicide and how my father was an alcoholic and how my mother didn't love me pretty much everything that she heard from Paige. What Kelly was saying didn't faze me, but what she whispered in my ear affected me. Kelly told me how she knew that I knew about Hunter and Paige and didn't tell Luke. Kelly said that she was going to tell him at that seventies party tomorrow. I don't even know how she knew about the party. I guess word of mouth has been getting around, and if she runs into Luke tomorrow night, she might try to start some shit between us. I felt like the biggest piece of shit in the world as I rode back home; all I could hear was Kelly's voice in my ear. I was already depressed as fuck, but she made it even worse. I know all the drinking and pills I did only exacerbated my depression, but I just wanted not to feel anything. Once again, I was in my room with a gun in my hand. Just like I was last weekend, but this time I decided I'd play a game of Russian roulette. I pulled the trigger three times, and nothing happened. I don't even know why, or how the fuck I'm still alive, but here I am! I woke up the morning of April 6th, still intoxicated from the night before. I picked up a beer that sat on my nightstand and started drinking it. I took it in the bathroom with me and used it to wash down my prescription pills that I've been on for the past year. They got me on Prozac, Klonopin, and Adderall. I brushed my teeth, grabbed another beer, and hopped in the shower. I've been running every morning consistently since I got out of the hospital, and I did this morning as well. The run was arduous, I threw up half a mile into it, but I managed to get through it. I stumbled into the house, grabbed a half a blunt that was in my ashtray, and then plopped down on the floor. I started smoking, and then that's when I realized that I would have to take another shower. After I took an additional shower, I got dressed, took my phone off of the charger. I sat down at the kitchen table, eating a breakfast sandwich that I made yesterday morning. I checked my unread text messages. The first message was from Luke, and it read. **"Yo, I know I was supposed to get good, but you're gonna have to do that too."** The second message was from Caden. **"Castro, I haven't seen you since I been back in town, come and hang out if you can!** The third message was from my therapist Dr. McCaster. **"Adrian, you know I don't like to text, but it's been a month and a half since our last session, and you haven't returned any of my calls. I have an open slot today and would like to see you, please respond! You mustn't continue to go backward!"** And the last message was from my father. **"Mijo, I need you to run something to your storage unit for me, don't take too long, Jr. Love you!"** I finished reading and responding to those messages and then sent one to my boy Giovanni. **"Aye, bro, I'm trying to slide through and holla at you. Let me know what's good!"** I finished up my sandwich and made my way to my father's house. When I got to his house, I didn't see his car; he must have run to do something. I started to text him, but he sent me a message as I was typing mines up. **"Mijo, I had to run and take care of somethings. Grab the trunk that's in Manny's room and take it to your storage unit. If Jalon gets there before you leave, give him his folder that he left on the table."** When I walked inside my pops crib, the T.V. was still on with a soccer game playing on the screen; soul music played over the living room speakers. I walked over to the coffee table and saw the folder that Juice had left. Even though I wanted to see him, I wasn't about to wait around for him to show up. I had too much to do. I drink the rest of the whiskey glass that my father left on the table and then ran upstairs to Manny's old room to get the trunk that my father was talking about. I don't know why he wants me to take it to my storage unit, but whatever it's not like he ever ask me for much, so when he does, I just do what he asks without too many questions. I can't even remember the last time I was in his room. Manny never lived with us, but he had a room, and My father has pretty much kept it the same since he died. All of his old clothes and pictures are still in the room. There's an old picture in a frame of Manny and two other kids. He had to be like eight or nine in that picture. They all look so happy. I wish I could be that happy again! I cleaned up some before I left my father's spot because I can't stand when his house is dirty. As I was outside loading the trunk into my car, Juice pulled up and said. "Yo, Blue take a ride with me real quick!" Even though I had shit to do, I rode with him because I haven't seen him in like six months, and I rarely tell Juice no. I don't know why I said what I did, but Juice told me how proud he was off me on the promotion I just got at my job at the top of the year and I told him. "I ain't gone lie bruh. This corporate shit just ain't right. Man I've been working this job since I was twenty one, I'm not gonna be able retire till I'm in my 60's, I don't wanna work for forty years. I got to fake with these people every day, the shit gets depressing!" Jalon rubbed his chin, looked at me and said," Well you're making enough money I don't know if you're saving it, why don't you be your own boss if you feel like this?" "It's not that simple for me Juice!" "Shit ain't never simple for people who always got excuses." And that's when I made the dumb ass statement! "Man sometimes I wish I would have took the route, and moved like you!" Jalon looked at me offended that I would even let some shit like that cross my mind. "Blue you could never in a million life time's move like me. Even if you were me, you better stop being dumb like everybody else looking on the other side of the fence, and not recognizing what you got." Jalon shook his head and paused for a second. "But anyway you a grown ass man, you gonna think how you think, and do what you do! I ain't seen you in a minute, no reason to waste time on already knows, I got other things I wanna talk to you about. Matter a fact I was just gonna sit down and have a beer with you, but I see we got other things we need to address. You don't have anything you have to do right?" "Nah! I got time for you big brother!"

The first location we went to was some construction spot I just sat in the car on my cell phone while Jalon talked to some overweight white guy inside of a trailer. After that we went to some strip club in Prince Georges County. I'm pretty sure this is where the stripers came from that were at my house, like four years ago. I sat and watched some of the girls dance sipping a screwdriver while Jalon was in the back office talking to the owner I guess. Jalon came out of the back room pulling me away from the ATM as I was about to withdraw some money. The next spot we went to was a lawyer's office I think. Matter a fact it definitely was a lawyer's office! After me and Luke graduated from high school, Jalon, gave both of us a card with this law firms number on it name on it, and he told us if we ever got caught up in some serious shit to not say shit and just call that law firm on the card.

The same name was on the card that was on the sign of the building. We stayed at that spot the longest. The secretary flirted with me as I sat outside in the lobby waiting for Juice. The second before last spot that we went to was Boogie's tobacco shop. I stayed down stairs and talked to Donnie and Lisa who worked there as Juice talked out back with Boogie. After staying at Boogie's smoke shop for a little over twenty minutes we pulled up to an Ice cream spot that was in Old Town Alexandria Virginia. "Aye Blue you trying to run in the Ice Cream shop and get us something real quick?"

"Yeah I got you what do you want?"

"A mango smoothie."

"Aight bet!" Juice proceeded to hand me a roll of money. It had to be over five grand! I was shocked and told him. "Fuck bro, I don't need all of this!" What are you trying to buy-out every flavor?" Juice looked at me like boy you better take this money, so I did and went inside of the Ice cream shop to get our orders. The shop was lightly crowed eighties music played over the intercom. While I scanned the menu a little red head girl that was in line in front of me with her family turned around and started talking to me. "Hey Mr. me and my brother Alex were good at the dentist, so my mommy and daddy are getting us some ice crème! Oh really that's awesome what kind of ice cream are you getting? Well I'm getting rainbow sherbet, it's the very best"! The little girl hopped up and down rubbing her hands together. "My little brother is getting mint which is gross, yuck! My daddy is getting coffee flavor, and my mommy is getting cookie dough. What kind are you getting Mister?" I was smiling ear to ear as I looked down at the little girl replying to her question. "A mango smoothie, and I haven't decided what else I'm gonna get? "Eww mangos nasty! You like mango? Why are you getting mango?"

"Well it's not for me! Well who's it for? It's for my big brother!" The little girl's mother turned around gently grabbing her daughter and telling me, "I'm sorry about that mister. Mary we told you about that, there's being polite and social, and then there's being rude and intrusive what you're doing right now!

"Oh no ma'am it's ok!" I said.

Her father who was wearing a lime green shirt also turned around as he held his sons hand, "Yeah sorry about that sir."

"No you guys are good! She's such a sweetheart!" The father got their orders and apologized to me an additional time as he exited the shop caring his energetic daughter in his arms. The family left out and I took my spot at the register and placed my orders. I walked back to the car waving at the family that was in the ice cream shop as the load into the car, Juice was just getting off the phone as I hopped in the passenger side! "Here you go bruh! What did you get Blue? Berry Chocolate Bonanza!" Juice shook his head amused and called me a fucking hipster! "Yo Blue I'm about to take you back to your car now. Who was you waving at when you got out of the ice cream shop? Oh nobody it was just this family that was in front of me in line, Jalon they had the most adorable little girl, she was so cute, makes me want one." I was laughing as Jalon smiled backed and told me. "Yeah kids are a gift, or they can be a gift, but I'm glad you adjusted your schedule to chill with me for a second Blue, hope you remember all the shit we talked about today." "I heard everything you was saying bruh, shit I'd adjust my schedule anytime just to parlay with you big brother." "When we were riding earlier, you said you wished you would have moved like me!"

I looked down, "Juice that was some loose tongue shit I was out of pocket for that."

"Nah listen Blue cause this is important. You remember that cute little girl you was just talking about right?" He asked.

"Yeah! Well that little girl is about to be half an orphan!" My heart dropped into my stomach when Jalon looked me in my eyes and told me that. Why the fuck would he say something like that to me. Jalon continued on with what he was saying. "Her daddy, who we'll call Dean Dot! No better yet well call him D.D.! Word on the streets is D.D is gonna get his brains blown out in the next couple of days, maybe even in front of the babies!" My eyes started to water as I looked at Jalon's stone cold eyes. "This is all shit allegedly heard of course, and allegedly I could stop it". He shrugged his shoulders as he smiled at me. You know niggas be talking a lot of times, but a lot of times niggas be dead accurate, but that's type of shit you live with

221

when you move like me, you know how important Manny was and how I always felt." We pulled up in front of my dad's house and Jalon condescending said. "Oh shit we're already back at Seniors house!"

I started to leave out of the car feeling horrible about what Juice just told me. He smiled as I looked at him through the passenger side window. "Be safe Blue for real, I know how you get down. Come by your pops spot more you might see me"! I dapped Juice up before he drove away from my father's house. If he was trying to show me what it was like to move like him today he did a good job. I don't know how a human being could be cool with taking another life. I love both him and Manny but I could never be evil like them to take another life and sleep at night. I could never imagine taking another life under any circumstance and be cool with it. How the fuck could you live it. Even if you weren't the one who pulled the trigger!

GIOVANNI'S HOUSE

I had to drive back over the bridge to meet Giovanni at his crib in Virginia. I got out of my car, smoking a Newport cigarette, reading a text message from G that said. "Come in, the doors open"! I threw my cigarette out before I walked inside of G's suburban Virginia home. *Dirty Work* by Steely Dan played as I walked through the front door hallway trying to locate him. I walked through the front hallway calling his name. I went into the living room. I looked to the left and located G sitting at the kitchen table looking down at his phone, chopping up cocaine lines on a plate. He looked up from his phone, smiling, saying. "Oh, hey, what's up, Kemosabe! How are you doing?" G walked over and gave me a gigantic hug. I meet Giovanni back in the summer of 2014 through my job.

My company was doing some security for him and his partner's company. Giovanni and I really hit it off. I remember Luke asking me about a connection for some coke on labor day weekend before he moved to California, and besides Boogie's people's Giovanni was the first person I thought about. We went out one night while I was trying to secure the account, and he had the best coke I ever had in my life, and ever since then, we have built a relationship. G has been my go-to for cocaine and psychedelics. I think Giovanni is around the same age as Jalon, but he carries himself like he's a hippy from the seventies. From his long brown hair to the way he talks and the music he listens to, Giovanni acts like he was born at Woodstock! I smiled, hugged G back, and told him. "I'm good dude, I'm good! I see you already got the party started! The party always started on this side, brother, come test the slopes before you take a night at the lodge!" I sat down at the table, and G slide me the plate of cocaine. "Well, thank you, Sir, don't mind if I do. I never been one to turn down a free…Well, a free anything!" "Well, come and take a ride on the sugar express bud." I took a line of coke off the plate that G passed to me. He flicked hair behind his ears and asked me. "So what kind of havoc are you misfits getting into tonight? You already have the disco tunes curtsey of yours truly!" I rubbed my nose and responded. "Well, since you mentioned disco!" G leaned forward, intrigued by my response, and asked. "Ok, what're the grooves?"

"This cat my boy Luke is cool with is throwing a theme seventies party." "No kidding! It sounds like my type of vibes, bro."

"Yeah, he's thrown a theme party every year, and every time it's cool as fuck, I got one-half of my party supplies now, I'm almost ready to go!" Giovanni threw his hands up shouting. "Hold on amigo, don't rush out of here just yet! For one, you're going to take a couple of more lines with me, two you're going to take a shot with me of this killer ass rum my partner Dean brought me back from Asia! And then you're going to take a couple more lines and a couple of more shots with me, because if you're going to go into 70's you gotta have your dancing shoes on Buster Brown"! Giovanni has such a chill cool demeanor that I told him. "Ok just one more drink and then I gotta roll out to meet my boy Caden and my homegirl Sarah for some drinks!" I sat at the kitchen table numb, not able to feel my face. This coke is really, really fucking good! Giovanni came back in the kitchen, holding up some rum that he got from Asia proudly telling me, "This shit is killer, bro!" He grabbed two glasses out of the kitchen cabinet and poured two drinks, proudly holding his glass up as he toasted his glass with me. " To being two beast ass kick in the balls dudes." I smiled and told G. To being two beast ass dudes"! G passed me the coke plate again, and then I slide him the money for the eight ball that I was buying. G told me about a trip that he just took to Greenland. He told me how he and his girlfriend took some mushrooms under the Northern Lights on their trip. He asked me if I wanted another shot and a line to which I responded. "Nah, I'm cool, bro!" To which he replied. "Aww Adrian, come on, dude, don't be a killjoy."

"I'm not dude. I have to meet my boy Caden up for some drinks," I said.

"Hey Kemosabe, you said you we're going to the seventies tonight, I just was trying to be you're Lizard King!" G did the rock and roll sign with his left hand and licked his tongue in between it. I just laughed and told him. "Thanks! But no thanks, dude. I will take some water, though!"

"There's bottled water on the fridge's side and cups in the cabinet above the microwave if you want to drink out of the faucet instead," Smacks himself softly in the face three times and say. "I'm such an idiot."

"Why did you say that G?"

"I just thought about my boy Dean is sending some guys over to fix my AC unit so that you would have to leave anyway. But you're my boy Adrian, and I want to do one more line."

"It's all good, Gio! Hey bro, where's the bathroom at again?" I asked.

"It's going to be your third door on the right Kemosabe!"

"Aight bet!" I said as I headed that way.

"And you have to jiggle the toilet handle, are else it will just run, so take a second after you tinkle to make sure it's all copasetic."

"Ok, will do, dude! And I'm going to have another line waiting for you when you get out of the Lou!" Gio says with a British accent.

"Ok, if not more for me." I made my way to the bathroom and had to double back to the kitchen for my phone. As I did, Giovanni asked me. "Did you change your mind, Kemosabe?"

"Nah! I'm just grabbing my phone, dude."

"Well, the slopes await, bro!" I made my way back to the bathroom, feeling happy. Maybe it was the coke, or perhaps it was Giovanni's vibe, but I felt at peace for the first time in a long while! I took a piss and then ran the sink. I put some water in my palm and then sniffed it to flush the coke in my nose and started to fix my hair in the mirror. That's when the conversation from outside caught my attention! Whoever was supposed to fixing G's AC came to the house. Everything was cool until I heard a ruckus outside the door. When I stuck my head outside of the bathroom, G crawled on all fours towards the back door. Lord, why would you put me in this position! Why would She end my life like this? From the tone of old boys, voice yelling, and the gun pointed at Giovanni's head, I knew this was going to end badly! I closed the bathroom door and looked for something to use from under the sink to protect myself. I grabbed a bleach spray bottle. I figured if he came in the bathroom, I could at least spray him in the face and maybe blind him for a second. I don't want to die like this. I see all that suicide shit was me just not wanting to feel depressed because I want to live. I don't want to die in this bathroom. Hopefully, he'll just rob the house, and he won't kill me or G. I put the spray bottle down in the tub and got out to put my ear against the door, so I could try and hear what was said outside. All I could hear for a few minutes was music playing, and then I heard G cry out, "Jesus Christ, he's in the bathroom, don't shoot me, bro! Don't shoot me, bro!" The dude must have had a partner with him. I can't believe G gave me up so quick this mothafucka! Oh, God, what am I going to do? When this mothafucka comes back here, I'm going to blind his ass with this bleach. I could hear him walking through the hallway kicking in the doors looking for the bathroom. He already kicked in the first two. I know I'm next. The bathroom door got kicked open, and my heart just about jumped out of my chest, he positioned himself in front of the shower, and that's when I heard gunshots coming from the living room. I don't know what came over me, but I just jumped at the dude like I was a crazed animal. I was fighting for my life. The dude was taller than me and definitely outweighed me, but the bleach actually worked, and I was able to wrestle the gun out of his hand onto the floor. We both battled for the gun on the bathroom floor. I don't know how but the gun ended up in my hand and before I knew it. I let off three shots! Blood covered my white shirt and parts of my face and neck. All I could do was stare in the mirror, looking into my bloodshot eyes. My mother always said I would end up being a piece of shit criminal like Manny, and now she was right! I committed the worst sin that a human being could commit. I took another human life! I've always felt like a Misfit in this society, but now! I'm that without question. If I didn't come here to buy cocaine, I wouldn't even be in this position. I felt like such a fucking fool. I guess April is for fools, and right now. I'm the biggest one in the world!

I'm not saying I'm gonna
change the world, but I
gurantee that I will spark
the brain that will change
the world.

— 2pac

To: KC

From Aaron Cheles

I appreciate the
support black man.

Made in USA - Kendallville, IN
1213583_9780578822914
12.15.2020 0858